Murder Is Not a Girl's Best Friend

Murder Is Not a Girl's Best Friend

The Diamond District Mystery Series

Rob Bates

Kenmore, WA

A Camel Press book published by Epicenter Press

Epicenter Press
6524 NE 181st St.
Suite 2
Kenmore, WA 98028

For more information go to:
www.Camelpress.com
www.Coffeetownpress.com
www.Epicenterpress.com
www.robbatesauthor.com

Cover and interior design by Scott Book and Melissa Vail Coffman

Murder is Not a Girl's Best Friend

ISBN: 978-1-94207-818-0 (Trade Paper)
ISBN: 978-1-94207-819-7 (eBook)

Printed in the United States of America

*To Susan and Mikey, for companionship,
support, and love in the time of COVID.*

CHAPTER ONE

Mimi Rosen felt terrible. She felt like crap. She was overcome by guilt—the kind that gets lodged in your throat and stays there.

Her day at the "Social Responsibility and the Diamond Industry" conference had been draining and dispiriting, as one speaker after another grimly recited the industry's ills. They acknowledged that conflict diamonds—which fueled civil wars in countries like the African Democratic Republic, or the ADR—were far less of a problem, and many diamond mines benefited local economies.

Then came the "but." As Mimi's father said, "in life, there's always a but."

"Beautiful gems shouldn't have ugly histories," thundered Brandon Walters, a human rights activist known for his scorching exposés of the ADR's diamond industry. "This—" he aimed his finger at the screen behind him, "is how ten percent of the world's diamonds are found."

Up popped a photo of an African boy, who couldn't have been older than sixteen. He was standing in a river the color of rust, wearing nothing but cut-off jeans, bending over with a strainer. Mimi could see his vertebrae under his skin, feel the sun beating down on him, sense the stress and strain on his back.

"That kid is paid two dollars a day for his labor," Walters declared. "If you sell diamonds, this may not be your fault." He paused for emphasis. "But it is your responsibility."

Walters had sandy-blonde hair, high cheekbones, a perfectly trimmed goatee, a ponytail that flopped as he talked, and a South African accent was so plummy it sounded affected. He looked to be in his mid-twenties but had the bearing and confidence of someone ten years older. Unlike the other activists, who delivered their speeches in whispery monotones with their eyes glued to the podium, Walters planted his feet firmly at the center of the stage and stood on it like he owned it. He peppered his talk with splashes of theater, dropping his voice to signal despair, or cranking it up to roar disapproval.

Mimi didn't want to close her eyes to his message, but knew she might have to, to preserve her sanity. Diamonds were now how she made her living. She had been working at her father's company for over a year—a fact she sometimes found hard to believe. She occasionally dreamed of again working as a reporter—the only thing in life she had ever wanted to be. But journalism had become an industry that people escaped from, rather than to.

She had hoped the conference would inspire her. She had even convinced her father, Max, to come. Instead, the sessions made her feel depressed and sorry for herself—which didn't feel right, as she was hearing about extreme poverty in a plush New York City auditorium with the air conditioning cranked, while the summer sun broiled the streets outside.

She also knew the industry's problems weren't so easy to fix. When Mimi started working at her dad's company, Max seemed intrigued by her idea of a socially-responsible diamond brand. She was excited to help change the industry.

Then the project ran into roadblocks. She never quite determined what a "good" diamond was. What if it was unearthed by one of the diggers Brandon Walters talked about, who earned two dollars a day? Human rights activists condemned that as exploitive. Yet, they also admitted those workers had few other sources of income and would be far worse off if the industry vanished. They didn't want to kill the business; they wanted to reform it. Mimi wasn't an expert on any of this—and even those who were didn't always agree.

Mimi spent many nights and weekends researching these issues, and ended up frustrated, as the answers she sought just weren't there.

When her project began losing money, her father started losing patience. Mimi hoped that dragging her father to this conference would reignite his interest. Nope.

"These people act like everything is our fault. All minerals have issues." Like many in the diamond business, Max believed his industry was unfairly picked on. He fixed his *yarmulke* on his bald head, so it stayed bobby pinned to one of his side-tufts of hair. "I haven't done anything wrong. I'm only trying to pay my rent."

Max spent most of the conference with his arms crossed, his face toggling between bored and annoyed. If he had a phone, he'd probably spend the day staring at it. But he didn't, which was another issue.

Following Walters' talk, he leaned over to Mimi. "I should call Channah for my messages."

Mimi gave him her mobile and a dirty look. He had already borrowed her phone six times that day. She considered lecturing her father to get over his stupid aversion to buying a cell phone, so he didn't constantly pester the receptionist to see who called. But she'd also done that six times that day.

Besides, she was intrigued by the day's final speaker.

Abraham Boasberg grabbed the crowd's attention the moment he stepped on stage. "I believe there is a reason that God put diamonds in the poor countries and made rich countries desire them," he bellowed, puffing out his barrel chest. "And I'm going to prove it."

Mimi sat up and thought, *who was this guy?*

She soon found out. Boasberg was six feet tall, stocky, bearded, with a bright red yarmulke capping a salt-and-pepper mop of curly hair. He worked in the diamond business, and his words came fast and forceful. Like Brandon Walters, he seemed to savor being the center of attention. He had a mike clipped to his suit and prowled the stage like a panther. His presence filled the auditorium.

"This whole conference, we have heard about the problems of our trade. They are real. The people who dig diamonds are part of our industry. They deserve to be treated fairly.

"But we must do more than just complain," he declared, holding up his index finger. "We need solutions!

"What if diamonds, which once helped rip the African Democratic Republic apart, could put it back together? What if they built new roads, schools, and hospitals?" He stopped and took a breath, his chest heaving. "What if diamonds became symbols of hope?"

Max returned to his seat and handed Mimi back her phone. She was so entranced with Boasberg, she barely noticed.

"A few months ago," Boasberg proclaimed, "a local Reverend in the African Democratic Republic found a one-hundred-and-seventeen-carat piece of rough on his property. It has since been cut into a sixty-six-carat piece of polished, about the size of a marble. It has been graded D Flawless, the highest grade a diamond can get. It's the most valuable diamond ever found in the ADR. It's worth twenty million. Easy."

A giant triangular gem appeared on the screen behind him, gleaming like a sparkly pyramid.

Max's eyebrows shot up. This guy was talking diamond talk, a language he understood.

"But that is more than a beautiful diamond." Boasberg declared, sweat beading on his forehead. "That is the future."

"Here's what usually happens with diamonds in the ADR. In most cases, miners hand them over to their supporter, who's basically their boss who pays their *bupkis*. Or, if they're freelance, they'll sell them to a local dealer, who pays them far below market value. The miners don't know how much the diamonds are worth, and they're usually hungry and just want a quick buck.

"And since the ADR has no money to police its borders, most dealers smuggle diamonds out of the country to avoid taxes. As a result, the ADR gains little from what comes out of its soil. Its resources are being systematically looted.

"When I met Reverend Kamora, I told him, consumers are turning away from diamonds because they believe they don't help countries like yours. That further hurts your people. Now, instead of working for two dollars a day, they'll do the same work for even less.

"But what if we can flip the script? What if this diamond helps your country? And what if we let people know that? That will *increase* its value. It's documented that people will pay extra for products that do good, like Fair Trade Coffee. It's the same reason kosher food is more expensive. It's held to a higher standard.

"If we get more money for this diamond, soon every gem from the ADR will be sold this way. We'll do an end run around the dealers who have robbed the country blind. We'll turn ADR diamonds into a force for good."

He pivoted to the screen. "Let's talk about this gorgeous gemstone. We wanted to call it the Hope Diamond. That name was taken."

A few members of the audience tittered.

"We're calling it the Hope for Humanity Diamond. Four weeks from now, we'll auction it from my office, live on the Internet. We want the whole world to watch. We'll even sell it in a beautiful box produced with locally mined gold." On screen, a glittering yellow box appeared. The diamond sat inside it, perched like a king on a throne.

"What celebrity wouldn't want to wear a diamond called the Hope for Humanity?" Boasberg asked. "It will make them look glamorous *and* morally superior."

The audience laughed.

"This diamond—" he exclaimed as spit flew out of his mouth, "will transform a continent." He stretched out his arms, revealing pit stains the size of pancakes.

"So many conferences talk about Africa, but you never hear from people who actually live there. And so, I've flown in the Reverend who found the diamond, to talk about what it can do for his country. Reverend Kamora, can you come here, please?"

The auditorium grew quiet as small middle-aged Reverend Kamora shuffled to the front. He walked slowly, gripping the guardrail as he climbed the stairs to the stage. When he finally arrived at the microphone, Mimi could barely hear him; his voice was low and delicate, with the soft cadence of a bell.

"For years," he began, "blood diamonds were a curse on my country. Things happened that were hard to describe. They haunt us still." He paused, as he momentarily got choked up.

"The African Democratic Republic has known two decades of peace, but not one minute of prosperity. Like many people in my country, I dig for diamonds for extra money. It's hard work. I don't make much from it. But I have no choice.

"Many people who work in my country's diamond fields don't understand why people in the rich countries buy diamonds. Some believe they are magic. And when I found this gem in a riverbed, sparkling in the sun, I thought God had blessed me with a bit of magic.

"But God's real gift came when I met Mr. Boasberg. He told me that we could hold an auction for this diamond, receive a better price for it, and ensure the proceeds benefit the people of my country.

"I hope you tune into the auction of the Hope for Humanity Diamond four weeks from today. Together, we can change my country's diamonds from a curse to a blessing. That will really be magic."

After a tough day, Mimi felt a smidgen of optimism. When Reverend Kamora finished speaking, her eyes were filled with tears. She peered at her father. He was asleep.

After Reverend Kamora toddled from the stage, Boasberg bounded back to answer questions.

A man approached the microphone in the middle of the audience. "Mr. Boasberg," he asked, "what are you getting out of this?"

"Nothing," Boasberg smiled. "I'm not even taking a commission. I see this as the way forward for the business that I love, and a country I care about."

"Mr. Boasberg," a second person asked, "how do we know the money will go where you say it will?"

"Our accounts will be posted online and completely transparent. We'll account for every penny."

On it went, Boasberg swatting back every question with the grace of a tennis pro. Maybe it was the journalist in her, but Mimi was growing skeptical. Boasberg's almost-Messianic tone struck her as too good to be true.

Just then, she heard a familiar voice at the microphone. It was Brandon Walters, the activist who spoke earlier.

"Mr. Boasberg, I'm intrigued by your new initiative," he said.

Mimi braced herself for the "but."

"But when you talk about dealers who've robbed the country blind, you didn't mention you were once partners with the worst offender."

Boasberg's nostrils flared. He looked down at Walters like he wanted to kill him.

The young activist plucked the mic from its stand and spun around to address the audience.

"For those unaware, Mr. Boasberg used to own a company with Morris Novak. During the civil war in the African Democratic Republic, Morris Novak was one of the biggest dealers in blood diamonds. He remains a significant player in the industry, though his main business today is money laundering. Diamonds are kind of a sideline.

"For years, I've sought to expose Morris Novak's corruption. In response, he has repeatedly threatened to sue me. Our friend Mr. Boasberg could help by supplying information about Novak's business dealings. He won't."

He circled back to Boasberg. "So, while it's admirable you want to play a role in the ADR's future, maybe first, you should come clean about your past."

There was a smattering of applause.

Throughout Walters' speech, Boasberg appeared ready to erupt, and when it ended, that's what he did. "First of all," he boomed, "you are correct, Morris Novak is my *former* partner. Let me emphasize *former*. I haven't worked with him in six years. Is that long enough for you?

"Second, who the hell cares? This is old news. The problem with you non-government organizations, you NGOs, is you're always pointing fingers. Maybe if you stop the holier-than-thou B.S., you could help do something good."

Walters seemed to relish this reaction. "I'm just saying," he shot back, "that given your history, and that of certain of your, shall we say, 'associates,' you're an unlikely savior for the ADR."

This sent Boasberg into a fury. The bickering grew so loud, even Max woke up.

The moderator—a middle-aged woman with silvering hair wrapped in a bun—hurried to the stage and declared question time was over.

"Thank you, Mr. Boasberg for that inspiring presentation," she said, with a jittery squeak. "The conference organizers would like to present you this humanitarian award for your efforts."

The award was likely pre-arranged and came off as awkward with Walters' question hanging in the air. The moderator rushed through her praise of Boasberg, while he impatiently fingered the marble statue. When she finished, he stormed off the stage.

The moderator gamely tried to end the meeting on an upbeat note, saying it had many "impactful takeaways" and "urgent calls to action," and reminding everyone to attend the post-conference cocktails in the next room. No one listened. They were digesting that final spectacle.

So was Mimi. Walters' question had transformed Boasberg from a passionate plain speaker to another defensive diamond dealer, like her dad. Maybe he was too good to be true.

CHAPTER TWO

MAX HAD NO INTEREST IN ATTENDING the cocktail reception, but Mimi felt, to get her project off the ground, she needed to make contacts. Yet, she spent the first ten minutes standing against the wall, not talking to anyone, nursing a glass of white wine.

Mimi didn't consider herself a shy person, though when she was, she hated it. It made her feel lonely and weak.

She made a deal with herself. She wouldn't leave the cocktails until she met five new people. She gulped down her wine and shifted into social mode.

Most of the attendees were dressed in swank cocktail attire. So was Mimi, though she was probably the only attendee who bought her sundress off eBay. One guy wasn't honoring the dress code: he sported a t-shirt, jeans, and a bandana, as well as long hair and a free-flowing beard—seemed like a good person to talk to.

He gave his name as Rafi. He appeared in his late twenties. He had a gravelly voice and a friendly puppy-dog manner. "So," he asked, "what did you think of that presentation at the end?"

Mimi tapped her wineglass. "It sounded great. But that Boasberg guy got so defensive, it made me doubt he's for real."

"I can assure you he's for real," Rafi said with a smile. "He's my father."

Mimi spotted the yarmulke hiding under his bandana. "Sorry. I didn't—"

"It's cool, man," Rafi laughed. "You were just expressing how you feel. Why don't you talk to my dad, get a sense of where he's coming from? I'll introduce you."

He walked her over to Boasberg, who was holding court at the center of the room. Rafi waved at him to meet Mimi.

Up close, Abraham Boasberg was a formidable, almost overwhelming presence. Everything about him was big, from his meaty hands to his booming voice to the scope of his ambition.

"Miss Rosen here doubts that you're for real," Rafi chuckled.

"Oh yeah?" he barked. "Why?"

Mimi thrust her weight from one foot to another. "The Hope for Humanity diamond sounds like a great idea—"

"Yeah, yeah, yeah." He folded his arms across his chest. "What's your issue with me?"

"You got very defensive when that activist asked his question," Mimi said quickly. "You know, the one about—"

"I know the question!" Boasberg stared at her for a few interminable seconds. He expelled a breath and his tone softened. "Rafi told me the same thing. Maybe you're right.

"That Walters kid is a *putz*." His voice climbed to its familiar volume. "I'm trying to do something good, and he's just dredging up old *chazeri*. Does he want to hurt this project?

"I'll take of care of it," he grumbled. "Have you met Reverend Kamora? If you don't trust me, maybe you'll believe him."

Mimi tried to clarify that she never said she didn't trust Boasberg, but he had already left to fetch the Reverend.

Reverend Kamora marched up to Mimi, bowed his head, and offered his hand. "Lovely to meet you, Miss Rosen. I believe God has a reason for me to meet every person."

He was smaller than Mimi—who, at five feet, four inches, wasn't exactly tall. He looked to be in his late fifties, with clear muscle tone, probably from his work in the diamond fields. He stood in front of Mimi, yet his voice was so soft—with a chiming, almost musical quality—that she strained to understand him over the surrounding din.

"Will you be bidding on the diamond?"

"No," Mimi laughed. "My company doesn't have twenty million lying around."

"It's true, we are asking a good deal of money." Lines appeared on his forehead. "And frankly, that has me rather concerned. This diamond has captured my country's imagination. The entire population may tune in to the livestream. I am worried people's hopes have gotten too high."

Just then, a young man began excitedly talking with Reverend Kamora, and he politely excused himself. Rafi and his father were also engaged in another conversation. This round of socializing was over.

Not bad, Mimi thought. She had met three new people, all of whom were interesting. Just two to go.

Mimi spied her next target: a brunette woman, standing against the wall, lugging a movie camera on her shoulder; an observer, like Mimi.

Mimi introduced herself, and the woman set her camera down with a grunt of relief. She gave Mimi a polite, formal handshake, and offered her card.

It read: "Anita Vaz. Award-Winning Documentarian," and listed three movies she'd made.

Anita was thin, with a long intense face, framed by a pair of a librarian glasses. She sported a light summer dress and appeared to be in her mid-twenties. Mimi was impressed by how much she'd accomplished at such a young age.

Mimi would have loved a career like hers, but that dream was probably out of reach now that Mimi had turned forty—another fact she sometimes found hard to believe.

"I'm getting footage for my latest film," Anita said. "It's a profile of Brandon Walters."

"You mean the activist who asked the last question?" Mimi said. "He turned the conference upside down."

"Oh yeah. That was great footage." Anita smiled and patted the camera. "Brandon's an amazing subject. He's young, attractive, and charismatic. Plus, he's a Rhodes Scholar and has fifty-thousand followers on Twitter." It was hard to know which she considered a more impressive accomplishment.

"He's done amazing work exposing the diamond industry's dark underbelly," Anita said. "So, what do you do?"

Mimi's body grew stiff. "I work for a diamond company."

Anita's expression turned blank, and her eyes dashed around the room.

"I used to be a newspaper reporter," Mimi said, trying to win her back. "I'm just doing this temporarily."

Anita pulled a recorder from her pocket and held it to her mouth. "Idea for future documentary: What happens to old journalists? Do they take other jobs? Do they feel like they are selling out?" She put the recorder down. "Sorry. I do that sometimes."

Mimi forced a grin. "I'm very interested in responsible sourcing. And I feel like I'll always be a journalist—"

Just then Brandon Walters sauntered over, introduced himself, and pointed his blue eyes at her. "Did I hear you say you're a journalist?"

"No," Anita said. "She works in the diamond business."

"I was a newspaper reporter for nine years," Mimi added hastily. "And I edited a website for five."

Brandon considered this. "I'm looking for journalists to help with research. Have you done any investigative reporting?"

"Definitely," Mimi chirped.

"Like what?" Anita asked. She seemed warier now that Brandon was talking to Mimi. Mimi was beginning to suspect that they were more than filmmaker and subject.

"Well," Mimi said, "I once solved a murder."

Brandon tilted his head. "I'm sorry. Did you say you solved a murder?"

Mimi forgot. Nobody believed her when she said that.

She quickly relayed how, the year before, she'd caught her cousin's killer. Yosef was a diamond dealer engaged to Channah, the office receptionist. The police believed he was murdered by jewel thieves. Mimi proved otherwise.

As she unspooled her tale, Walters seemed impressed, amused, and a little skeptical. He also didn't take his eyes off her. When she finished, he unleashed a crooked grin.

"That's some story. I've met many journalists, but never one who solved a murder before." He put his hand to his mouth. "I might be able to use you. I am looking for someone to keep tabs on Morris Novak."

"He's the person you asked about, right?"

"The one and only," Brandon said. "He has become an obsession of mine. I've exposed a lot of bad actors in the ADR, and they've all lost their licenses. Not Novak. He's the biggest and dirtiest fish in that pond, but for some reason, the government protects him. I've made it my mission to bring him down. I need someone to watch him in New York. But I can't pay much."

"I'm a journalist," Mimi smiled. "I'm used to low pay."

"This would be no pay."

"What I figured," Mimi said. "That's fine, I guess."

They traded numbers and agreed to meet for drinks the next night.

Mimi walked away, thrilled. An internationally recognized human rights activist—*a Rhodes scholar*—wanted her help with research. She'd be using her reporting skills and industry knowledge in the service of a larger cause. Attending this conference finally felt worth it.

Mimi had fulfilled her new-person quota, but she felt energized and in the groove. It wouldn't hurt to meet just one more.

She spotted a lanky man, leaning against the wall, gripping a glass of water. He was quite tall, over six feet, with hawk-like features, deep brown eyes, and well-coiffed gray hair, topped with a *yarmulke*, which meant he was probably in the diamond business. But he wasn't socializing, only scoping out the crowd—another observer.

Mimi extended her hand. "I'm Mimi Rosen. I work at Max Rosen Diamonds."

"Nice to meet you." He looked her over and nodded, but didn't smile, and didn't offer his hand. A bodyguard hovered nearby; this man was important enough to need one.

"And your name is—"

His eyes narrowed. "I saw you talking to Brandon Walters. Are you an associate of his?"

"No, we just met," Mimi said. "But I'm going to work for him."

He raised his head forty-five degrees. "I wouldn't do that if I were you. And I wouldn't trust him. He's about to land in a good deal of trouble."

"What do you mean?"

He gave a tight smile. "You'll see."

He and his companion walked away. He didn't say anything more, including his name.

CHAPTER THREE

THE NEXT MORNING WAS HOT AND HUMID. As Mimi walked down Forty-Seventh Street to her father's office, the early summer heat made her clothes stick to her back and turned her brown hair into a damp, messy mop.

Even with the swamp-like weather, the Diamond District was characteristically packed. The roadway was clogged with armored cars, which were continually loaded and unloaded by big men with big guns. Drivers unlucky enough to get stuck behind them could only pound their horns in frustration.

The sidewalks were just as jammed, with the standard mix of workaday smokers, gaping tourists, and harassing hawkers; plus, plenty of diamond dealers.

Mimi noticed that regulars on the Street—as they called it—walked at two speeds: They rushed, or trudged.

The Rushers were propelled by an unshakable conviction that they had somewhere to be and everyone else was in their way. They charged down Forty-Seventh Street like they were a bull, and the world was the matador.

The Trudgers were the old timers. They had long beards and long faces. They had spent their life toiling on Forty-Seventh Street and were still there because they had nowhere else to go. They walked slowly, staring at the ground, like a weight was attached to their ankles.

Perhaps, Mimi mused, today's Rushers would end up tomorrow's Trudgers. They'd devote their youth and middle age to some urgent goal, then spend their final years wondering why.

This morning, the middle of the block was dominated by the Mitzvah Tank—a long white trailer, about the size of a bus, adorned with Hebrew letters and the crinkled face of a *Rebbe*.

Hasidic teenagers stood outside it, sporting *payis* and the traditional black hats and suits, even though it was summer and a little too hot for that. They spent their day asking male passers-by—and only male passers-by—if they were Jewish. If the man said yes, they'd grab his arm and try to drag him in the van to put *tefillin* on. They were known for being persistent. "I've told you a million times, I don't want to pray," one man shouted at them.

They didn't approach Mimi. She was a woman, and they weren't interested in her *davening*. Sometimes, on Fridays, they would offer women *Shabbos* candles, which Mimi eagerly scooped up, since she could always use free candles. So, she told them she was Jewish—which she was, at least by birth. But she had little interest in religion—certainly not the strict version she'd been raised in, never mind the stricter version touted by these folks.

In a way, it was fitting the *Haredi* called their van a "tank"—the people inside it were hunkered down, seeking protection from the outside world, hoping for small gains in hostile territory.

But that was also true of the Diamond District. It sat nestled in one of the most forward-thinking cities in the world, but clung to the past. On Forty-Seventh Street, deals were still sealed on handshakes, everyone moaned about the old days, and no one was phased by the Mitzvah Tank.

Yet, change was coming, even to the Diamond District—as shown by its sea of hollowed-out storefronts. A developer planned a lavish new skyscraper in the middle of The Street, causing many long-term tenants to lose their leases.

While the new building was meant to revitalize the block, for the moment the empty spaces made it look gloomier and uglier. Forty-Seventh Street had once been home to an unbroken chain of jewelry stores. Now, there was noticeable gaps, like a child with missing teeth.

Even Max's building had been modernized. The lobby had been given a sleek modern makeover; its elevators no longer resembled cattle cars; and some of its décor looked like it originated in this century. Max was happy to see the changes, though he grumbled the new landlord would likely use them as an excuse to jack up the rent.

When Mimi arrived at her father's office, her best friend Channah sat at her standard spot at the receptionist desk, talking on the phone. She waved at Mimi—sending her long black curls flapping—then buzzed her through the double security doors. Like many religious women, every day Channah stuffed her full figure into a blouse with long sleeves, a skirt that stretched to her ankles, and black stockings to cover any parts that might peek through.

Mimi walked to her desk, which was bare, except for a picture of her ten nieces and nephews. (Her two religious sisters didn't mess around.) Max's office was such a mess that Mimi kept her workstation an oasis of order, as a silent rebuke.

Her dad sat a few feet over, his desk submerged in papers, tweezers, jeweler's loupes, and boxes of diamonds. As usual, Max's dealer friend Sol was visiting, and they were squabbling over a diamond deal. Max and Sol had been friends for decades—and they'd spent most of that time squabbling over diamond deals.

"This stone is beautiful," Max said of the two-carat pear-shape he had just plucked from its parcel papers. "Its price is even lovelier."

"Sorry, Maxie, there's no market for this item," Sol said in his thick Israeli accent, as he peered at the stone through a loupe. He was tall, wrinkled, and his hair was dyed a rusty shade of brown not found in nature. "I've seen better-looking rocks at the bottom of fish tanks."

Of course, if Sol was selling that diamond, he'd talk about how beautiful it was, while Max would call it ugly, and they'd be just as vociferous about it.

Finally, Sol said he'd "be generous" and buy the stone for far below what Max offered. Max responded with an umbrage-filled speech about how his first price was extremely reasonable—however, as he was "also generous," he'd go down a few percent. Following a few more rounds tossing numbers back and forth, they stalemated at four hundred dollars apart.

"Maxie, I'm doing you a favor, taking this dog off your hands," Sol said. "Why don't you just say *Mazal*?"

Mazal was short for *Mazal und Brucha*—the magic words that sealed deals in the diamond business.

"What are you, nuts?" Max scoffed. "You want to put me in the poorhouse?"

"You're the crazy one!" Sol yelled. "You're killing a deal over four hundred dollars!"

"No." Max rose slightly from his chair and pointed his finger at Sol. "*You're* killing a deal over four hundred dollars."

Actually, you're both nuts, Mimi thought. Four hundred dollars wouldn't make or break either of their bottom lines, but haggling was part of the game, and neither could stop playing. After a few more minutes of fruitless bickering, Sol stormed out.

Channah popped her head out of the reception area. "Sol was really mad," she said. "He said he's never coming back."

"Don't worry," Max responded. "We'll see him by Friday."

"So Channah," Mimi asked, "how was your date last night?"

Before she could answer, Max piped up, "are you seeing somebody, Channah? Should I get a new suit?"

After the tragedy with her former fiancé, Max longed to see his receptionist happy. He was constantly prodding her to get married, and joking about a new suit. Channah handled this with customary good humor, though it made Mimi roll her eyes.

"No, Mr. Rosen," Channah moaned. "It wasn't a match. Not even close." She pulled up a chair, rested her elbow on Mimi's desk, and cradled her head in her hand. "The guy was nice and all, but we had nothing in common. The only thing I wanted to talk about was Yosef. And who wants to hear about someone's dead boyfriend?" She sighed. "My parents are starting to get worried."

Channah was twenty-five, which, in her community, was enough to bring on whispers that she was getting past prime marrying-age. Mimi always said that shouldn't bother her. Clearly, it did.

"What do you expect?" Max said. "Parents worry. That's their job. There's an old saying: 'Parents can have a dozen children, and each is the only one.'"

Channah exhaled. "I know. They just don't understand what I'm going through. The guys they set me up with, there's nothing wrong with them. They're just not Yosef."

That was the pattern: since her fiancé died, no suitor could live up to his memory.

Mimi took her hand. "You're still grieving, Channah. It'll take time."

For once, Max didn't comment. He was still grieving, too. He hadn't dated anyone in the three years since Mimi's mom died.

Mimi could understand why, at seventy-four, Max wasn't seeking a new romantic partner. She certainly couldn't picture him on a date. Yet, after working with him for a year, Mimi knew he often felt lonely. He still lived in their old family home, which once housed their family of five, and now just held him. Mimi wished he had a companion, someone to talk to, who wasn't someone he traded diamonds with.

"Anyway," Channah turned to Mimi, in a clear attempt to change the subject, "how was the diamond conference? I missed you yesterday." A grin played on her lips. "I didn't get a chance to miss a certain someone because he kept calling me, checking for his messages."

"Yes." Mimi raised her voice and looked at her father. "It would be nice if that person got a cell phone, so he didn't constantly bother Channah."

Max didn't look up from his computer; he either didn't hear her, or was pretending not to.

"The conference was okay," Mimi said. "It made me think about things."

For instance, that pear shape Max and Sol were arguing over. Where did it come from? Who dug it up, and under what conditions?

"I made a good contact," Mimi said. "This human rights activist wants me to help with his research. We're meeting tonight to discuss it."

Channah's round face burst into a smile. "That's so cool." Even though she was twenty-five, there was something girlish about Channah, from her loud, hearty laugh, to the way even minor surprises could make her eyes grow comically wide.

"What's this?" Max said from his desk, his hearing having magically returned. "You're not helping that Brandon Walters, are you?"

"Yes," Mimi groaned. She knew her father wouldn't approve.

"What are you crazy, helping that guy? He's out to kill our industry."

"No, Dad. He doesn't want to hurt the legitimate trade. He's only targeting bad actors, like Morris Novak. You don't do business with him, do you?"

"Novak?" Max frowned. "No way. I knew him years ago. Never cared for the guy."

"So, is it so bad if I look into him?"

"Actually," Max sat up on his seat, "yes, it is. Novak is buying real estate all over the city, including on Forty-Seventh Street. He's a big *macher* now. He can crush a guy like me. Walters should worry, too. He probably won't, the *shmuck*."

Mimi's body tensed. "What do you have against Brandon?"

"Besides him trying to destroy my business?"

"Which he isn't."

"He has a ponytail. Guys with ponytails have attitudes."

"That ridiculous," Mimi scoffed. "And it's not your business how I spend my free time."

Max leaned over his desk. "All right, here's something that *is* my business. We need to stop this responsible sourcing project of yours. It's a waste of time and money."

"Seriously?" Mimi asked. "Why?"

Mimi had put her heart and soul into that project. It sounded better to tell friends "I'm marketing a socially-conscious diamond brand" than to say, "I'm working for my dad's diamond company." It also sounded better to herself.

"At that conference, I realized this whole responsible sourcing thing, it's too idealistic. I run a small business. I can't do everything these people want. All the audits, the tracking, it's too much. Maybe a big company can handle it. Not mine."

Bringing her father to the conference had completely backfired.

Mimi felt a headache come on, right behind her eyes. "Dad, didn't you listen yesterday? Don't you feel bad for those people who dig for diamonds and barely get anything for it?"

"Sure, I feel bad for them," Max said, with a feeble shrug. "I feel bad for a lot of people. I can't go around feeling bad all day. I'll never get anything done."

He leaned back on his chair. "Unfortunately, this is how life is. We're on top of the food chain. Those people aren't. I didn't set it up that way. I'm just one person. I can't change everything."

Mimi wanted to tell him what a ridiculous, insensitive comment that was, but held her tongue. He might forget this decision; he often did. If they argued, he'd surely remember. So, she stewed in silence, trying to forget that someone she loved had just said something she hated.

AROUND FIVE, BRANDON WALTERS PHONED, saying something important had come up, and he might be late for their meeting.

"Do you want to reschedule?" Mimi asked.

"No," he said. "The appointment's on Forty-Seventh Street at a quarter to seven. It shouldn't take more than twenty minutes. I'll call you when it's done.

"By the way," he added, sounding chipper, "it looks like I'm about to get a motherlode of information on my friend, Mr. Novak. I'll need your help sorting it out. You'll have plenty to do."

"Sounds good," Mimi said.

After she hung up, Mimi mused that working for Brandon might open certain possibilities. "Human rights researcher" would look good on her resume—especially for Brandon Walters, future documentary star. Sure, it didn't pay. But it might lead to more.

Mimi could use a change. She didn't hate working for her father—in fact, she liked it, particularly the steady income. She just didn't care for the work.

She had already attempted most of what she set out to do, with mixed results. She'd upgraded her father's computer systems. She wanted to hook him up with a jewelry designer, but they couldn't agree on one they liked. And her socially-responsible diamond project was about to get junked.

Max occasionally made noises about teaching Mimi to trade diamonds, but she had little interest in quibbling with Sol over four hundred bucks. Most days, she was a glorified office manager. Which was fine. She just wanted more.

Mimi still believed she had something to contribute. Brandon's offer may have come at exactly the right time.

Mimi stayed in the office after Max and Channah left, luxuriating in the air conditioning, and surfing the Internet.

Brandon told her he'd call when his appointment was through. At seven-fifteen, Mimi hadn't heard from him, but figured his meeting was running late. By seven-thirty, he still hadn't phoned. She started growing antsy.

Eight o'clock came, with no word from Brandon. He could be blowing her off. Which didn't make sense. He'd sounded excited when he called before.

Perhaps something happened to him. Her father had warned that Novak could crush a guy like Brandon. Mimi flashed to that terrible day when Channah came to her desk, wondering why she hadn't heard from Yosef . . .

At eight-fifteen, she texted Brandon: "Running late?" He didn't text back. Fifteen minutes later, she called, got voice mail, and left a message: no response. Five minutes later, she sent another text, and left another message. Again, no answer. At nine, she gave up, though she checked her phone all the way home.

Mimi arrived back in New Jersey, feeling deflated. She spent the rest of the night binging on reality TV and ice cream, and chocked the whole thing up to a learning experience, though she wasn't sure what the lesson was.

Around eleven, just as Mimi was going to bed, she got a phone call from an unknown number.

The voice was flat. "Hi, Mimi. This is Anita Vaz, the documentarian. We met yesterday at the Social Responsibility conference. I understand that you've sent bunch of texts and messages to Brandon Walters."

"Yes. I was supposed to meet him tonight."

"He told me to call and say that he can't make it." Her tone was cold and clinical.

"Why? Has he been hurt?"

"No. Nothing like that."

"Good." Mimi took a breath. "Then why couldn't he make it?"

Anita emitted a low moan. "He just couldn't."

"Can I talk to him?"

"No."

Mimi clenched the phone. "Why not?"

"Because you can't," Anita barked. "I have to go, but there's a very good reason why Brandon can't talk right now."

"I'd like to know what it is."

Anita inhaled. "Abraham Boasberg has been killed, and Brandon has been charged with his murder."

Mimi's mouth dropped. "That's a good reason."

CHAPTER FOUR

MIMI BARELY SLEPT THAT NIGHT. BOASBERG was such a *force,* such a powerful presence; it was hard to imagine him dead.

It was even harder to imagine Brandon killed him. Not only was he a human rights activist, but he was also supposed to meet Mimi that night. A person wouldn't commit murder, then go for a drink.

At five a.m., Mimi checked her phone for news reports of the murder. There were plenty.

"Hard Rock", blared one headline, and "Diamond Dealer Found Dead."

A well-respected diamond industry luminary was found bludgeoned to death at his office last night, and a prominent critic has been charged with the crime.

Police say Abraham Boasberg, 57, was killed around 7 p.m. last night after he received a blow to the head with a heavy object, possibly a humanitarian award he had received the day before.

Brandon Walters, 28, a human rights campaigner famed for exposing gem industry corruption, was charged with first-degree murder after surveillance video showed him entering Boasberg's office shortly before the crime.

Police said that the two had clashed the day before at an industry conference, where Boasberg announced a plan to sell a 66-carat diamond and use the proceeds to benefit a local community in Africa.

The top-quality gem, dubbed "The Hope for Humanity," is currently missing, police sources said.

Cops believe that Walters murdered Boasberg so he could steal the diamond, which has been valued at $20 million. The mega-rock had been locked away in Boasberg's office, but police think the killer was able to break into his vault using a welding torch Boasberg had on hand to craft jewelry.

MIMI LAID HER PHONE ON THE NIGHTSTAND and tried to sleep. She suddenly remembered the man at the cocktail party, who told her Brandon would get in trouble soon. He said that one day before Brandon did.

That was strange. It could be a coincidence—but maybe not.

WHEN MIMI ARRIVED AT THE OFFICE a few hours later, she was dripping with sweat from the hot summer morning and exhausted from her sleepless night. Channah wasn't at her standard spot at reception, but sitting on a chair in front of Max's desk. Mimi's father had a newspaper spread out in front of him, open to a story about the murder.

"You see the news?" Max asked Mimi, the minute she walked in.

"Of course," Mimi growled. This was looking like a long day.

"It's shocking," Max said, his eyebrows bouncing up his forehead. "Just two days ago, we were watching Boasberg give that whole *spiel* at the conference. And now this." He shook his head. "Did you know that Channah's family was friendly with his?"

Channah nodded sullenly. "My father knew him from *shul*."

There was a pause.

"I guess you saw they arrested—" Max said.

"Of course," Mimi snapped. She was in no mood for this.

"That's crazy, Mimi," said Channah. "Weren't you two supposed to meet?"

"Yes, last night." She dropped her purse on her desk, not looking at either of them. "We didn't, obviously." She fell into her chair.

"I'm not surprised," Max said. "I never trusted the guy."

"Dad," Mimi said, "this is hard for me. Please don't say, 'I told you so.'"

"I would never say that."

"You *live* to say that!"

Max held up his hands. "It just so happens my comment was correct. There was something not quite right about the guy."

Mimi's face curdled. "You never said that. You said you didn't like his ponytail."

"Same thing."

"That is not the same thing! You were critiquing his hair!" Mimi's fists clenched. "I don't want to discuss it."

Max dipped his head. "All right. We won't. But if you ever need to talk—"

Mimi cut him off. "I'll speak with Channah."

"I was just thinking," Channah chimed in, "have you considered that this Brandon guy could be innocent? He sounds like a good person, trying to help Africa and stuff." Her eyes turned into saucers. "Maybe you should investigate this murder, like you did Yosef's."

"*Oy,* Channah!" Max barked. "No, she should not do that. Do not suggest that, even as a joke. You remember what happened last time. Do you want her to get attacked again?"

"You're right." Channah's hands fluttered. "I know that was a difficult experience."

"Yes, it *was* difficult," Max pouted. "Very difficult." He wagged his finger at Mimi. "I've told you, many times, never to do anything like that again."

"And I've told *you*, many times," Mimi lashed back, "I don't want your opinions on my life."

Max folded his arms. "On that subject, I will never keep quiet."

Mimi would have to accept that. He never would.

"Dad, this is stupid." Mimi said. "I'm not investigating this. There's no mystery. The police know who did it."

"You're right." Channah said. "Although last time—" She stopped mid-sentence.

"Last time what?" Mimi said.

Channah looked panicked. "Never mind. I should go up front. I'm sorry to hear about this, Mimi. Let's talk later." She sprung from her chair and scurried to the reception area.

Max and Mimi both exchanged glances but didn't say anything. Max turned his eyes to his computer.

Mimi knew what Channah was going to say. Last time the police thought they knew who did it. And they were wrong.

FOR MOST OF THE MORNING, the thought haunted Mimi: What if the police were wrong again? What if Brandon Walters *was* innocent?

As much as she hated to admit it, her father was right. It *would* be crazy to investigate another murder. The last one was trying enough. Besides, last time, Channah requested her help. No one was asking her now.

Mimi tried not to think about Boasberg for the rest of the day, and for the most part, she didn't.

That afternoon, she received a mass email from Anita Vaz, touting her GoFundMe for Brandon's defense.

"As many of you know," it started, "I am filming a documentary about Brandon Walters, an amazing human rights activist who has exposed massive corruption in the African Democratic Republic's diamond industry. His efforts have been internationally recognized, including by me.

"Brandon's commitment to social justice is unwavering, but he has made powerful enemies along the way. He always feared one day those entrenched interests would come after him. I am sad to announce, THAT DAY HAS COME.

"Last night, Brandon Walters was accused of a murder HE DID NOT COMMIT. The evidence against him is circumstantial and EXTREMELY flimsy. It's a clear set-up.

"If you have any money to donate to his defense, I urgently need it to clear Brandon's name. Right now, I don't have enough for bail. I'm also interested in hearing from anyone with information that might prove relevant to the case."

At the bottom, she left her number.

Mimi was about to donate, when she realized Anita might be interested in the man's comment at the cocktail party. That still struck her as strange.

She didn't call until her father left the office. He would go nuts if he knew she was getting involved in this, even in this limited way. Not that she considered what she was doing a big deal. She was passing on information; it would be wrong not to.

Anita sounded surprisingly friendly when she picked up the phone. "Good to hear from you," she said. "I was thinking of calling. It might be good to talk. At the cocktails, you said that you solved a murder once."

"Yeah," Mimi said, dragging out the word.

"I plan to investigate Abraham Boasberg's murder. I'd like your help. Maybe we can get together tonight. What do you think?"

Mimi thought: *Oy.*

CHAPTER FIVE

Mimi agreed to meet Anita that night—then spent the rest of the day thinking she should cancel. It might be better to just send her an email and call it a day.

Mimi didn't, though. She *couldn't.* She needed to know why Anita believed Brandon was innocent. She was too damn curious.

Curiosity was a good quality in a journalist. Mimi sometimes considered it a bad quality in her. She was always vacuuming up gossip, data, every stray morsel of intel. She always wanted to know who, where, why. The world was so strange. She longed to make sense of it.

Before she left, Mimi Googled Anita and had found that, yes, she was an award-winning filmmaker. One of her films had been named "best documentary" at the Central New Jersey Film Festival, which may not be the most prestigious award in the world, but—well, she could probably end the thought there. At least it was *something.*

Mimi was more impressed with the subjects she tackled: one film examined the lives of the homeless, another showed how the education system was failing underprivileged youth.

Mimi's interactions with Anita hadn't been all that pleasant. Those documentary subjects made her hard to hate.

Mimi met Anita at a nearby coffee shop, which had a fancy French name that Mimi could never figure out how to pronounce. Anita sat at a wooden table on a cushioned bench against the back wall, her hands circling a cup of tea. She looked far less put together than the first time they'd met. Her glasses sat on the tip of her nose and her bangs drooped on her forehead. There were obvious bags under her eyes.

"I'm just beside myself," she told Mimi. "I've spent my life documenting injustices, and to see something so wrong happen to a friend of mine is just horrifying. Brandon is completely innocent. Of everything."

"It's crazy." Mimi shook her head. "I reached out to you because I heard something that might be relevant to Brandon's case."

Anita squinted through her glasses.

"At the reception after the conference, I talked with this man, and told him I might do work for Brandon. He said, 'I wouldn't if I were you. He's about to get in a lot of trouble.' I asked him what kind of trouble, and he just said, 'you'll see.'"

"Do you know who he was?"

"No. But he was very distinctive looking. Tall. Elegant. Wore a *yarmulke*."

Anita opened her laptop and angled it toward Mimi. She clicked a video of the cocktail reception and fast-forwarded through the footage until she found the tall man, lurking in the corner, his bodyguard beside him.

"Is that him?"

"Definitely."

Anita's eyebrows rose. "Do you know who that is? That's Morris Novak. He's the person Brandon talked about at the conference, the one Boasberg used to be partners with, the guy involved in all those corrupt deals in the African Democratic Republic. Did he tell you anything else?"

"No," Mimi said, slightly shocked. "That's it."

"There was a rumor that Novak was at the conference, but I wasn't sure until I reviewed the footage later. It was a big deal he was there. He rarely appears in public. That was why Brandon asked that question, to get his attention."

"That's strange," Mimi said. "Brandon called me last night and said he was about to get a lot of information on Novak."

"I just spoke to Brandon," Anita said. "Boasberg texted him yesterday and said he had important information to share. Brandon figured Boasberg was ready to spill the beans on Novak. Perhaps Boasberg winning a humanitarian award convinced him it was time to start acting like a true humanitarian.

"So, Brandon went to Boasberg's office and found him dead. He immediately called 911. The police came, and asked him a bunch of questions, Then, at the end of the night, they arrested him, totally out of the blue. He's been in jail ever since."

"Why did they arrest him?"

"According to them, the building security footage showed he was the only person to enter Boasberg's office that night. Which, by their weird logic, automatically means he's guilty."

"Let me play devil's advocate," Mimi said. "If security cameras recorded Brandon entering Boasberg's office right before the murder, that's pretty good evidence, isn't it? What makes you sure Brandon is innocent?"

Anita's mouth became a straight line. "Because I know. I know *him*."

Time for the big question. "Is it possible," Mimi asked, "your personal feelings are playing a role here?"

Anita's face turned to stone. "What do you mean?"

Mimi sighed. Anita wasn't making this easy. "When we first met, you and Brandon seemed like you were, you know, involved."

"Is that germane to what we're discussing?"

"It might be. You don't have to answer."

Anita let loose a long gust of air and turned her eyes to the table. "It's fine. I've never been particularly good at hiding my feelings, and I guess I wasn't when we met at the cocktails.

"After college, I backpacked through Africa and visited the ADR. I was shocked by the poverty there. This is the twenty-first century; there were people living in huts, with barely any electricity, sometimes without clean water. I think about it all the time. I've always wanted to make a movie about it.

"After I won that award, I figured I'd get my chance. I had meetings with producers, but they weren't interested. They said the idea wasn't commercial enough. One told me, 'we barely care about poor people in *this* country.'

"Then I met Brandon. He was so charming and committed, I got the idea to build the movie around him. He was the perfect subject. It would be kind of a 'Western man saves Africa' thing. A few producers have expressed interest, but I'm basically funding this on my credit cards."

Anita gazed at the inside of her teacup. "I was always attracted to Brandon. But I figured we would keep everything professional, at least while making the movie. But sometimes, when you spend a lot of time with someone, things begin to shift. At least they did with me. We hooked up a few times. It meant something to me. I don't think it did for him. He told me he didn't have time for a relationship. His life was devoted to the cause.

"And I get that. I make documentaries. I don't have time for a personal life. It's been years since I've had a boyfriend. But—" She scowled. "I know a load of crap when I hear one."

Mimi laughed.

She twirled her teacup. "So, yeah, it's been awkward at times. When I make movies, I ask a lot of people. At one point, Brandon called me a pain in the neck." She shuddered, as if talking about it hurt her all over again. "The kind of thing men always say about ambitious women. You'd think a human rights activist would know better than to act like a garden-variety male asshole.

"I could talk about this for a long time, though I might need a few margaritas." She half-laughed, then snatched her recorder from her purse and lifted it to her mouth. "Possible documentary subject: Famous documentarians who had personal relationships with their subjects. Is it ethical? Does it make them less objective?" She stuffed the recorder back in her purse.

"Look," she said, "I may still have feelings for Brandon. I don't know. At this point, it doesn't matter. The important thing is, he's been framed for murder after speaking out against powerful people. We can't let that happen."

"But if Brandon didn't kill Boasberg, who did?"

Anita almost rolled her eyes. "It's obvious! Morris Novak! Don't you see? It was a total set-up.

"Novak must have found out that Boasberg was going to blow the whistle on him. So, he killed Boasberg and set up Brandon for the crime. He got rid of two birds with one stone. It's brilliant. Evil, but brilliant."

"That makes sense, I guess," Mimi said. "But do you have any evidence of that?"

"Not until now. You just provided it."

"I did?"

"What Novak said to you at the cocktail party. That's huge. It shows he was out to get Brandon." Anita gnawed on her fingernail. "You should tell the police." She fished around in her green-and-yellow crocheted purse and yanked out a card. "Here's the detective investigating the case."

Mimi was shocked to read the words, "Detective Michael Matthews."

She nearly jumped out of her seat. "Remember I told you I investigated a murder? That's the cop I dealt with. Detective Matthews."

"He's a jackass," Anita sneered. "He's sure Brandon is guilty, and you can't convince him otherwise. Brandon thinks he's on the take."

Mimi wrinkled her nose. "Matthews and I had our differences, but he seemed straight to me."

"Novak is a powerful man," Anita intoned. "He has a lot of money and influence. Don't underestimate how far that goes. Didn't you say that the police got everything wrong in your case?"

Mimi shifted in her seat. "Pretty much. But by the end, Matthews admitted he made mistakes and I was right. That showed me he was a good guy, and good detective."

"Big deal," Anita scoffed. "He screwed up and he admitted it. We have pretty low standards for cops these days." Anita fingered a bag of sugar. "When you told me you solved a murder, I didn't believe you. But I found an article that said it was true."

Funny. Anita had scoped out Mimi, just like Mimi had checked on her. They were both journalists.

"I'm launching an independent investigation of Abraham Boasberg's murder. I'm going to need help."

Mimi tensed up. "You want me to investigate?"

"Actually. I was hoping you could give me advice." Her face brightened. "But if you could help investigate, that would be amazing."

"No, it wouldn't." Mimi's underarms grew damp. "That would not be amazing. I am still getting over my last investigation. You need someone who specializes in this. Like a private detective."

"I've considered that." Anita scrunched her face. "They are way too expensive. And I'm basically broke. Brandon doesn't have any money and has to use a public defender. The entire burden of proving him innocent has fallen on me. I can't do it alone."

"Look, I feel terrible about this," Mimi said. "But I don't know if I can help."

Anita regarded her through slitted eyes. "At the cocktail party, you said that investigative reporting was your specialty."

Mimi cringed at her wine-driven bragging. "Yeah—"

"You also said that you cared about social responsibility."

Mimi felt put on the spot. "Well, sure—"

"I can give you a credit on my documentary. I'll name you the head of research. If you ever want to get back into journalism, that'll look great on your resume."

Mimi had to admit, that was tempting. It represented as good an opportunity as working for Brandon.

"Though," Anita added, "until we get a distributor, I can't pay you."

"Brandon's rates," Mimi said.

"Yes, but this could help your career. I hate to say it, but Boasberg's murder will make this film a lot more commercial. True crime is hot right now; this would be documenting the aftermath of a murder as it happens.

"This could be my breakthrough. And if you're part of it, it will be your breakthrough, too. I don't know what your future plans are, but you don't want to work for your father's diamond company your whole life, do you?"

Mimi bristled at the way Anita said, "your father's diamond company," with a sneer in her voice. She was finding Anita easier to dislike.

"Let me think about it," Mimi said. "A murder investigation is a big deal. I want to be sure it's the right thing."

"Of course, it's the right thing!" Anita said with sudden force. "Brandon is rotting in jail, while Morris Novak, the real criminal, is walking around free. It makes me sick."

Anita reclined against the cushions. She looked exhausted. "These have been the worst two days of my life. Last night, I went to sleep, hoping I'd wake up and find this was all a dream. But today, I got up, still living this nightmare.

"If we don't get these charges dropped—" The corners of her eyes grew red. "That's it. Novak will win and Brandon will go away forever. We have only one chance at this. Brandon's life is on the line."

She grabbed a tissue from her purse, and for a few seconds, quietly wept.

Mimi studied her hands until the sobbing stopped.

Anita gazed at Mimi, her eyes pink, the tissue crinkled in her fist. "I can't do this by myself. Won't you help? Please."

Mimi didn't know what to say. She did not want an innocent man to go to jail. She did not want to spend her life working for her father—particularly now that he was killing her pet project.

Plus, Anita was right; this *could* be a great opportunity. If Mimi ever returned to journalism, it wouldn't be through a newspaper job. Those were gone. It would be with something like this.

Perhaps if she got a credit on this film, she could get more. She might even learn to make documentaries herself. She fantasized about becoming a director, travelling the world, looking for worthwhile subjects—

Until a stark fact jolted her back to Earth: She did not want to investigate another murder. The idea scared the hell out of her.

CHAPTER SIX

LATER THAT NIGHT, MIMI RETURNED to her one-bedroom apartment in New Jersey. It had never been a pretty sight.

In the last year, Mimi had tried to spruce up the place, hanging new curtains and pictures on the walls, and adding a cool 1940s-style lamp she bought at an antique shop. Yet, whenever she came home, she experienced fresh feelings of disappointment. Despite all her efforts, it was still the same drab box where she'd lived in the two years since her divorce. The carpet remained frayed, the walls were painted a strange color somewhere between orange and yellow, and the toilet clogged every month, as if on schedule. At least she liked the lamp.

When Mimi started working for her father's company full-time, she hoped the regular income would let her move to a nicer place. One year later, she was still climbing out of debt. She wouldn't be going anywhere anytime soon.

Luckily, the air conditioning worked. She needed it this hot night. Her favorite lounge chair was as comfy as ever. She'd discovered some new Edith Piaf on Spotify and poured herself a glass of chilled white wine. That always helped her think.

Mimi had left the coffee shop without agreeing to investigate. She was tempted to flat out tell Anita no, but that's not easy when someone is sitting in front of you, begging for help.

The days Mimi spent probing her cousin's death were some of the best and worst of her life. She relished the challenge of solving the mystery, feeling like she'd finally found a purpose, and experiencing the thrill of being a journalist again.

But so much of that period continued to haunt her: the threats, the anxiety, the times she was nearly killed. When it was all over, Mimi lay in bed for weeks, trying to banish the investigation from her mind, but unable to think of anything else. Even old sitcoms, her standard comfort food, didn't help; the characters' problems seemed so alien. Who cares about a bad date? She had seen such darkness, such evil. She didn't live in that world anymore.

The first day Mimi went back to work at her father's company, she was walking down Forty-Seventh Street when a short, bearded man in a black hat and suit spotted her. He changed direction and ran towards her.

"Miss! Stop!" he yelled.

Mimi froze. Every hair on her body shot up. The man must have noticed, because he stopped in his tracks, turned pale, and stammered a quick apology.

"Sorry, I didn't mean to startle you," he said. "I was a friend of your cousin. I just wanted to thank you for what you did. It was truly a great deed."

Mimi stared at him, wide-eyed.

"Sorry to upset you." He vanished into the crowd before Mimi could respond.

That should have been a nice moment. Mimi was too messed up to appreciate it.

Mimi knew she'd accomplished something important. She'd brought to justice someone who might not have been caught otherwise, and risked her life doing it. That made her feel proud. She just felt the other stuff more.

Mimi had dreamed her whole life of landing a big story. Now, she had, and it just left her scared and scarred and wanting to get on with her life.

She was doing better lately, thanks to medication and therapy. Yet, one year later, she still relived the scariest moments in dreams. They inevitably jarred her awake, her pillow soaked with sweat, and she knew she wouldn't be getting back to sleep that night.

As much as Mimi tried to move on, she couldn't. The memories continued to plague her. They made it hard to hang out with friends. They distracted her from free-lance work. And they wreaked havoc on her love life.

For the last year, Mimi kept telling herself that she needed to get "out there." She tried online match sites, but hated the format. She felt like she was looking at a "person catalog."

She did go out with a few guys, but each time she did, instead of the standard lighthearted banner about jobs or Netflix, Mimi talked about the investigation. Her dates never knew how to react. Some didn't believe she solved a murder. A few found it "cool"—which annoyed her, because she'd lived through it, and there was very little cool about it. She rarely went on second dates.

Her therapist told her this was normal. Just as it would take Channah a long time to get over her grief, Mimi shouldn't expect an immediate end to her post-traumatic stress disorder.

Now, she was on the verge of being dragged into a new investigation. Her therapist would probably tell her she was crazy to even consider it. Then again, therapists probably weren't allowed to say that kind of thing.

THE NEXT MORNING, MIMI CALLED DETECTIVE MATTHEWS, as she'd promised Anita she would.

Just the way he answered the phone, with a brusque "Matthews," set her nerves on edge. He'd always struck her as a gruff bulldog of a man, who turned almost every conversation into an inquisition. Mimi believed they had arrived at a place of mutual respect by the end of the last investigation; yet, simply hearing his growl rattled her.

"Hi, Detective. This is Mimi Rosen. I don't know if you remember, we met during the Yosef Levine case."

"Of course, I remember," Matthews said—a surprisingly friendly greeting. "You were a reporter of some kind."

Mimi laughed. "Fair description."

"How are you doing?" he asked. "I remember you got into some pretty nasty scrapes last year."

"I'm okay, thank you for asking," said Mimi, genuinely appreciative that he did. "Some days are better than others."

"It can take a while to get over something like that." He cleared his throat and switched to official-voice. "How can I help you?"

Okay, Mimi thought. *I guess small talk-time is over.*

"I know you're investigating the murder of Abraham Boasberg. I have some information I'd like to share."

Mimi told him how, one day before Brandon's arrest, Morris Novak declared that he would get into trouble soon.

"Well, he was right about that," Matthews replied.

That was it: no questions, no follow-ups. She didn't know what reaction she expected, but it wasn't that.

Mimi didn't want to let this go. "Don't you think that's suspicious? Morris Novak said Brandon Walters would get in trouble, and the next day, he did."

"I'll make a note of it, but I don't feel comfortable characterizing beyond that. I appreciate you bringing it to my attention." His voice grew sharper. "You're not writing an article on this, are you?"

"No," Mimi said.

"Good," Matthews pronounced.

"I might investigate though."

"What?" Matthews nearly shouted. "Why would you do that?"

"It wasn't something I planned on." Mimi felt suddenly defensive, though she wasn't sure why. "Someone asked me to."

"You're going to investigate a murder, because someone asked you to?" He sounded appalled. "With all due respect, Miss Rosen, we are talking about violent crimes committed by dangerous criminals. You don't investigate them as a favor. I don't want to see a repeat of what happened last time, when, frankly, you got in over your head."

"Hey!" Mimi sputtered. "You told me I was helpful!"

"I said, 'somewhat helpful' and that was only after a drink."

"Good memory."

This seemed to temporarily fluster him, and he emitted a few scattered grunts. "I'm a detective. I need a good memory. And I hope you remember that during that investigation, you nearly got killed."

"Of course, I do. And I hope *you* remember that if it wasn't for me, the actual killer might have gone free."

"Now listen here, Miss Rosen—"

"You can call me Mimi."

"Miss Rosen, Mimi." He took a breath. "I appreciate it when members of the public supply me with information, like you just did. But that's as far as it goes. Investigations should be left to the professionals.

"This isn't just about you," he continued. "I look online, and I see retirees trying to solve cold cases, like they're—" He paused for emphasis. "*Crossword puzzles.*"

Mimi sensed he was on the verge of a much longer rant. "Come on," she said. "I'm a little more qualified to investigate than they are."

Matthews seemed annoyed to be even discussing this. "I'll grant that you've been a reporter, and last time you helped a bit. But that doesn't mean you should keep investigating homicides. Why do you think you're qualified to do that?"

Mimi waited a moment to answer. "I don't know. I'm very analytical, and good at putting things together. When I set my mind to something, I usually do it. And I'm generally able to get people to open up. That's probably because I'm pretty open myself. Sometimes I don't have much of a filter. Like when I'm nervous, I tend to babble."

"Actually, come to think of it, I might be babbling now. You make me nervous sometimes. I'm not sure why. You just do."

There was a long pause.

"Okay," Matthews said. "Even if I allow that you have certain skills, you still don't know anything about detective work."

"I wouldn't say that," Mimi protested. "I've heard a lot of true crime podcasts."

Matthews audibly moaned. "Listen, Miss, um, Mimi—you appear well intentioned. But it would be foolish and extremely dangerous for you to conduct another so-called murder investigation. We have thoroughly examined the facts of this case, and we are confident that we have apprehended the perpetrator.

"There must be other things that someone with your talents could investigate. I just heard on NPR that there's all these issues with hot dog vendors. The way the city licenses them, it's a mess. Look into that."

Mimi wasn't sure how to take that comment. "Are you suggesting that because I'm a woman, I can only investigate people who sell hot dogs?"

"No, of course not! I work with lots of woman cops. But you don't have the training to investigate violent crimes. I don't want you getting hurt again. So, I'm asking you nicely, for your own good, do not investigate. I repeat: please, do not investigate."

"I'll think about it," Mimi said and hung up.

Mimi was surprised at Matthews' forcefulness. She was also surprised that he listened to NPR.

Mimi's curiosity then got the best of her, and she spent the next few hours reading about the issues with licensing hot dog vendors—which, she had to admit, was kind of an interesting subject.

She also knew Matthews had a point: he understood solving crimes far better than she did.

But here's something Matthews didn't understand: when a bunch of men told her not to do something, that made it far more likely that she'd do it.

CHAPTER SEVEN

The next day, Mimi and Channah grabbed lunch at Kosher Gourmet, a Diamond District fast-food place that proved Boasberg was right when he said kosher food was more expensive, but wrong about it having higher standards. Kosher Gourmet specialized in greasy, oily pseudo-Asian food, served on bright orange trays. Its ambiance was one step down from McDonalds, at twice the price.

During the summer, Mimi and Channah escaped its grimy confines by eating at nearby Bryant Park. Bracketed on all sides by visible skyscrapers, the four-block park was both a green respite from Midtown Manhattan and a reminder it was always there.

On this day, as Mimi focused on the always-arduous task of properly grasping the cold kosher sushi with plastic chopsticks, while keeping her napkins from blowing away, she updated Channah on recent events.

"So, you won't believe it. Someone asked me to look into Boasberg's murder."

"Really?" Channah tittered, bouncing on her chair. "I knew that would happen! Who?"

"The woman making a documentary about Brandon Walters. She's convinced he's innocent. She has a bit of a bias, obviously. But she seems pretty certain."

"Wow, Mimi. Another investigation."

Mimi looked at her food. "I probably won't do it. I didn't commit to anything."

Channah's lips formed a wry smile. "I bet you will. I know you. You can't resist something like this." She chuckled, then noisily slurped her diet soda through a straw. "I can give you background on the Boasbergs. My father knew them from *shul*."

Mimi dipped her sushi in the cup of soy sauce that was stationed on the ground. "What were they like?"

"Mr. Boasberg was always loud. When he spoke at *shul*, you could hear his voice all the way down the hall. Everyone treated him like a big deal because he worked for Morris Novak. And then—" She released a long sigh. "Things changed."

"What do you mean?" Mimi asked.

"It was a big scandal in my community. The Boasbergs got divorced, and a year later, Boasberg's wife married Novak, his former partner."

"Ooh." Mimi lifted her eyebrows in mock horror. "I had a no idea this was so scandalous."

"It broke up two families. It definitely gave the local *yentas* something to talk about. Everyone considered Mrs. Boasberg a gold digger because Novak was so rich. I just feel bad for his son, Rafi."

"I met Rafi at the conference. Kind of a hippie, right?"

Channah looked surprised. "Hippie? When I knew Rafi, he was your typical *frum* boy."

"Really?"

"Yeah. When we were younger, he was the local golden child. All my friends wanted to date him, since his father was a big businessman. I had a crush on him, too, but he was out of my league." Channah thrust out her lower lip. "Then he had issues."

"What issues?"

"From what I hear, he was so upset when his parents split, he disappeared for a while. No one knew where he went. There were rumors he'd gotten into trouble."

"Wherever Rafi went, he's back." Mimi popped a piece of sushi in her mouth. "He seemed like a nice guy. Did the Boasbergs have any other kids?"

"Nope, just Rafi." Channah speared a piece of chicken with her fork. "See, you're investigating already!"

Mimi squirmed. "I'm just asking questions."

"I think you're doing more than that. I'm going to Boasberg's *shiva* tonight with my parents. I'll let you know if I find out anything. I can be your assistant detective."

"Channah, I'm serious. I'm not sure if I want to do this." She looked her friend in the eye. "You're not the only one still scarred by Yosef's death."

They were both quiet for a moment, and the conversation turned to other things.

THAT AFTERNOON ANITA TEXTED, "Made up your mind?"

Mimi didn't write back. She remained torn. Part of her was leery of investigating another murder. Another part wanted the credit on Anita's documentary. And a third said all these logical arguments didn't matter; Channah was right, Mimi couldn't resist this kind of thing. She couldn't let an innocent man be charged with murder. That went against everything she believed in.

Three hours later, Anita reached out again. "Decided yet?"

Mimi replied, "not yet. Sorry."

That was not what Anita wanted to hear. "How about this?" she replied. "Let's meet tonight at the coffee shop. I have someone who wants to speak with you."

"Who?" Mimi asked.

"It's a surprise," she wrote back.

Anita was poking at Mimi's weak spot—her curiosity.

Mimi realized Anita would not let up until they met again. She now understood how Anita had accomplished so much, so young. She *was* a pain in the neck.

Mimi texted, "Fine."

Okay, she thought. *This better be good.*

CHAPTER EIGHT

When Mimi arrived at the coffee place with the French name she couldn't pronounce, Anita was sitting at the same spot along the back wall as before, her hands cradling a teacup. Next to her was Reverend Kamora.

Mimi shook his hand and asked how he was.

His glum expression said it all. "I am alive, thank God. That is about it."

Mimi remembered how proud he was of his big diamond at the conference. Now, he just seemed sad.

"What's the matter?" Mimi said, while sliding into the chair across from him.

"What do you think? It's missing. The Hope for Humanity. The diamond I believed would uplift my country. No one knows where it is."

"The police must be looking for it," Mimi said.

"They *say* they are. I ask and ask, and they don't know where it is. For all I know, one of them has stolen it. It is so frustrating."

"The problem," Anita interrupted, "is that the police are looking in the wrong place. They think Brandon took it. They searched him thoroughly and he didn't have it. They need to use their brains and start investigating Morris Novak. But they're too afraid of the big bad billionaire."

Reverend Kamora ignored what Anita said; he'd likely heard it before. "I just know that we must get it back," he said. He banged his fist lightly on the table, as if he wanted to demonstrate his resolve but was reluctant to hurt an inanimate object. "It is the property of my country.

I can't imagine how people back home will react if they find out that the diamond has been stolen."

"They don't know?" Mimi said.

His mouth flattened. "The government is keeping it quiet. This diamond has become a big deal in my country. They are concerned its disappearance could cause serious social unrest. Even riots."

"I can even imagine people saying that I stole it. Never mind that I was the one who found it and donated it for the greater good. This will give rise to all sorts of conspiracy theories. I don't care what the gossips say but I do worry about violence. I have a wife and daughter."

He took a moment to compose himself. "I'm sorry, I shouldn't burden you with this. I believe God knows the best path for all of us. I have faith we will get the diamond back by the time of the auction."

Mimi wasn't sure what she just heard. "Hold it. The auction hasn't been cancelled?"

"No."

"But it's happening three weeks from now. You might not get the diamond back. You should call it off."

A look of horror crossed his face. "Oh no. I couldn't do that."

This baffled Mimi. "But you have to. You have no diamond!"

"I believe God will return the diamond in time. He is the one led me to it in the first place."

"Of course, Mimi," Anita interjected, "you are welcome to help find it."

"I'd love to." Mimi crossed her arms. "But I don't know how much help I can be."

Reverend Kamora aimed his eyes at Mimi. "Miss Rosen, when we first met, I said God has a reason for me to meet every person. I feel there is a reason I met you. Anita tells me that you once solved a crime."

"Yes." Mimi straightened her back. "My cousin's murder."

"Really?" he said. "You solved a murder?"

Jeez, Mimi thought. *Even Reverend Kamora doesn't believe me.*

"It's a long story," Mimi said.

"Speaking of stories," Reverend Kamora said, "have I ever told you how I become associated with Mr. Boasberg?"

"No."

"After I found the diamond, I had no idea what to do with it. A million options presented themselves, but none seemed to realize its potential. I prayed to God for guidance.

"The next day, I was walking down the street, and I saw a newspaper on the ground. Something told me to pick it up. There was an interview with Mr. Boasberg, discussing his plans to market our country's diamonds as a symbol of hope. When I saw that, I knew that God had led me to that article, and that diamond, for a purpose. As Mr. Boasberg said, it was *bashert*."

That earned a smile from Mimi. "Seems like it."

"Now that he's gone, I can't let his dream die too. Mr. Boasberg wouldn't want that. The people back home wouldn't want it either. Have you ever been to my country?"

"No," Mimi said.

Reverend Kamora's normally soft voice rose a notch. "It is very different from here. A lot of the time, people go hungry. When I enter a beautiful shop like this, and I see people leaving large plates of food uneaten, it feels like a place of fantasy.

"I always thought finding that diamond was a miracle. So, I'm praying for miracle number two. This diamond is not just important to me. It is important to the citizens of my country. They are poor people, desperate for help. Whatever assistance you can provide, I would be eternally grateful."

There was no way Mimi could resist his plea—or him. Reverend Kamora sure knew how to press her guilt buttons. He should get together with her dad.

"All right," she sighed. "I'll help."

He smiled. "That warms my heart, more than you'll ever know. May God bless you."

Anita's face took on a look of grim determination. "So, what do we do now?"

Mimi thought for a second. "A friend of mine, Paul Michelson, owns a grading lab. He might be able to shed light on how to track a stolen diamond. And of course, we need to interview Morris Novak."

"He won't talk," Anita said. "I tried to get him for my documentary. I couldn't even figure out how to reach him."

"You know who might know?" Mimi said. "Boasberg's son, Rafi. Novak's his stepfather."

"How do we talk with Rafi?" Anita asked.

"My friend knows his family and said they're sitting *shiva* tonight," Mimi said.

"What's a *shiva*?" He asked.

"It's a Jewish mourning ritual," said Mimi. "It's when the local community gets together to comfort people who have suffered a loss. Let me find out where it's happening."

She dialed Channah and told her she'd agreed to help investigate Boasberg's murder.

Channah laughed. "I knew you would!"

"You said you were going to Boasberg's *shiva* tonight. I'd like to go, too."

Channah texted her Boasberg's address in Brooklyn. Reverend Kamora was too tired to attend, but Anita was eager to tag along. "It's right near my apartment in Williamsburg," she burbled.

This gave Mimi pause. "Do you really think you should come?"

Anita looked puzzled. "Why not?"

"This is Abraham Boasberg's *shiva*. Brandon has been arrested for his murder. And you're making a documentary about Brandon. Don't you think that will be awkward?"

Anita brushed this off with a flick off her hand. "Not at all. Brandon is innocent."

Mimi didn't press the point. But she thought, *this could get weird.*

CHAPTER NINE

THE SUBWAY RIDE TO BROOKLYN took forty-five minutes. On the way, Anita and Mimi didn't talk much about Brandon or the murder—though Mimi could see that was weighing on Anita's mind, as it was on hers. Instead, they talked about their reporting careers—even if, in Mimi's case, it was her old career.

They both lamented how journalism had become faster, clickier, and shallower. And it had, though Mimi recalled having the exact same conversations with her newspaper colleagues a decade ago. They had both encountered their share of sexism. And they both agreed that, for all its faults, reporting was a great way to make a living because it involved constantly learning, and what could be better than that.

At one point, Mimi declared that she got into journalism to change the world. That was true, though Anita responded with a not-particularly-discreet smirk. This upset Mimi—though it took her half the subway ride to figure out why: Anita was just like her—the old her.

Back in the day, Mimi was just as idealistic. She was determined to change the world and was convinced the world couldn't stop her. If someone from a diamond company had told the old Mimi what she'd just told Anita, she'd probably snicker, too.

Over time, Mimi had grown more practical, less judgmental. She better understood the need for compromise since she'd been forced to do it so many times. In the old days, she'd scoff and crack wise when she visited her father's office. Now, she worked there.

While she still wanted to make a difference, most days, she wasn't trying to change the world. She was just trying to survive.

A year of working on the ethical diamond project had left her mostly frustrated and dejected. And while Mimi used to volunteer for good causes, that had lately skidded down the priority list, and become something that she *wanted* to do, rather than something she did, like vacuuming behind her couch or taking up tennis.

Mimi believed she was a good person, and a caring one. She was kind to the people in her life. She tried not to hurt anyone. Wasn't that enough? She thought so. Then she'd listen to Reverend Kamora, and think: maybe not.

Boasberg's *shiva* was held at his two-story brownstone. It was an impressive house, considering only one person lived there—and while it wasn't overly ostentatious, it sent the clear message that its owner had money. It had a bigger, lusher garden than the houses surrounding it, a larger front door, higher gates.

Inside, the walls were studded with pictures—mostly shots of Boasberg with local dignitaries, interspersed with the occasional shot of Rafi. No doubt the humanitarian award from the conference would have occupied a particular place of honor.

As they entered, Anita pulled out her tape recorder. "Possible documentary subject: Grieving rituals. Are they outdated? Have they adapted to changing times?"

Mimi spotted Channah's parents. Her short stout mom gave her a tight hug. Her father was dressed in a suit and looked dapper in his silver *yarmulke* and trimmed white beard.

They talked a little bit about Mimi, and a lot about Channah.

"She's doing better, *Baruch Hashem,*" her father said. "Much better than last year. That's one less thing to worry about."

Her mother gave a knowing grin. "Actually, tonight, she's doing better than we ever thought."

"What do you mean?" Mimi asked.

"She's in the other room," said her father, "having a long conversation with Rafi Boasberg. A *very* long conversation."

"She's more than talking," the mom said. "She appears to be—" She hesitated a second, as if she couldn't believe what she was saying. "Flirting."

IN THE LIVING ROOM, RAFI SAT GLUMLY on a low chair, while a sea of visitors milled around him, eating, and talking. The side of his shirt was ripped, in line with the customary rending of garments when a family member dies. Channah was perched on a folding chair next to him, excitedly chatting, her hands flapping in the air. She *was* flirting—and not being subtle about it.

Mimi was happy Channah had found someone she liked. But was a *shiva* the right place to show it?

Anita and Mimi walked over to Rafi and offered their condolences. Anita gave Mimi a small shove, so she was standing right in front of him.

"I'm Anita Vaz. I'm an award-winning documentarian. I saw your father speak at the responsible sourcing conference. I'm making a film about the problems in Africa."

Well, Mimi thought. *That's one way to put it.*

Anita crouched down so she was face-to-face with Rafi. "I'm sorry to hear about your loss. How are you doing?"

"I'm okay," Rafi shrugged. "It's weird thinking that my dad is no longer with us. It hasn't sunk in. I'm going to miss him."

"I'm sure it's hard," Anita said. "At the conference, the two of you seemed close."

"Actually," Rafi rubbed his forehead, "we only recently reconciled. We didn't talk for years."

Anita kept her focus on him. "I'm sorry to hear that."

"I'm sorry to hear it, too," Channah added, visibly upset that Rafi was no longer paying attention to her.

"We used to be close," Rafi said. "It's a long story."

"If you want to talk about it, I'm happy to listen," Anita said.

"I'm happy to listen, too," Channah added, craning her neck to make sure Rafi was aware of her existence.

Rafi's eyes didn't leave Anita. "My father used to be partners with Morris Novak, the big diamond guy. Morris would source the goods from Africa, and my father was responsible for selling them.

"My dad insisted I come into the business after college. After a year or so, they sent me to the African Diamond Republic on a diamond-buying trip. They acted like I was getting the keys to the castle. Instead, it opened my eyes.

"We came to the ADR with these big suitcases of cash and bought every diamond super-cheap. We took advantage of those poor miners who had no idea how much their diamonds were worth. Novak was thrilled. He couldn't believe how much money we were making. I couldn't believe the poverty I saw. I had never seen a country like that. And we were zipping in and out of there on private jets, staying at five-star hotels, and leaving richer than we came. The flight back was seventeen hours, and I didn't sleep the whole time."

"At the airport, Novak ordered me to hide the diamonds in my coat. He said because we didn't export the goods with the proper Kimberley Process paperwork, we had no choice but to sneak them through Customs. That was the last straw. On top of everything else, he wanted me to commit a crime. I let Novak know what I thought about him and got fired on the spot.

"When my father asked me what happened, I told him I hated how they did business, and I never wanted to speak to him again. He looked so hurt by that, I thought he was going to cry. I didn't care. I was so angry."

He took a breath. "Then came the divorce." His head turned down, then his eyes floated up to Anita's, like he wanted her to ask about it.

"My parents also split." Anita said. "It wasn't easy."

"While my parents are together," Channah declared, "I'm sure if they divorced, I'd find it difficult."

"Their divorce was particularly painful," Rafi sulked. "I caused it."

"You shouldn't blame yourself," Anita said.

"Yes, don't blame yourself," echoed Channah, though by that point, no one was listening.

"But I *did* cause it," Rafi said. "After I was fired, my father had a huge fight with Novak, and they broke up the partnership. My mother thought he was crazy to leave such a successful business, so she tried to patch things up between the two of them. She reached out to Novak, and let's just say they hit it off. They got married a year later.

"It's crazy. When I worked for Morris Novak, I hated his guts. Now, he's my stepfather." Rafi's mouth formed a semicircle. "I didn't speak to my parents for years."

Mimi felt a sudden stab of guilt. She had considered the story of Boasberg's wife marrying Novak as a juicy soap opera. Now, she saw it as a sad event, which happened to real people, with real consequences.

"You don't know what was happening behind the scenes," Anita said. "In the end, people are responsible for their own behavior."

Mimi was impressed by the way Anita was slowly, methodically, getting Rafi to spill his guts.

Channah, on the other hand, regarded her with hard eyes. Mimi felt for her friend; Rafi was the first guy she'd showed any interest in since Yosef died. And here was this chic, pretty woman, swooping in and stealing him.

"For a couple of years," Rafi said, "I travelled around, being a bum. I didn't want my parents' money. I considered it tainted. So, I worked different jobs. It was weird; I was the stepson of a billionaire, and to make money, I'd wash dishes and sleep outside."

"When I got really desperate, I sold pot. It was just like the diamond business: buy low, sell high. Literally." He cackled. "But I wasn't careful and got arrested. The cop told me I was the first drug dealer he'd arrested with a *yarmulke*.

"Fortunately, my mom hired fancy lawyers, and I got a slap on the wrist. But I came close to screwing up my life. It was scary for a while."

"It's okay. You made a mistake," Anita said, in soothing maternal tones. "We all make mistakes. It's nothing to be ashamed of."

Rafi lifted his shoulders to his ears. "It's nothing to throw a party about, either. It caused a lot of pain for my parents." He leaned back on his chair. "Anyway, you can't change the past. You can only work to make things better. That's what my father tried to do."

"Is that why he did the Hope for Humanity Diamond?" Anita asked.

"I think so," Rafi said. "My father was a complicated guy. I can't say I fully understood him. When he first started talking about it, I thought it was just a ploy to get on my good side, to stick it to my mom and stepfather. And maybe that's what it was, originally.

"But he became real passionate about it. You saw how he was at the conference. He was like that all the time. That diamond became everything to him. It gave him the chance to do something truly meaningful. And how many times do you get that in life?"

Rafi rested his hand on his chin. "It's weird. I inspired my dad to do this project. Now, it's up to me to carry it out. And I don't know if I can match my father's passion or energy." He frowned. "It doesn't help that my stepfather hates the idea."

"Why?" Mimi asked.

Rafi clicked his tongue. "Think about it. When my father talked about dealers robbing the country blind, who was he talking about? Guys like Novak. The Hope for Humanity is a direct threat to his business model.

"He knows that if the diamond makes more money for the local community, a lot more ADR diamonds will be sold that way. And Novak isn't interested in diamonds that benefit Africa. He only wants diamonds that benefit him.

"Novak even came to the conference to try to talk my father out of it. They hadn't spoken in years. Of course, my father told him to shove off."

Anita inched closer to him. "Rafi, you seem to have a contentious relationship with your stepfather."

"That's putting it mildly," he laughed.

"Have you ever considered that your stepfather may have had something to do with what happened to your dad?"

He perked up. "I've more than considered it. I believe it."

Anita's face flashed surprise. "Really?"

"Not many people hated my father more than Morris Novak. Maybe my mom." He let out of a small cackle.

"Did you tell the police this?" Anita asked.

"Of course, I did," Rafi pouted. "But they told me there's no proof that my stepfather was involved. They said all the evidence points to Brandon Walters. They didn't even care about the money I wired."

Mimi's antenna perked up. "What money?"

"The day my father died, he asked me to send money to this company in the ADR, Merlano Resources. He said, 'make it look like it didn't come from us.' I said, 'isn't that counter to all the stuff we've been preaching, about openness and transparency?' He said, 'in this case, we have to keep it secret.'"

"Have you ever dealt with that company before?" Mimi asked.

"Me? No."

"Do you know who owns it?"

"Nope." He lowered his head. "But the only person I know who owns companies in the ADR is my stepfather."

"Rafi, I have something to tell you," Anita said. "I am friends with Brandon Walters. I don't believe he killed your father. I think your stepfather set him up. I just can't prove it." She let this sink in.

"I don't know if you're aware, but the day your dad died, he texted Brandon and said he had information for him. So, Brandon went to his office, figuring he would get dirt on your stepfather. Then, well, you know what happened. That's a huge red flag. Your father is killed, just as he's about to spill the beans."

"Wow!" Rafi said, his eyes wide. "Have you told the police this?"

"Brandon did, a million times," she said. "They didn't care. They believe they've caught their killer, and you can't convince them otherwise."

Anita leaned forward. "Rafi, you said you wanted to carry on your father's legacy. Your father was about to tell what he knew about Novak. You saw Novak engage in rampant smuggling. Would you be interested in discussing that in my documentary?"

Rafi's face became cloaked with fear. "No way. I don't want to cross my stepfather. He's a powerful guy. And vindictive."

"I always thought Novak married my mother to get back at my dad for breaking up their partnership. His pride couldn't handle anyone walking out on him. When Novak and my mom got married, it completely destroyed my father, not that he ever talked about it."

"I would never want Novak as an enemy," Rafi continued. "Especially not after what just happened."

"I understand that but—" Anita looked ready to push him, then reigned herself in. "Any information you could provide would be really helpful. Right now, Brandon's sitting in jail, and he's completely innocent. He doesn't even have money for bail or a lawyer."

Rafi scratched his forehead. "I can help with that."

"Really?" Anita's eyes almost popped.

"Sure," Rafi said. "I'll put up his bail. I'll even fund his defense."

Anita was taken aback. "I can't ask you to do that. That might be a lot of money."

"It's no big deal," Rafi shrugged. "I'm my father's only heir. I'm loaded now."

Before they left, Mimi told Rafi that she wanted to speak with Morris Novak. Rafi didn't have his stepfather's phone number, but provided his mom's. Mimi called her the second she left the house.

When Rafi's mother picked up, her New York accent was so loud and piercing, Mimi had to move the phone from her ear.

"Hello, Mrs. Novak," Mimi said. "I was wondering if you could put me in touch with your husband, Morris."

"He's not here," the voice said. "Who's this?"

"I'm Mimi Rosen, a friend of your son, Rafi."

"And what do you want with my husband?" the voice demanded.

"I'm working on a documentary—"

The minute Mimi uttered the word *documentary*, Rafi's mom hung up.

CHAPTER TEN

THE NEXT MORNING, Mimi called Paul Michelson. That always made her nervous.

Paul was a childhood friend that Mimi had reconnected with when she investigated her cousin's murder. They went on one short, but sweet date. He was the only guy she'd been interested in since her divorce.

Yet, things never gelled, and Mimi could never understand why. Right after the case wrapped up, Paul launched his own gem lab, which consumed his days and nights. That didn't leave time for Mimi.

They periodically called each other, just to check in. That made Mimi think—or maybe just hope—there was still something between them.

This morning, she hoped he'd tell her how to find the missing diamond.

"Hey Mimi," Paul said brightly. "I was just thinking about you."

"You were?" Mimi asked, her voice rising.

"Yeah, I was reading about this murder on Forty-Seventh Street," he said. "And of course, that made me think of you."

Mimi suddenly realized something she probably should have grasped long ago. Yosef's murder was a scary time for Paul. That was his main association with Mimi. Which might be why they kept making plans, and he kept cancelling. He wanted to forget.

"That's what I'm calling about," Mimi said. "This big diamond was stolen from that guy's office."

"Yep. A sixty-six carat D Flawless. You don't see those every day." Even after all his years in the industry, Paul still geeked out about gemstones. Mimi found that charming.

"I've talked to the Reverend who was selling it, and he's beside himself. Do you have any advice on how he can get it back?"

Paul snickered. "Not really. It's tough to do. By now, that stone's probably been cut into smaller pieces."

"But doesn't that make it less valuable?"

"Of course. But it also makes it harder to trace."

"So, there's no way to find it?"

"Even if you do, if it was recut, you have to prove it's the same stone in court. So, what usually happens is the lawyers hire experts to testify that it's the same diamond, or that it isn't. The case drags on for about a year, and by the end, the lawyers get rich and everyone else is so exhausted and angry they just split the money and go home." He paused. "Why are you interested? You aren't trying to help find the diamond, are you?"

A wave of stress came over her. "Kind of."

"But isn't that—" said Paul, his tone sharper. "You told me you weren't investigating murders anymore."

Jeez. Mimi groaned to herself. *Why does everyone have that reaction?*

"I wasn't planning on it," Mimi said. "Someone asked me to."

"Right," he scoffed, adding a bitter chuckle. "Another murder investigation just fell in your lap."

"It did!" Mimi said.

"You realize that doesn't happen to normal people?" He sounded exasperated. "I would never get involved in another murder investigation. I've had my fill, thank you. But do what you want. It's your life."

For a moment, neither said anything.

"You're right," Mimi said. "It is."

And with that, Mimi hung up. She no longer cared if there was something there between her and Paul. It was no longer there for her.

When Mimi arrived at work, she gave Channah her customary hello hug. It was Friday, and as Max predicted, Sol was back. The two of them could be heard squabbling from the reception area.

"They won't stop arguing about that pear shape." Channah pointed her eyes skyward. "I swear, if there was a nuclear holocaust and they were the only two survivors, they'd still be negotiating the price of that diamond."

Mimi laughed. "It never ends." She felt a little awkward broaching this next subject, but knew she had to. "Last night, it seemed like you were flirting with Rafi Boasberg."

A blush crept up Channah's neck. "Was I that obvious?" she laughed. "My parents noticed, too."

"Rafi's a nice guy. I'm happy you found someone you like, but—" Mimi hesitated.

Channah sighed. "There's always a but."

"I feel bad saying this, but are you sure it was appropriate to act that way at a *shiva*?"

Channah's eyes flicked down. "You're right. I was so excited to see Rafi again, and it was so nice catching up, I felt like we were back in high school, when I had a crush on him. I guess I got carried away." She frowned. "I'll cancel our date."

This threw Mimi for a loop. "What date?"

"Rafi asked me out after you left."

"But it seemed like—"

"Yeah, I thought he was blowing me off, too. He seemed into that Anita girl. In the end, he's a *frum* boy. He wouldn't go for her. He may not love his family, but he doesn't want to get disowned.

"Besides, it turned out we have a lot in common. After you left, we had this long talk about grief, how hard it is to accept when someone close to you dies, how they feel always present and always absent. It's not how I dreamed I'd bond with a guy, over depression and intense grief." She threw up her hands. "But hey. Whatever works." She picked up her phone. "Anyway, I'll call it off."

Mimi reached out to stop her. "No, no, if he asked you out, that's okay." She smiled. "It's more than okay, it's great. Let me know how it goes."

The office phone rang. Channah answered, then passed the call over to Max. As Mimi walked to her desk, she saw her red-faced father screaming on the phone.

"You people are criminals! You're thieves!" Veins bulged in his neck. "Yeah, yeah, yeah. Have a rotten day." He slammed down the receiver.

Sol, sitting on a chair in front of Max's desk with his legs crossed, watched this in horror. "That was strong, Maxie. Who was that?"

"The *ganefs* who own the building," Max said. "Neighborhood Properties. They've jacked up the rent twenty percent."

"Twenty percent!" Sol said, disgust wafting over his face. "That's highway robbery, Maxie."

"No kidding. I knew something like this was coming, but that's just nuts. I asked the woman if they would cut the price twenty-five dollars.

She said, 'I won't go down twenty-five cents.'" Max stared into space. "There's no way I can afford what they're asking."

Mimi's stomach turned. If her father couldn't pay his rent, she'd be out of work again. She'd have to go back on unemployment, back to living on credit cards, back to struggling to pay bills. Working on Anita's documentary now seemed a much more enticing option.

"What are you going to do?" Sol asked.

"Who knows? I'll figure out something."

"Of course, you will, Maxie," Sol said. "You're a survivor. You've been in this game for how many years?"

"Too many." Max waved his hand.

"Worse comes to worse, I have space in my office," Sol said. "You can work out of there."

"I appreciate the offer, but we'd kill each other."

Sol nodded. "That would be a downside."

"Besides, they'll kick you out next."

"We gotta face it, Maxie," Sol said. "Forty-Seventh Street's changing. Morris Novak's gonna kill us all."

Mimi's ears perked up. "What does Morris Novak have to do with this?"

Max scowled. "He's become a major player in real estate. The word is, he's bought a lot of property on The Street. People say he bought this building, but no one really knows."

"So, you don't know who your landlord is?" Mimi asked.

"Guys like Novak, they use a million shell companies to hide everything," Max said. "They don't like people knowing how rich they are. Particularly tax people."

Sol turned toward Mimi. "You see those boarded-up stores downstairs? According to the grapevine, Novak bought all those buildings, then kicked everyone out. He promised he'd build this beautiful new skyscraper that would be nothing but diamond companies. But no one could afford the prices he was asking."

"So, all of a sudden, he had an excuse to change plans. Now, he's going to build a fancy hotel. Right in the middle of the block. And if that's successful, I guarantee, the whole street will be hotels. And that'll be the end of the Diamond District. No one will be here but the largest companies."

"It's sad," Max said, leaning back on his chair. "When I was a kid, New York had a toy district, a flower district, a photography district. They were communities like Forty-Seventh Street, where everyone knew each other. Then the developers drove everyone out. Now, they're just blocks, like any other."

"That'll happen to Forty-Seventh Street eventually. We're right in the heart of midtown Manhattan. This is prime real estate. They can make a lot more money renting out offices to fancy law firms than they can to guys like me."

"They need those law firms, Maxie," Sol said. "Someone has to handle the evictions."

"Can't the industry fight him?" Mimi asked.

"*Eh*, we can't do anything," Max said. "We're the *schnooks* who invited him in. He only got control of those buildings because he had connections. Everyone thought, he's a diamond guy. He'll do right by us. Now, we know he's just another lying *mamzer*. His old friends mean nothing to him. He thinks he's too high-class."

"You see him today, he goes around with this ultra-polished speaking style, like he went to some private academy. I've known him for years. He was a kid from the Bronx. He went to a *yeshiva*, like the rest of us."

"When he was young and starting out, I helped him get established. Now, I'm just another *pisher* he wants to kick out on the street." Max chewed his lower lip, mulling his new place on the bottom of the food chain.

Sol hated seeing his friend so sad. He sat forward on his chair. "Maxie, since you have to make this big rent payment, you want to meet my price on the two-carat pear shape?"

This stirred Max back to life, as it was intended to. Max aimed at finger at Sol. "Actually, now I'm *less* likely to meet your price. I'm being robbed by my landlord. I'm not gonna be robbed by you, too."

They were off to the races, again.

Mimi's weekend would now be spent updating her resume. She had another project, which she was far more excited about: discovering if Morris Novak was her father's landlord.

That night, Mimi scoured Google for info on Morris Novak. Two things became clear. First, he was quite rich; one list called him the world's six-hundred-and-second richest person. Second, he was quite good at avoiding the spotlight. He seemed to have no firm home; he was supposedly based out of London, Switzerland, Dubai, Israel, Russia, and New York. He apparently lived on a plane—a private one.

When Novak first started buying diamonds in Africa, he styled himself as a reformer, a socially enlightened alternative to the Vanderklef cartel, which then had a stranglehold on the world's diamond supply. He promised to bring jobs and benefits to the countries where he did business.

Then, human rights groups soured on him, especially one persistent critic—Brandon Walters.

Novak was the subject of Brandon's first exposé—released when other activists were too scared to visit the ADR. It noted that one of Novak's employees was arrested trying to smuggle diamonds into the United States, leading the ADR government to temporarily crack down on local dealers sneaking stones over the border.

"What was striking," Brandon wrote, "was that even though one of Novak's people was caught in the act, the ADR authorities didn't arrest anyone connected with Novak, or any of his shell companies. They only nabbed his smaller competitors, effectively driving them out of business and out of the country."

"That had the twin effects of making the government look like it cared about corruption in the gem sector—which, of course, it didn't—while serving Novak's interests, by removing his competitors. Since Novak was the one caught doing something wrong, we must ask: why does the government protect him like it does? Why is it so deferential to the most corrupt player in its midst?"

Novak did appear to be making some rudimentary attempts at damage control. When Mimi Googled his name, up popped ads for the Morris and Sonia Novak Foundation, which featured glossy pages detailing his charitable works, accompanied by photos of smiling African kids. Reading it, you'd think he'd given all his money away. He must have some left over for those private jets.

New York newspapers periodically printed stories that the "shadowy press-shy billionaire" was snatching up prime Manhattan real estate. But they added, just like Max did, it was impossible to determine what he actually owned.

Mimi decided to give it a shot.

She started with Neighborhood Properties, the new owner of her father's building. She couldn't find much information on it, though a lot of people hated it on Yelp. Its website called it a "family business" that managed several properties on Forty-Seventh Street. It didn't say what family.

She looked up her building's address at the New York City Department of Buildings. It listed Neighborhood Properties as a division of another company, Northside Projects. She checked state business records, and found that Northside Projects was owned by another company, Nexus Partners. All these bland, nondescript names had to be hiding something.

Mimi searched New York State court records and saw that Nexus Partners frequently tried to evict tenants. On one rare occasion, a renter fought back, and Nexus Partners was forced to disclose that its corporate owner was New Prometheus Consultants, based on the Caribbean island of Nivens.

Why would a family real estate business be based in the Caribbean? She became even more suspicious when she called up New Prometheus' website.

"We are a financial planning service for high net-worth individuals with special needs looking for discretion," it said. "We are not regulated and do not intend to seek regulation."

My God, Mimi thought. *This company's address might as well be Welaundermoney.com.*

She tried to look up New Prometheus in Nivens' company registry—and discovered Nivens didn't have one. She hunted for clues on the New Prometheus website. She Googled its IP address. That led her to an IP directory, which listed a cluster of sites that shared New Prometheus' server.

One, for a company named Natural Promise, had an almost-identical website to New Prometheus, and touted similar financial shenanigans. It was also based in the Caribbean, in the Caspian Islands, but listed a branch office on Nivens, with the same address as New Prometheus. Their sites were registered the same day. Looked like a match.

The Caspian Islands did have an online business registry, but it made users cough up thirty-five dollars per search. That wasn't a huge chunk of change, but Mimi wasn't exactly feeling flush lately. Spending that would mean she'd have to skip a takeout lunch or two. She ponied up the cash regardless.

That listing said Natural Promise was owned by yet another company, Noble Pegasus, based in Panama. Mimi felt trapped in an endless maze designed to confuse her. Every time she switched on the light in one dark room, it led to another.

Mimi called up the Panama Papers, the massive leak of a law firm's ledgers that listed the previously hidden owners of offshore companies.

Noble Pegasus was in there. *Thanks, anonymous person, who stole all that data!*

The Panama Papers linked Noble Pegasus to another company, and then another, which was connected through an intermediary to a third, which—at last—showed the name she was looking for: Morris Novak. The marathon game of hide and seek was over, and Mimi had finally discovered her quarry, crouching behind the curtains.

She stretched and checked the clock. It was two in the morning. She had been at this for six hours and ended up just where she expected.

Mimi's back felt stiff from all that time hunched over a laptop. She craned her arm over her shoulder to give herself a self-massage, which wasn't exactly satisfying. She did feel a small sense of accomplishment; she had uncovered a vast, secretive world from her kitchen table. She just had no idea what to do with this info.

She knew Novak was her father's landlord. So what? There's no rule that building owners have to speak with their tenants. Maybe all her work was for nothing.

Then it hit her: all that work would be her way in.

CHAPTER ELEVEN

MIMI GUESSED NOVAK WAS THE KIND OF GUY who came to the office early. Monday morning, she dragged herself out of bed at six a.m. An hour later, she was sitting on a bench in front of the sleek blue skyscraper that housed Neighborhood Properties. Which was just in time.

At seven-fifteen, a black sedan pulled up. The driver opened the rear door, and Novak stepped out, one spaghetti leg after another. He briskly walked into the building, tailed by his bodyguard.

Mimi hopped off the bench and scurried behind them, but they were walking too fast for her to catch up. She cried out "Mr. Novak! Morris!" He may have turned his head; she wasn't sure. In any case, he kept walking. Mimi pulled out her phone, snapped a picture of the back of his head, and followed him into the building.

There, she lost him. He was nowhere to be found in the vast, cavernous lobby. Maybe he had his own private elevator.

In any case, Novak was in the building. Time for Plan B.

THE OFFICES FOR NEIGHBORHOOD PROPERTIES took up three floors and were way too lavish for a family business that just owned a handful of buildings on Forty-Seventh Street. The sign on the door read, "NP Inc." That could stand for Neighborhood Properties. Or New Prometheus. Or Novak's Playthings.

The reception area was large, sterile, and quiet. Its walls were adorned with large black-and-white photos of the New York skyline. It offered few clues to what the company did. It was designed to both intimidate and obfuscate.

A middle-aged receptionist sat behind a glass window, wearing a gray dress and thick glasses. A telephone headset was wrapped around her skull, and a strand of pearls hung from her neck. She reluctantly slid opened the glass to talk to Mimi.

"I have a question about my rent," Mimi said. "I'd like to speak to Morris Novak."

The woman tilted her jaw upward, so she was literally looking down her nose at Mimi. "I'm sorry. There is no one here by that name."

"Morris Novak doesn't own the company?"

"Neighborhood Properties is a family-owned company," she said, sounding rehearsed.

"What family owns it?"

The receptionist sniffed. "I am not authorized to provide that information. We're a private company."

"It's okay. I know Morris Novak owns it."

"Ma'am, I told you cannot say—"

"You don't have to say anything. I know he's the owner. I can show you proof."

She plucked a folder from her purse. Mimi methodically laid documents on the receptionist's desk, narrating her journey from Neighborhood Properties to New Nexus Whatever to the Panama Papers to the doorstep of Morris Novak.

The receptionist's eyes bulged but she said nothing.

"Morris Novak owns this company," Mimi declared with a touch of pride. "And I want to talk with him."

The woman kept her cool. "While I cannot confirm or deny that Mr. Novak has a stake in this business, I can tell you that no one by that name is currently in the office."

Mimi scooped up the documents and stuffed them back in her purse. "And I can confirm that you're lying. I've been waiting outside this building since early this morning. I saw Morris Novak come in an hour ago. Unfortunately, I didn't get a chance to say hello." She pulled out her phone. "But here's the picture I took. Along with the time- and date-stamp."

The receptionist stared at the picture, baffled. "That's just the back of someone's head."

"It's the back of Morris Novak's head."

"You can't prove that."

"Look at the picture. That's a red and yellow *yarmulke*. Isn't that what he wore this morning?"

"Ma'am, I don't know the color of his *yarmulke*."

Mimi smiled. "You just confirmed he's in the office."

The receptionist offered no response.

"I want to talk to Morris Novak," Mimi insisted, surprising herself with her firmness.

The receptionist picked up the phone. "I'm calling security."

"Go ahead. And I'll call the media. Reporters might be interested why a so-called family real estate business is owned by offshore companies that don't want to be regulated."

The receptionist mulled this over. "I'll call the executive office. Please note that, my placing this call does not constitute any acknowledgement that anything you have said is accurate."

Mimi rolled her eyes.

With obvious annoyance, the receptionist pressed a few numbers. She muttered into her headset, "Can I speak to—" She dropped her voice. "Mr. N.?"

There was a pause. "There's a woman in the reception area. She has all these documents that says he owns this company, and wants to speak with him, and says otherwise she's calling the media." Another pause. "I told her that, but she claims she has a picture of him entering the building this morning." She lowered her voice further. "She knows the color of his *yarmulke*."

After a moment, the receptionist gazed up at Mimi. "What is your name and purpose of your visit?"

"I'm Mimi Rosen. I work for the Max Rosen Diamond Company at Four-Sixty Fifth Avenue. I have an issue with our rent increase."

The receptionist listened intently to the voice on the other end, avoiding Mimi's gaze. "Our chief operating officer will be right with you," she said finally.

"I don't want to talk with him." Mimi had no idea if the chief operating officer was a man, but that seemed a safe bet. "I want to speak to Morris Novak," she declared, as loudly as possible, "I'm also interested in his corrupt diamond dealings in the African Democratic Republic."

The voice on the phone must have caught that because Mimi heard screaming coming from the headset.

The receptionist hung up the phone, and declared with a snarl, "please wait on the couch."

Mimi settled on the leather sofa . . . where she waited . . . and waited. As time dragged on, she worried she'd stay there all day. But after forty-five minutes, Novak's executive assistant strode out to greet her. She was young, bleach-blonde, and moved with speed and purpose. She didn't offer her hand, just said in the most businesslike voice possible, "follow me, Miss Rosen," then spun around.

Mimi trailed the assistant as she wordlessly walked out of the reception area, then marched through the endless maze of an office, her ID electronically opening one door after another. They climbed down a staircase, rushed down a hallway past clusters of offices, along with a glass-enclosed bullpen, filled with benches of people sorting diamonds.

Finally, they arrived at a giant executive office. It held a mahogany desk, which a petite woman sat behind, and a metal door, guarded by a burly man. The walls were dotted with paintings in heavy wooden frames. Mimi couldn't really see the artwork, but the selection seemed odd and random: some pictures were modern art, others old, a few vaguely familiar. All were, undoubtedly, expensive.

The executive assistant nodded to the woman behind the desk, who nodded to the guard, who unfolded his arms and slowly opened the door. Mimi felt like she was in Oz, about to meet the Wizard.

CHAPTER TWELVE

MORRIS NOVAK STOOD AT HIS DESK in a brown tailored suit. Like everyone else at Neighborhood Properties, Novak wasn't acting particularly neighborly this morning. After the guard closed the door, Novak wordlessly motioned to Mimi to sit on the couch in front of his desk. Then he sat down, stretched his long torso over his desk, and clasped his hands together.

"Miss Rosen, I wish I could say I'm happy to see you again. But I don't appreciate people making baseless charges to my receptionist."

"I wanted to get your attention."

"You've gotten it." He swerved his chair toward his computer and typed on his keyboard. "I'll certainly remember it when your father's rent comes due, and he begs for an extension. I hope this isn't some hairbrained scheme to lower your father's rent by threatening to reveal my building ownership."

"No," Mimi said, stunned. "I didn't think of that. But now that you mention it—"

"It would be considered blackmail," he said icily. "I'd have you arrested, instantly."

"Yes, of course." She shifted on the couch. "That's not why I'm here. Mr. Novak—can I call you Morris?"

He didn't blink. "No."

"I am investigating the murder of Abraham Boasberg."

He inclined his head. "Are you a private investigator?"

"I'm a journalist." She fished her notebook from her purse, and threw it open, so she'd look more reporter-y. "I'm the head of research for a documentary on—" She hesitated. "—the problems in Africa."

"Is this a documentary for a studio?"

"For now, it's independent." Mimi smoothed her skirt. "It's directed by Anita Vaz. She's an award-winning documentarian."

"I don't know her. What awards has she won?"

"One of her films was named top documentary at the Central New Jersey Film Festival."

"I've never heard of that."

"It's a film festival in Central New Jersey."

"Thanks for clearing that up." He reclined on his chair. "When we first met, you told me that you worked for your father's diamond company. It doesn't seem like you are affiliated with any reputable or established journalistic organization. So, it's kind of a stretch to call yourself a journalist, isn't it?"

Mimi's throat constricted. "I might not be working as a journalist right this moment, but I have good credentials. I worked for a newspaper for nine years. I once solved a murder."

"Oh please. You solved a murder? That's a little far-fetched."

"Why doesn't anyone believe that?" Mimi snapped. She took out her phone. "It's true! I can show you clips!"

Novak gave a self-satisfied smile. "No need. I've looked you up. I read all about the case. Impressive work."

Mimi blinked hard. "So, how come—"

He cut her off. "Why are you here, Miss Rosen?"

"I was curious about something you told me at the diamond conference. You said that Brandon Walters would soon get in a great deal of trouble."

He half-shrugged. "Sounds like something I'd say."

"I thought it a little strange that you would say that, and then, one day later, Brandon gets arrested for murder."

His eyebrows climbed. "How so?"

"It's a pretty big coincidence."

"Not really. Brandon Walters is an obvious bad seed."

"Why did you think he was about to get into trouble?"

"I was planning to sue him for defamation. I've had my lawyers threaten him on numerous occasions but his question at the conference was the last straw. Of course, now that he's been arrested, there's little point in a lawsuit. He's saved me a lot of time and money. If it wasn't for the fact that he murdered my ex-partner, I'd probably be grateful."

Mimi tapped her pen against her notebook. "So, let's talk about your ex-partner, Abraham Boasberg. You worked together for a long time."

"Almost twenty years."

Mimi was about to follow up, then held off. Her old editor used to preach that silence was a journalist's best friend. When reporters don't talk, sources feel compelled to fill the gap. And, to Mimi's surprise, Novak began filling this one.

"For a while, Abraham and I did quite well together. Mind you, I did most of the real work. But as you may have surmised from that little show he put on at the conference, Abraham can be quite a passionate and effective salesman. You know the old expression: he can sell ice to Eskimos. Abraham could do that. The problem was, afterward, he'd buy himself the biggest freezer."

"I understand that in recent years, you didn't get along with him. Why was that?"

"I married his former wife. Generally, that's enough."

Mimi clicked her pen. "Can you tell me where you were when Mr. Boasberg was murdered? It happened on Wednesday night, at around seven p.m."

"Let me see, Wednesday night at seven?" Novak brought his finger to his chin. "I believe I was in the conservatory."

"The conservatory?"

"Yes. I was with Professor Plum. We had just killed Colonel Mustard with a candlestick."

Mimi glared at him. "I guess this is a joke to you."

He steepled his fingers before his face. "I can't see why I should treat your questions as anything but. The police have arrested the murderer."

"The police don't always get it right."

"True. Why do you think they have it wrong here?"

"They may have been paid off. By someone rich and powerful."

"Intriguing theory." Novak snickered. "Do you have proof of it?"

"No," Mimi said, almost under her breath. "I didn't say I believed it. That's Brandon Walters' theory."

"Hmm." He massaged his chin. "This may surprise you, Miss Rosen, but it's not uncommon for murderers to blame others for their crimes." He scribbled on the white pad on his desk. "In any case, I would urge you not to believe the conspiracies peddled by Mr. Walters and his friends. That's how people like him make their living, holding ridiculous conferences like that one last week, which portray legitimate businessmen like me as monsters, when our only sin is making money."

"If that conference was so ridiculous," Mimi asked, "why were you there?"

"I wanted to hear the talk by my former business partner, *olav ha-shalom*."

"And what do you think?"

"I was not impressed, sadly," Novak said. "I expect a certain low level of rhetoric from speakers who have no idea what it's like to do business in a country like the ADR. But I was a little put off by the preening from Abraham, who knew better."

Mimi rubbed her pen between her fingers. "I understand that, at the conference, you tried to dissuade Mr. Boasberg from selling the diamond as the Hope for Humanity. Is that true?"

He appeared surprised by the question. "Not exactly. I simply warned Abraham that by making such a spectacle, he was opening himself and others close to him to criticism from folks like Mr. Walters. He wouldn't want Walters releasing information about certain events that are, shall we say, a little sensitive."

"What events?"

"Given I just described them as 'sensitive,' I don't think I'll be discussing them with a journalist. I will say that if people knew that particular diamond's real backstory, they might not find it such an inspiring tale."

"What do you mean?"

Novak flashed a wolfish grin. "I see they've also kept it from you." He rested an elbow on his desk. "Did you know that dear saintly Reverend Kamora first tried to sell that diamond on the black market to one of those fly-by-night companies that specialize in smuggling? That would mean the diamond would garner no taxes for the country, no benefit for the community he professes to care about, and no money for anyone other than him."

"Oh, come on." Mimi folded her arms. "He told me something completely different. How do you know that?"

"It's a small community over there. When a big diamond is up for sale, word gets around. From what I understand, he even said *Mazal* on the deal, then changed his mind." He sat up on his chair. "And here's something else you may not know about the good Reverend Kamora. He was a commander during the ADR civil war."

"Now I know that you're BS-ing me," Mimi said. "I can't believe that sweet man was in the military. He wouldn't hurt a fly."

"He hurt far more than that," said Novak. "He was quite vicious. Arguably, a war criminal. He has since claimed to have reformed himself. Let's just say he has quite a lot to repent for."

Mimi silently processed this.

"Miss Rosen, there are no angels in this world. Only in the Heavens."

"Look," Mimi said, "let's say I agree those facts might have hurt the diamond's sale. What did you plan to do with that information? Leak it to the press?"

"Absolutely not. I talk to the media as little as possible. I'm not exactly sure why I'm talking to you."

"But wasn't it in your interest to hurt that sale? If the diamond was sold successfully, wouldn't all the ADR's production be sold that way?"

"That was Abraham's grand fantasy," Novak sniffed, "that he could magically change how the ADR works overnight. I assure you, my position there is quite secure."

He pointed to a picture on his wall. It showed Novak in short sleeves and slacks, standing next to an African man in a silk suit and dashiki. They had their arms around each other's shoulders and were smiling broadly, showing lots of teeth.

"That's me and the minister of mines for the African Democratic Republic. We were at his compound, Windcliff Estates. Mr. Walters has long accused me of quote-unquote exploiting the ADR. If that were true, would I have such an excellent relationship with one of its most important officials?"

"The fact is, the Honorable Minister knows that I have done quite a bit for his country. I've donated large sums of money to local charities. Of course, Mr. Walters and his ilk never talk about that. Mind you, that is not the only good cause I support. Have you ever been to the Coltura Garden in Central Park?"

Mimi had heard of it but never visited. It was one of those places that turned up on lists of "New York's hidden treasures."

Novak gestured at a photo of it, hanging on the back of his door. It looked lush and green and full of color.

"It's one of my favorite areas of the city. I pay for its upkeep, almost singlehandedly. I suppose I could just build a private garden for myself, but I prefer to share it with the public at large. I go there sometimes to clear my mind. I enjoy watching the children play. You see, I am a human being, despite what Mr. Walters and his friends might have told you."

Novak turned his face to his computer. "Is there anything else? Didn't you tell the receptionist you wanted to complain about your father's rent?"

"As long as you brought it up—"

He rolled his eyes. "Oh, here we go."

"You raised it twenty percent!"

He swiveled his chair back to face Mimi. "Correct. And even with that, his rent is extremely reasonable by midtown Manhattan standards. From what I hear, a lot of small diamond companies are in dire straits. I knew your father long ago, and I recall him as a very decent man. Even so, I don't see why I, as a landlord, should subsidize a failing business model."

"But don't you think a twenty percent increase is outrageous?"

"Not at all. We've renovated the building. You don't think that happens for free, do you?"

He played with a gold pen. "It's curious. I've met a few journalists in my life, as well as some former journalists like yourself. One thing I've noticed, as smart as they are—or, perhaps, as smart as they think they are—they are often quite naïve about the world of business." He paused and lifted his chin slightly. "Maybe that's why so many have to call themselves former."

After Mimi left Novak's office, she decamped to the bench in front of his building, trying to process what she'd just heard. She had to know if what he said about Reverend Kamora was true.

She couldn't find any info online that placed Reverend Kamora in the rebel militia; there wasn't much on him, period,. It was only after she Googled "commander" and "Reverend Kamora" that she found his picture, at the bottom of a news story about child soldiers.

He had a different first name then. He was with a group of boys, all of whom looked about fifteen. The story described him as part of a "notorious" battalion called "The East Side Kids."

He stood in front of the others, the clear top dog. He brandished an AK-47 that was thicker than his arm. He was at an age when his eyes should shine with innocence, but they blazed with so much anger, it burned through the screen. That so upset Mimi she shut the browser.

That picture was taken twenty-five years ago. Which, according to some quick mental math, meant Reverend Kamora was about forty—around Mimi's age. She'd always thought he was close to sixty. It showed the toll everything had taken on him.

Now that she knew this information, she didn't know what to do with it. Matthews probably wouldn't be interested. Anita might be.

Mimi called her and explained how she had tracked Novak to his office.

"Wow," Anita exclaimed. "That's amazing you talked to him. He never speaks to anyone. You must be a good investigator."

Anita's appraisal of Mimi's detective skills dwindled, however, as Mimi relayed the gist of their conversation. Anita seemed disappointed that Novak didn't confess to the murder then and there, in a puddle of tears on the floor.

"He did tell me something interesting," Mimi said. "Did you know that Reverend Kamora was an officer in the ADR rebel militia?"

Anita was momentarily struck speechless. "He never mentioned that to me."

"Probably not something you bring up in casual conversation," Mimi said. "Novak called him 'arguably a war criminal.'"

"Novak would know. He was arguably a war profiteer."

"I can't believe it. He seems like such a sweet man. I don't know what it means."

"You should ask him about it. He's staying at a hotel in Midtown. Maybe you can meet him tonight."

"I guess so, but would you mind coming along? I could use support."

"I'd love to, but can't. We secured bail for Brandon on Saturday. We're talking with his new lawyer tonight." She sounded excited, like meeting with a criminal defense attorney was her idea of a good time.

Mimi called Reverend Kamora, and said she had something to discuss. They agreed to meet at the place with the French name she couldn't pronounce. Mimi was a little nervous about having coffee and a biscotti with a war criminal. Reverend Kamora was scarier to her now than before.

On the other hand, perhaps he *had* changed. He sure seemed like it. Something told her not to give up on him.

CHAPTER THIRTEEN

MIMI ARRIVED AN HOUR LATER at the confusingly named French place, and grabbed Anita's usual spot at the back.

As Reverend Kamora approached her table, Mimi noticed something she hadn't before—he walked with a limp. He gripped chairs and tables to steady himself as he made his way to her table.

"So, what's your big news?" he asked, his eyes shining. "Has the diamond been found?"

"No," Mimi said. "It hasn't."

His demeanor instantly changed. His face sagged, and he clutched the table while lowering himself into the chair.

"Were you expecting it had?" Mimi asked.

He looked sheepish. "I certainly hoped so. As you know, the auction is less than three weeks away."

Mimi gave a sorrowful sigh. "I hate to say it, but you shouldn't expect that diamond to show up in time. I just spoke to someone who works for a diamond lab. He said, in most cases, stolen diamonds get cut into pieces, and become unrecognizable. Chances are, the diamond you want to sell doesn't exist anymore. You should probably cancel the auction."

"I cannot do that," he said, his reedy voice jumping an octave. "People in my country will think I sold the diamond and kept the money for myself."

Like you nearly did, Mimi thought.

"Reverend," Mimi said slowly, "I need to speak to you about something. I just met with Morris Novak. He told me something that I hadn't heard, but I now know to be true." She took a breath. "He told me that you fought in the rebel militia during the ADR civil war."

Reverend Kamora's expression became blank. He looked down at the table and murmured a few words Mimi couldn't hear.

"I'm sorry." She brought her head forward. "I didn't get that."

He mumbled something inaudible.

"Reverend, please. I can't hear you."

He lifted his chin, bared his teeth, and for a moment, Mimi felt she was getting a glimpse of his old, hard self. "That's because," he nearly screamed, "I hate talking about it."

He slumped in his seat, looking crushed. "I didn't choose to be in the militia. I was conscripted when I was fourteen. They tore me from my family, separated me from everything I knew."

Mimi tried to stay skeptical, but as someone who had dealt with trauma, she recognized the pain on his face, the anguish in his voice. Those couldn't be faked.

"We were all children," he continued. "They sent us into battle. They gave us pills that they called vitamins but were really amphetamines. They told us lies, said we were heroes fighting for freedom, when we were little more than thugs. They stripped us of our humanity, turned us into killers. Every day, our lives were on the line. It was a constant struggle to survive."

Mimi's stomach lurched. A sick feeling swished around her throat. She fought the urge to burst out in tears.

"I'm so sorry that happened to you," she said, her voice barely a whisper. "I feel awful bringing it up. Please accept my apology."

He had a faraway look. "It is not something that I ever forget. Even now, as we sit here in this lovely coffee shop, in this beautiful city, I see it all, just as I'm talking to you. Once you've experienced the horror of war, you never leave it behind."

Mimi was flooded by guilt. "Sorry if it sounded like I was judging you. That was wrong of me. The things you did were not your fault."

"You are correct," he said. "Most of what I did was not my fault. However, some of it was. And that is very difficult to live with." He was quiet for a moment. "I am no longer the person I was. I also know that some things can never be repaired.

"I am just grateful that God led me to the Church. I can't change the past; I can only try to do better. That is why I believe God led me to that diamond. So, I can finally make a positive contribution to my country."

Mimi grimaced. That led to her second question.

"Novak told me something else. He said that when you first found the diamond, you tried to sell it to a local company, and planned to keep the money for yourself."

Reverend Kamora fidgeted in his seat. "Mr. Novak told you many things. What is the expression Mr. Boasberg used to say? *Oy vey.*"

He rubbed his face with his hand. "After the war, I pledged to be as good a person as possible. Occasionally, I fall short of that. That was one of those times.

"I am a poor man, with a poor family. I run a poor church. When I saw that diamond, my mind went wild. I dreamt of a better life. The diamond was all I could think about. I even slept with it.

"I brought it to a local company and agreed to sell it for a very large sum. I remember, when I was sitting in the buying office, the man behind the desk kept stacking bills in my hands, one after another, and it felt like he would never stop. I had never seen such a large pile of money. My hands shook holding it. At one point, I caressed it, as if it was a baby.

"This wave of euphoria swept over me. I realized I had felt that way before. In the militia. When they pumped us full of drugs and sent us into battle. Back then, I lived only for myself."

"Until that moment, I'd believed that part of me was gone. Now I know, it is something I must always struggle against."

"I put the money down, and told the man I needed to walk outside, to think a moment. When I returned, I cancelled the sale. The man was furious, but since I hadn't given him the diamond, I told him to keep the money and left."

"For days, I didn't know what to do. Part of me wanted to put the diamond back in the ground, forget I ever found it. But I believed there was a reason God led me to it. I contacted our local paramount chief. He had talked with Mr. Boasberg a few months prior. He connected the two of us, and we came up with the idea for the Hope for Humanity."

His Adam's Apple bobbed. "I realize that is not the story I told you, that I prayed and saw the newspaper on the ground. Mr. Boasberg said we needed a dramatic tale to interest the media. That is what he came up with, but I never felt comfortable telling it."

"When you said you were unwilling to help, I panicked and relayed that fiction to you. I apologize. I realize the truth is far less flattering."

Mimi flashed back to her newspaper days, when her editor would rail against stories that were "too good to check." Those were tales that were so perfect, so compelling, reporters would rush them into print, without verifying the facts. They often got their authors in trouble, as the reality behind them was usually more complicated than it first appeared. Reverend Kamora's story was too good. It should have been checked.

Mimi was not thrilled about being lied to, but had more to ask.

"How much were you offered for the diamond?"

"Two hundred and fifty thousand dollars."

"Way less than it's worth," Mimi said.

He nodded ruefully. "It is quite a large amount of money in my country. It would have been all cash."

His voice rose on the word *cash*, and Mimi sensed some part of him regretted not taking it.

"So, who did you nearly sell it to?"

"A local company. Merlano Resources."

"Merlano Resources?" Mimi was stunned. "Boasberg had his son wire money to that company the day he died."

"Really?" Reverend Kamora looked puzzled. "Why would he do that?"

"I don't know. Did Boasberg ever deal with them?"

"Not to my knowledge. He knew I nearly sold them the diamond. He was always worried they would lay claim to the sale. But they never did."

"Can you tell me anything about the company? Who owned it?"

"Like many local companies, it's connected to an overseas player that has hidden their identity. I only knew their local contact, Farhad Sultan."

Mimi wrote down the name. "What do you know about him?"

"We used to be friends. But that was the first time I had seen him in years."

Mimi took out her phone. "Let me Google him."

She gasped at the first result. It was an ADR newspaper article, accompanied by a photo. She passed the phone to Reverend Kamora. "Is this him?"

Reverend Kamora's eyes grew wide, then red. He dropped the phone onto the table. "Yes."

Mimi picked it up and read the story. It was from the day before.

LOCAL DIAMOND DEALER MURDERED

Farhad Sultan, 41, a father of three who worked for a local diamond company, was killed last night by an unknown assailant, police say.

Authorities said Sultan was walking on a local road to his home when a man came up to him and stabbed him brutally all over his body. After the man ran away, Sultan called out to nearby villagers who came to help. They ferried him to a nearby clinic where he died upon admission.

The police said they had no idea of a motive, but believe Sultan was deliberately targeted.

"We don't know why anyone would do this," said a member of his grieving family.

When Mimi finished reading, she slammed the phone on the table, face down. She couldn't even look at the story; it was awful beyond words.

Reverend Kamora's mouth hung open. "Do you think this has something to do with what happened to Mr. Boasberg?"

"I don't know. But it's possible. The murders happened pretty close together."

"This is a terrible tragedy. When I said Farhad and I were friends, that was only part of the story. We were in the militia together. We fought side by side. He survived all the horrors of that period, only to end up like this."

"I do not understand what is happening." Reverend Kamora sank in his seat. "This diamond was supposed to offer hope for humanity. Now it is just another blood diamond. It has caused nothing but death."

CHAPTER FOURTEEN

THE NEXT DAY AT WORK, Max went out to lunch with a friend, which meant he'd be gone for at least an hour. That would give Mimi plenty of time to research Merlano Resources. That company seemed like the key to this case.

It had no presence on Google. She played with the spelling, eventually coming across MerlanoResource, one word, with no "s", based on the Caribbean island of Saint Phoebus. Seemed like the same company.

Unlike Nivens, Saint Phoebus had a corporate database, but it wasn't easy to use. She first had to identify fire hydrants for a CAPTCHA. It took her three tries, which annoyed her, since obviously she knew what fire hydrants looked like. When she entered MerlanoResource in the database, it spit out dozens of companies with the word "resource" in them. After wading through ten pages, she found a listing for "MerlanoResource," which contained only its ID number.

She then had to plug that number into a second database, after completing another CAPTCHA, which made her pick out taxis. She nailed that easily, which gave her a brief moment of pride.

Up popped another long list of documents. This process was needlessly, and perhaps deliberately, confusing. She now understood why rich guys hid their money offshore.

She finally found the registration for MerlanoResource, but it lacked the info she sought—who owned it. It did say that it had been open for six years. But the most interesting thing was it closed two days ago, right after the murders of Boasberg and Farhad Sultan.

As Mimi jotted this down, Channah stuck her head in from the reception area.

"Sol's on the phone. He can't get ahold of your father, and he's demanding he speak to you."

Mimi gripped her mouse in frustration. "Tell him I can't reach my father either. He has no cell phone."

"He knows that. He's really insistent. Can you at least talk to him? He sounds real upset."

Mimi didn't have the patience to argue. "Patch him through," she grumbled.

When she picked up, Sol barely said hi. "I need to reach your father," he said, speaking even faster than usual. "That man should really get a cell phone."

"I know!" Mimi groaned in frustration.

"I'm calling about that two-carat pear shape. You know the one I'm talking about?"

"Of course. You two have been arguing about it nonstop for the past week."

"He hasn't sold it, has he?"

"Not as far as I know."

If Max had, he'd crow that he'd finally found a buyer who had met his price—unlike Sol.

"One of my customers has a client looking for that kind of item. He's expecting a call back in the next five minutes. I don't have tons of time. I need that stone. I'm willing to increase my offer by one hundred and fifty dollars. Meet your father right in the middle. What do you say?"

Mimi couldn't believe he was bothering her about this. "You need to talk to him about that."

"I'd be happy to, but I just told you, I can't get hold of him."

Mimi gritted her teeth. "I can't either. I don't know what to tell you."

"How about I go up two hundred dollars? We were only three hundred dollars apart in the first place. That's just one hundred dollars less than he was asking. I've spent more than that on dinner."

Mimi was getting antsy. "Sol, I wish I could help you, but I can't. How about this? I'll make sure my father calls you when he gets in."

"I just explained, I don't have time. I have a customer waiting." He smacked his lips. "What if I meet his price? You can't not accept that."

"I can't accept anything."

"Why not? I'm giving your father everything he asked for. Which, by the way, is killing me, just on general principle."

"I'm sure it's fine, but—"

"Of course, it's fine. So, say it."

"Say what?"

"Say *Mazal*."

"I can't say that, Sol."

"Why not?" Sol said, talking louder. "I'm meeting his price. Even your father, the most stubborn man I know, would accept that. Just say *Mazal*, so I can tell my customer yes, and me and your dad work out the details later."

Mimi was desperate to get Sol off the phone, so she could get back to navigating the intricacies of the Saint Phoebus database.

"All right," she said. "*Mazal*. But you and—"

"Great. Tell your father to send the stone over in the next few days."

Mimi froze. She realized what she'd done. "No, that wasn't—"

"It was great doing business with you!"

"We did not do business!" she yelled. "I just said that to get you off the phone."

"It doesn't matter. You said, '*Mazal*.' In this industry, that's binding."

"That wasn't a real *Mazal*. It was a fake one."

"Too late. You said it. You can't go back on it now, or I'll take your father to arbitration, and he wouldn't want that. I'll let my customer know. Have your dad bring the diamond by Monday."

"Sol, please—"

"Gotta go. Give your father my best. And tell him to get a cell phone."

Mimi wanted to scream. "I have!"

She broke out in a sweat. She had just sold a diamond. Her father would be furious.

MAX RETURNED FROM LUNCH a half hour later. Mimi told him the whole story—interspersed with admonishments that he should get a cell phone, because it wasn't fair to put her in that position.

"I'm sorry," she summed up. "I sold your diamond. I didn't mean to. Maybe you can get Sol to change his mind. Tell him I wasn't authorized to sell it."

Max took this in. He was silent for a second. "Sol met my price?"

"Yes." She hitched a breath. "Is that okay?"

"Okay? It's fantastic!" He was grinning ear to ear. "It's almost a miracle. You know how hard it is to get Sol to budge on anything? He's the most stubborn guy I know."

Mimi exhaled in relief. "It wasn't anything I planned," she said. "He kept raising his price and I kept telling him I wasn't authorized to negotiate. Finally, he said he'd match your offer."

"You held your ground!" Max enthused. "That's exactly what you're supposed to do! I never thought you'd have a nose for this business. We'll make a diamond dealer out of you yet."

Mimi swatted this away. "Does this help with your new rent?"

"I'll have to run the numbers," Max said. "This should pull us through, at least this month. The next, who knows?"

At least my job is secure for another few weeks, Mimi thought.

Max pulled the pear-shape from his big diamond box, slipped it into an envelope, and scribbled "sold" on the outside. He seemed giddy.

"See," he smiled, "wasn't that more exciting than that social responsibility *mishigas*? Which reminds me. We gotta kill that project. It's a waste of time."

And just like that, Mimi switched from worrying that her father would be furious with her, to being furious with him.

CHAPTER FIFTEEN

LATER THAT DAY, Mimi received a call from Brandon.

"I hear that you're a free man," Mimi said. "Congratulations."

"Yes, indeed." He sounded happy, even joyous.

Mimi didn't know how to approach the next question, but she couldn't not ask. "How was jail?"

"It wasn't my idea of a good time, put it that way. Until you've been in there, you have no idea how slowly a day can pass. It's nice to be out. And I intend to stay out.

"Anita told me that you're helping her investigate. I'm eager to see these ace detective skills of yours."

Mimi didn't know if he was mocking or serious, so she laughed, to play it safe. "Speaking of which," she said, "if you have a moment, I want to ask you some questions."

"No problem. We should all meet tomorrow night. You, me, Anita, and Rafi. We'll crack this case together."

Mimi felt like she'd been drafted into some cool detective club.

"I plan to go hard against Morris Novak," he said. "And I could use your help. Remember I told you that Abraham Boasberg had all sorts of interesting information on Novak he planned to show me? It turns out Rafi has access to those files."

"Great."

"It should be. The problem is, Rafi is too scared to share them. He is terrified that his stepfather will come after him. We need to apply some not-so-subtle peer pressure to the boy. So, miss reporter, how good are you at convincing people to spill the beans?"

Mimi sighed. "I'm okay."

In her newspaper days, Mimi often had to cajole reluctant sources to reveal info. It was her least favorite part of the job. She never found a good way to do it; she usually just nagged them until they gave in, or—in most cases—hung up.

She didn't blame them. Getting caught meant consequences. Early on, one of Mimi's sources was sniffed out and fired. When she wandered into her editor's office, dazed and distraught, he patted her on the back and told her not to worry about it. Her source was an adult, responsible for his behavior, and she was reporting on an issue in the public interest. Ten years later, she barely remembered what that issue was, but never forgot that incident, which haunted her to this day.

She had no clue how she'd convince Rafi to leak documents about his stepfather, possibly putting his life in danger. This wouldn't be an assignment she relished.

Later, Brandon texted they were meeting the next night at Abraham Boasberg's office. "Unfortunately," he wrote, "the last time we were supposed to get together, we were rudely interrupted. But it'll be great to see you."

Then, to Mimi's surprise, he added a heart emoticon.

At lunch the next day in Bryant Park, Brandon's heart emoticon was Topic A.

"Yep," Channah said, after studying it for a few seconds. "That's a heart, all right, jumping up and down with a smiley face. What do you think it means?"

"I don't know. I suppose it means what we both think it means. But that makes no sense. There's nothing between us. I hardly know Brandon. He's way too young for me. Plus, he's accused of murder. That's kind of a turnoff." She wrapped noodles around her fork. "It'll be fine. Other people will be there."

Channah's eyes fluttered. "Like Rafi Boasberg?"

"I think so," Mimi said.

Channah twirled her long curls. "Remember I told you, Rafi and I were supposed to go out? Well, he never called. It's been almost a week. Why would he say that, then change his mind?"

"I don't know. He's going through a lot right now. His father just died."

"I get that," Channah lazily moved her chicken around her Styrofoam container. "But it wasn't me who suggested we go out. It was him. It's just so frustrating. After all this time, I find a guy I'm interested in, he asks me out, then he ghosts on me."

"So, call him."

Channah looked shocked. "I couldn't do that." She didn't say it, but she didn't think that a woman should pursue a man.

"Why not? It's common these days. You certainly took the initiative the night of the *shiva*."

Channah released a soft, mournful chuckle. "That's true. But will it do any good?"

"I don't know. It will help *you*. It beats waiting around. You want to know where you stand, one way or another."

Channah looked pained. "How about this? You're seeing him tonight. Can you ask him if he's interested?"

Another assignment Mimi didn't relish. "I guess."

"Where are you meeting him?"

"At Boasberg's office."

"Whoa," Channah said. "Isn't that where Mr. Boasberg was killed? That'll be weird."

This so stunned Mimi, she sat with her fork frozen over her Styrofoam container. She hadn't considered that, but it was a good point. She was meeting Brandon, the man accused of murdering Abraham Boasberg, at the same place where Boasberg was murdered—with Boasberg's son acting as host.

Rafi must really be convinced that Brandon was innocent. Or else he just didn't care.

CHAPTER SIXTEEN

MIMI ARRIVED AT ABRAHAM'S BOASBERG'S OFFICE at seven-thirty, as the summer sky was growing dark. The building was eerily quiet. The halls were empty; even the cleaning crew had gone home.

Rafi greeted her at the door with a wide smile, surrounded by acres of scruff. His beard was always bushy, but—following the tradition that mourners can't shave for thirty days post-burial—it was even wilder now, bursting from his face and crawling down his neck.

"Good to see you," he said. "Everyone's in the conference room."

Boasberg's office was modern, elegant, and—not surprisingly—much larger than it needed to be. The reception area was dominated by an oversized picture of Boasberg and Reverend Kamora, standing aside the Hope for Humanity, beaming like proud fathers. That diamond really *was* everything to him.

"Is the livestream still happening?" Mimi asked.

"Yeah, in three weeks. Though I don't know how we'll hold a diamond auction with no diamond."

"You should probably call it off."

"I would if I could, but Reverend Kamora keeps telling me not to. He believes the diamond will turn up. And I'm like, 'whatever, dude, it's your diamond, and your country.'" He cackled again. "I've known plenty of people with faith, but he's in another league."

Mimi spotted an office with Abraham Boasberg's nameplate, covered with bright yellow police tape.

She cocked her head toward it. "Is that where—?"

“Yep,” Rafi said, his face turning grim. “That’s where it happened. In what my father called his ‘executive suite.’

“It’s completely sealed off, and it’s so frustrating. I would love to go in there, just for a second, to grab some mementos of my Dad, and feel his presence a bit. But the cops say it’s off-limits because they might re-examine it. I pass it all the time, and it drives me nuts.”

Mimi turned to Rafi. “This might be a personal question, but is it hard for you to work here?”

“Sometimes,” he said with a shrug. “But I’m dealing with a lot of stuff, so this is just one more thing.” A nest of wrinkles formed on his forehead, illustrating just how much stuff he was dealing with. “I’ve been in this office all day, settling my dad’s affairs. It’s nice to have visitors.”

They had nearly arrived at the conference room, when Mimi remembered she’d been charged with a mission.

“This is kind of a personal question, so let me know if it’s out of bounds. You told my friend Channah you wanted to go out with her. She’s waiting for your call.”

Rafi’s head bobbed. “Yeah, tell her I’m sorry. The *shiva* week just ended, and today was crazy busy, but I do want to call her. Thanks for the reminder.” He seemed non-committal, but not disinterested.

They entered the conference room. Brandon was at the head of the table; Anita sat next to him, at an angle. When Brandon saw Mimi, he leaped from his chair, rushed to the door, and gave her a bear hug. Anita followed his lead.

“How are you doing?” Mimi asked Brandon.

Brandon looked tired but had lost none of his standard wry detachment. “I’m breathing free air. That’s an improvement.”

They all took their seats.

“Mimi,” Brandon declared, “Anita tells me you spoke to my friend Morris Novak. If you see him again, tell him I appreciate his little plan to pin this murder on me, but it’s not going to work. I’m going to expose everything he’s done.

“Fortunately,” he continued, “our friend Rafi here has access to many of his father’s files. Unfortunately, he’s reluctant to share them. We’re hoping he’ll change his mind. How about it, Rafi?”

Rafi’s lips curled down. “I told you no,” he said sullenly. “And stop giving me a hard time about it.”

This made everyone stiffen. Brandon smiled and said, "We'll revisit that later."

"Let's clear your name first," Mimi said. "Can I ask you a few things?"

"Fire away."

Mimi took out her notebook. "Tell me everything you remember about the day of the murder."

"That afternoon, I received a text from Abraham Boasberg," Brandon said. "Which, frankly, I found a bit odd. After my question at the conference, he wasn't my biggest fan, to put it mildly."

"Can I see his text?"

"Sure," said Brandon. He pulled out his phone and passed it to Mimi. It said, "Brandon, I have shocking information we need to discuss. Please come to my office, ASAP. Abraham Boasberg."

"That's interesting he used the word 'shocking,'" Mimi said. "What kind of information would surprise you about Morris Novak?"

"I have no idea," Brandon shrugged.

"Do you know, Rafi?" Mimi asked.

He shook his head.

"I was quite intrigued, as you can imagine," Brandon said. "So, I arrived at this building, buzzed Boasberg's office from downstairs, and was let in. I got to this floor, rang the doorbell, and was buzzed in again. When I entered, there was no one inside. The office was empty.

"I said, 'hello' but no one answered. Which didn't make sense to me because I'd just been let in. I have since learned that there's an app that lets you buzz people in from off-site. But at the time, I was baffled.

"I saw a light coming from Boasberg's office. I figured that's where he was, and maybe he didn't hear me for some reason. I knocked on the door. No answer. I knocked again. Again, no answer. The door was unlocked, so I figured, what the hell, I'd go in. And there he was, slumped over his desk, covered in blood.

"I walked over to see if I could revive him. I couldn't, of course. I'll spare you the details, out of respect for our friend Rafi here. But it made me sick to my stomach. I instantly called 911."

"The police came in about five minutes. They took me to the station for a statement. They kept asking me the same questions over and over. At some points, they seemed kind of hostile, but I figured, that's just how New York cops are. When the questioning ended, I thought I could leave. Instead, they told me I was under arrest."

"My lawyer said I never should have talked to them without counsel present, that answering questions was the worst thing I could have done. So that's been a costly lesson."

"Why did they arrest you?" Mimi asked. "They must have had a reason."

"According to them, the security video in the hallway showed I was the only person who entered this office that night. So, based on that, and that alone, they have judged me guilty.

"My lawyer said there's a fifty-fifty chance they'll drop the charges, since the case is entirely circumstantial. The only evidence they have is a video that we've so far been unable to see. That's why I think that Matthews may be on the take. It's quite possible someone else could have come in that night."

Mimi turned to Rafi. "Do you have any surveillance cameras in the office?"

"Nope," Rafi said. "Only in the hallway."

"That doesn't help," she said. "Rafi, were you in the office that night?"

"Yep."

"What time did you leave?"

"Six-thirty."

Mimi wrote that down. "Is that approximately, or exactly?"

"Pretty much exactly," Rafi said. "My father told me to leave by then. He said he had this private meeting he didn't want me there for."

"Did that happen a lot?" Mimi asked.

"No," Rafi said. "He'd never asked me to leave like that before. It was pretty strange."

Mimi scribbled in her notebook: *Why did Boasberg want the meeting with Brandon to be private? Because of the "shocking" info?*

"When you left that night, was anyone else in the office?"

"No. Just my dad."

"How about before that?"

"Reverend Kamora and Anita visited that afternoon. The only other person who was here was Zeke, the computer guy. He left a few minutes before I did."

Mimi scribbled Zeke's name on her notepad. She should call him.

"Did you speak with your dad before you left?" Mimi asked.

"Yep," Rafi said. "I popped my head in his office and said good night." He paused. "It's crazy thinking that was the last time I talked to him."

Mimi felt a surge of emotion but carried on. "What time do the police think your father passed away?"

"Around seven," Rafi said.

"Which," Brandon said, "is certainly convenient for them, given that's right after I arrived. My lawyer says that's just an estimate based on whatever science they have. The actual time of death can vary widely, by an hour or more."

That comment sparked an uneasy silence, as it could implicate Rafi.

Mimi chewed on her pen. "So, let's assume the video was correct, and Brandon was the only person who came in through the front door that night. The killer could have entered the office another way. Like through a window. Is that possible?"

"Anything's possible," Rafi said. "But that's not likely. The windows in this conference room don't open. They do in my father's office, but it would be hard to break in that way. We're thirty flights up."

"We should examine them." Mimi rose from her chair.

"We can't," Rafi sulked. "My father's office is sealed, remember? No one's allowed in."

"Oh yeah." Mimi sat down, disappointed.

They talked a little longer, and Mimi excused herself to go to the bathroom. On her way out, she passed Boasberg's "executive suite," and its door festooned with yellow tape. If only she could go in there, just for a second, to check for anything the police may have missed.

She approached the door to Boasberg's office, expecting it would be locked. Instead, it was slightly ajar. If not for the yellow tape, she could easily enter.

She crouched down. The yellow tape stopped a few feet from the floor. All she'd have to do is crawl under it, and she'd be in the office.

Which would be crazy, of course. That was a sealed-off crime scene. The police had warned Rafi to not go in there. Ordinarily, Mimi would respect that. But what if Brandon was right, and the police were on the take?

She wouldn't stay long—just scope it out, and leave. She wouldn't disturb anything. And there wasn't much chance she'd get caught. Everyone was in the conference room, and there were no cameras in the office.

Before she thought this through, she was moving the yellow tape with her arm, then pushing down the door handle with her elbow. To her surprise, the door swung open.

She could now peek inside Boasberg's office, but it was too dark to see anything. That made her more eager to take a look around.

She dropped to the floor. Lying perfectly flat, she crept below the tape, slowly and deliberately. She used her hands to pull herself forward, pushing the door open with her head. She stayed close to the ground—close enough that the carpet scraped her face.

The closer she got, the faster she moved. Before she knew it, she had wriggled inside the office. The sealed room had been breached.

She lay on the ground, both terrified and excited. She used her foot to close the door. It barely made a sound.

The office was dark, but she could make out its contours from the shards of light drifting in through the windows. She grabbed her phone from her pocketbook to use as a flashlight.

Not only was the office huge, but so was everything in it. Boasberg's desk chair could fit two people, and his desk was the size of three chairs. An imposing black vault stood in the corner.

She tiptoed slowly across the large dark empty office. The floor creaked slightly, and even those small noises made her heart race.

She arrived at the windows along the back wall and found one open a crack. Why a crack? Boasberg might have opened it the night he was killed. Yet, his office had perfectly good air conditioning; she could feel it. Plus, that night was *hot.* If he wasn't using the AC, he'd have opened that window way wider.

She flashed her phone around the window, searching for signs of a break-in. She couldn't find any. Rafi was right; entering the office through a thirtieth-floor window would be both difficult and dangerous.

She kept looking, until something caught her eye—a rag, stuffed in between two bricks, not that far from the window. The rag was the same color as the brick paste, making it easy to miss. It appeared to hold something yellow. Peering closer, she saw it was not just yellow, but gold. It could be the gold box that held the Hope for Humanity. She felt a sudden jolt of excitement.

She got into a crouch. She stuck her hand through the gap in the window, then angled her arm to pluck the rag from the bricks.

She had just about reached it when she heard a sound. She froze. She heard another noise, which seemed to be coming from the other side of the room. Mimi pulled her hand back through the window, stood up, and spun around. She was horrified to see the office door creaking open.

Her stomach heaved. She was about to have company.

CHAPTER SEVENTEEN

THE INTRUDER DEFTLY DUCKED UNDER the police tape, with far less care than Mimi did. He strode into the room, closed the door, then stood silently for what seemed like an eternity.

Mimi wanted to shine her light on whoever it was, but was too scared to do anything other than stand glued to the floor.

Finally, the visitor pulled a phone from his pocket, turned on its light, and held it to his chin, throwing a shadow on his face. It was Brandon.

"Is that Mimi?"

"Yes," she said, exhaling a bit.

"Well, well, well. Fancy meeting you here." He had a wide grin, and the light flashing on it made him look like a jack-o-lantern. "I'm impressed. I had heard you were a good investigator, but I didn't realize breaking and entering was part of the package."

"It's not something I do regularly."

Brandon laughed. "I figured that."

"I just wanted to—"

"I get what you're doing," said Brandon, "and I'm very happy you're doing it."

"How did you know I was in here?"

"I left the conference room because I wanted to give Anita and Rafi a little alone time. I thought maybe she could use her feminine wiles to pry those documents out of him. I was sitting in the foyer when I heard someone in here. Which, needless to say, piqued my curiosity. I figured I'd pop in and take a gander. And look what I found."

"Brandon," Mimi begged, "please don't tell Rafi I broke in here. He was clear that he didn't want anyone—"

"Don't worry," Brandon said, a certain glee in his voice. "We'll keep this our little secret."

Mimi felt relief wash over her.

"Did you find anything?"

"Possibly," Mimi replied. "There's something outside here."

Brandon made his way to the back wall, guided by his phone-light, until he stood next to Mimi at the window. He put his phone down, and suddenly it was dark again.

He was standing so close to Mimi, she could smell his breath. This didn't bother her; in fact, she kind of liked it. It had been a long time since she'd been that close to a man. She didn't move away, but found herself inching closer to him.

She flashed her phone-light around the window. "There's a rag stuck in the gap between those bricks. It looks like it's holding something gold. It might be the gold box that stored the diamond."

As she pointed to it, her arm brushed against his. Her skin broke out in pinpricks. That didn't make sense; she wasn't interested in Brandon. At least, she didn't think she was. Now that she stood close to him in the dark, in a place where they both shouldn't be, the moment held a certain charge.

"I see," Brandon leaned against the window, and again, his arm bumped hers. This time, her skin not only tingled, her breath got caught in her throat. She moved closer to the window, closer to him.

She felt his hand on hers, and then his hand on her arm—except he wasn't touching it, he was grabbing it. He gripped her other arm and yanked her close. His face approached hers. *What the—*

He was kissing her.

This both calmed her down and freaked her out. She didn't expect him to kiss her, nor did she want him to. It was too weird, too abrupt, too inappropriate. Even with all the buildup, there was no magic in the moment, just a pair of unwanted lips pressing themselves onto hers.

Mimi ripped her face away, and broke from his arms with her elbows, with enough force to make sure he got the message. She stepped back a few steps. It took her a second to catch her breath and regain the ability to speak. "I didn't expect you to—"

"Sorry," he broke in. "That just happened. I got caught up in the moment."

Mimi's heart hammered in her chest. "That came out of nowhere."

"You're right," he said. "I shouldn't have done that. It was wrong. I usually don't do things like that."

Then came a long awkward silence, while Mimi caught her breath.

"Are you okay?" he asked.

"Yes," she said, though she wasn't sure she was.

"Please understand, I'm not in my right mind right now. I am not always thinking straight. I certainly didn't think straight just then."

He spoke haltingly, his voice soaked in sorrow. "My life is enormously difficult. My freedom is on the line. I might not show it, but I'm scared. This is big stuff. I feel abandoned by everyone. My family, my colleagues. They've all deserted me. And I'm scared to death."

In the short time she had known Brandon, Mimi always viewed him as a fearless activist, who charged into every battle without a second thought. Now, he was admitting he got scared, too. That was probably not surprising, given the gravity of his situation. She found it striking all the same.

"I truly appreciate all you've done," he continued. "You've been amazing. The fact that you've stepped to the plate and offered to help means so much to me. That was my awkward way of expressing it. It was wrong. I apologize."

"I realize that we're just getting to know each other, but you seem like an incredible person."

"That's nice of you to say," Mimi said, her mind a jumble of thoughts. "But with everything going on, I can't—"

"I know," Brandon said. "We'll keep this professional from now on, I promise."

"Okay," Mimi took around. "As long as we're clear on that." She caught her breath. "We should check that rag."

"Ah, yes," Brandon said. He crouched down, put his hand through the window, and plucked the rag from the bricks. "There's definitely something in it."

He unwrapped it and flashed his phone on it. There was a gold box inside. He held it to his face and peered inside. "This might be what we're looking for. Care to take a gander?"

She plucked a tissue from her purse so she wouldn't get her fingerprints on the box, and he handed it to her. It certainly looked like the gold box that held the Hope for Humanity.

Mimi couldn't help but notice the irony. A man was giving a woman a box with a diamond—*the* dramatic moment the diamond business was based on. While this particular moment was different—to put it mildly—Mimi opened the box with fevered expectation, hoping to find a diamond inside. But there was nothing. It was empty.

She shined her phone around the box, even turned it upside down, but couldn't find the Hope for Humanity.

"It seems to be gone," she said glumly.

Neither spoke for a moment.

"What should we do?" Mimi asked.

"We should probably put it back," Brandon said.

That made sense. They couldn't leave with the box. They weren't supposed to be in there in the first place.

He took it from her, wrapped it in the rag, reached his hand out the window, and neatly stuffed it back between the bricks. He was silent for a moment, until his shadow turned to hers. "Sorry again about before. I feel horrible about that. But could you do me a favor? You asked me not to tell anyone that you came in here. Could you not mention what just happened between us?"

Mimi didn't answer immediately. She didn't have the mental energy to figure out the right thing to do. "Fine," she said.

"I am going back to the conference room," Brandon said. "If you don't mind waiting a bit before you come back, so it doesn't—"

"Okay," Mimi mumbled.

Mimi leaned against the wall for a few minutes, then left Boasberg's executive suite, carefully crawling under the tape, and making sure the door was propped open the exact same amount it had been previously. She walked to the picture of Boasberg and Reverend Kamora posing with the Hope for Humanity. The gold box in the photo was definitely the same one they had just found, and put back, in the bricks outside of Boasberg's window.

It didn't make sense, though. Why would someone hide the gold box without the diamond?

Her thoughts were interrupted by a sudden barrage of noise. Rafi was screaming.

CHAPTER EIGHTEEN

When Mimi re-entered the conference room, Rafi was standing and pointing his finger at Brandon, who was sitting on the windowsill.

"How many times do I have to tell you?" he brayed. "I am not giving you that information. Quit asking!

"In case you forgot, Morris Novak is my stepfather! Yes, he's a terrible person, but he's family. I don't know why you can't understand that." Rafi sat down, looking ready to cry.

Anita put her hand on his shoulder. "It's okay."

He turned around to face her. "It's only since my dad died that my mom and I have begun to patch things up. I don't think she'll be happy with me bringing her husband's business down. I've had enough family drama for one lifetime."

"I guess that settles that," Brandon said. "How about we all go to eat?"

"I can't," Rafi said. "It's against Jewish law."

"What law is that?" Brandon asked with a smirk.

Rafi shifted uncomfortably. "If you've lost a parent, you can't enjoy entertainment for a year. That includes going out with friends. It's one of those customs that's hard to explain."

"It's okay," Anita said softly. "You don't have to justify anything to us. You have to do what you feel is right."

She touched his shoulder. "I'm sorry I pressured you before. I know it's asking a lot to have you turn over those files. I just feel it's—" She groped for the proper word. "The right thing to do."

Mimi was impressed—right after Anita apologized for pressuring Rafi, she was back making her case. She'd break the guy in no time.

"Who knows what the right thing is anymore?" Rafi griped. His eyes darted around the table, until they settled on Mimi. "What do you think? You have family in this business. Even when they do messed-up stuff, they're your family."

"Yes, but—" Mimi was at a loss for words. "I can't tell you what to do. I've had disputes with my father. He's religious, and I'm not. My ex-husband wasn't Jewish. It was a pretty big deal when I married him."

"Oh yeah," Rafi chuckled. "That's a big one. My mom would freak out if I even dated out of the faith. How did you deal with it?"

"For a long time, it wasn't easy. At the time, I didn't think I had a choice. I just did what I felt was right."

"My case is a little more complicated," Rafi said. "You wouldn't understand."

"Actually," Brandon called out from the windowsill, "I do understand. I mean, I don't completely understand your particular situation. But I've dealt with similar.

"I come from a wealthy family. They made money mining oil—another oft-exploited commodity. My family expected me to join the business. They sent me to the ADR, and I saw the conditions on the ground, and decided it didn't have to be that way. I reinvented myself as an activist, to get on the right side of history."

"My family never liked what I was doing. I wanted their support to help change the business. They weren't interested. They are friends with the people I've called out. They think of me as a traitor, the prince who torched the castle."

Mimi felt like she had just heard Brandon Walters' origin story.

"It's been difficult," he continued, in a quieter tone than usual. "An activist's salary isn't exactly lucrative. My family hasn't donated one penny to my defense, though it would be nothing for them. And now I'm in the fight of my life. But I did what I needed to. Like Mimi said, I had no choice."

Anita beamed, no doubt imagining how that speech would play in their movie.

Rafi gently tugged on Anita's shirt, so she would pay attention to him again. "This is different. This material could put my stepfather in jail. That would be serious family drama."

"But Rafi," Mimi said, "you believe that Morris Novak killed your father, don't you?"

Rafi was quiet for a moment. "Yes. I do."

"That's already family drama, isn't it?" she said.

Rafi chuckled. "I guess."

"She has a point," Anita said. "We haven't nailed your stepfather for the murder. But if we can shine a light on the other things he's done, it might help."

"I know," Rafi said. "But—" He didn't say more.

"I understand this won't be easy," Anita said softly. "I know you want to be loyal to your family. But you know what? We're here for you. It might sound corny, but—" She waved her hand around. "We're a family, too. A family of young people trying to make a difference."

Mimi found something touching in that, though she wasn't sure that she qualified as a member.

Anita brought her voice down to a whisper. "Rafi, I know you're a good person." She looked at him with doe eyes. "Deep in your heart, what do you want to do?"

"I don't know!" Rafi yelled, rising from his seat. "I'm being pulled in a million different directions." He started pacing back and forth. Anita and Brandon watched him closely.

"What does your conscience say?" Anita asked. "What would your father do?"

Mimi worried that invoking his father was a bit much.

But it seemed to work. Rafi stopped pacing and leaned against the gray cabinet at the end of the room. "Even if I wanted to show you the files, I don't know what we have access to."

"How could we find out?" Brandon asked.

"I'll ask our tech person." He went to the door, and called out, "Hey, Zeke."

In walked the tech guy, who had apparently been working in an adjoining room as long as they'd been there. He was short and plump and sported a beard and *yarmulke*.

"This is Ezekiel. Or as my father used to called him, 'Zeke, the computer guy.'"

Zeke gave a small hand-wave which started at his waist and ended there.

Rafi asked him, "Do we have any documents from when my father worked for Morris Novak?"

"I believe so," Zeke said. "On our old server." He spoke with an anxious stutter, which reminded Mimi of her cousin Yosef. "But retrieving them presents a number of technological challenges."

He launched into a jargon-filled explanation of what happened to the company's files after Boasberg split from Novak, then segued into another long discussion of how some older documents might be in outdated formats, which could require special software to open—and by that point, Mimi didn't understand what he was saying, and had stopped paying attention regardless.

Rafi not-so-subtly cut him off. "My friend here likes to go into detail," he said, with an uneasy giggle. "Zeke. *Tachlis.* Can we get those documents?"

Zeke did some quick computations on his stubby, ring-less fingers. "I'd say we could retrieve about seventy-five percent of them. Give or take a few percentage points."

"I'll take it," Brandon crowed.

"Okay." Rafi said. "I'll talk with Zeke and see what's possible. Then I'll give you the documents and let the chips fall where they may." He looked deflated, but relieved to have made a decision.

Brandon and Anita high-fived each other and cheered. Anita gave Rafi a hug and said she was proud of him.

Rafi broke up their reverie. "Let me be clear on one thing." He held his finger in the air and his voice took on a sudden air of authority, reminiscent of his father. "I am only handing you the documents. I won't walk you through them. What I'm doing already puts me in serious danger. I don't want to be any more involved than I already am."

"Fine," Brandon said. "And don't worry. If you're concerned about security, we'll make sure you're protected."

Rafi smiled cryptically. "I'm not worried about that. If worse comes to worse, I have protection. My little friend here." He lifted his shirt and pulled out a black pistol from his belt buckle. It was small and stubby and made Mimi's blood grow cold. She had seen more than enough guns in her life.

Anita seemed to have never viewed one up close before, and it clearly freaked her out. "Rafi," she gasped. "Are you sure you need that?"

"Of course, I do. My life may be in danger. My stepfather knows I have access to the same files my dad did. You saw what happened to him. I won't let that happen to me."

Brandon, Mimi, Zeke, and Anita exchanged looks.

"Please, Rafi," Anita said. "Put that thing away. It scares me." She sounded ready to cry.

"All right," said Rafi. He stuffed the gun back in his belt and placed his shirt back over it.

"Hey, you know what?" Rafi chirped. "Since I'm going against my family, I might as well break the religious rule, too. Let's all go to dinner."

No one answered, which didn't seem to faze Rafi. "Who's in?" he asked.

Mimi headed home. She did not like knowing Rafi had a gun.

Just then, Mimi's phone buzzed with a text from Channah.

"Did you talk to Rafi?" it said. "What did he say?"

Mimi stared at the message, horrified.

CHAPTER NINETEEN

Mimi dreaded going to the office the next day, as she knew Channah would ask about Rafi, and she was no longer sure she wanted the two of them together. She just didn't know what to tell Channah.

She could say that Rafi wasn't interested. The problem was, Rafi had said he *was* interested, and planned to call. He even thanked Mimi for the reminder. Channah was so invested in this, she might never forgive Mimi for lying. Mimi opted to take the middle ground—be honest, but not encouraging.

Shortly after Mimi came in the office, Channah pulled a chair up to her desk, expecting an update. "So, what did Rafi say? Is he going to call me?"

"Hey," Max called from his desk. "What's this I'm hearing? Does Channah have a new fella? Should I—?"

"No," Mimi snapped. "You should not buy a new suit." She turned to Channah. "I spoke to Rafi last night. He said he might call, but he's been busy. He has a lot on his mind. He seemed non-committal."

Channah stuck out her lip. "Okay. That's better than him saying he's not interested."

"Of course, he's interested," Max roared. "You're a lovely girl. If he's not interested, he's stupid. And who wants a stupid guy?"

"Dad, please." Mimi's shoulders grew tight. "This is a little more complicated. The guy is Rafi Boasberg, whose father was just killed." She turned to Channah. "I've been thinking. Rafi seems perfectly nice, but I'm not sure he's right for you. He has issues."

"Everyone has issues," Channah said.

"Yes, but his seem serious," Mimi said. "I think he's in a bad place."

"His father just died," Max said. "What do you expect him to do, jump for joy? Don't butt in, Mimi."

"I'm not butting in, Dad," Mimi shot back. "You are."

"Actually," Channah said, "you're both butting in."

Mimi's temples began to thump. The subtle approach wasn't working. Time to lay it all out there.

"You know why I'm discouraging this?" she snapped. "Because Rafi bought a gun to protect himself. He's worried his stepfather is going to kill him. That's some serious family drama. You want to be in the middle of that?"

Channah didn't respond, but looked to Max

"All right, that's not great," he said. "But a lot of people on Forty-Seventh Street carry guns. Diamond people are often the target of criminals. It's a fact of life. Rafi's father was just killed. It's not unreasonable."

"It wasn't just that he got a gun," Mimi said. "He just seemed a little—off. I don't think he's ready for a relationship. Channah, you yourself said that he asked you out a week ago and hasn't called since. What does that tell you?"

Channah lowered her chin.

"Maybe Channah should call him," Max said.

Channah's face snapped up. "That's what Mimi said."

"No, no, no," Mimi all but shouted. "I no longer say that."

"From what I hear," Max said, "it's common nowadays for women to call men. They're taking more of an initiative."

"Yes, Dad, you're a great source of advice on modern relationships." She took a breath; her anger wasn't helping. "Look, I've talked with Rafi. He knows you're interested. Just be patient."

"But, yesterday, you said calling would be better for me. It would make things clearer."

"Makes sense," Max said.

Mimi couldn't battle them both. Time for her emergency plan.

"How about this?" she said. "The diamond auction is next Monday. That's about a week and a half from now. Send Rafi a text, volunteer to help. That way, there's no pressure. You two can spend time together and see if something's there."

While Mimi didn't say it, she preferred them meeting in a place where there would be lots of people around.

"Okay," Channah said.

Even Max didn't object.

Channah pulled out her phone. Her finger hovered over it for a minute. Then she started furiously pecking out her message. When she was done, she showed it to Mimi.

"Hi, Rafi, it's Channah," it said. "I hope you remember me from the *shiva*. Sorry to bother you, but I was wondering if, it's okay with you, I could help out with the diamond auction next week. If not, fine. Thank you, Channah."

Mimi didn't know if Channah needed so many hedges and apologies, but that was her style. Mimi nodded her approval.

Channah sent off the message with a flourish, then set down her phone. "Let's see what he says."

For a minute—which felt like an hour—Channah, Mimi, and Max fidgeted as they awaited Rafi's response. Finally, the phone dinged.

Channah nearly jumped. Her lips moved as she read the text, then she broke into a smile. "He wrote, 'Great. That would be perfect. You should definitely come.'"

"That's encouraging," Max grinned.

"I know!" Channah almost floated off her chair. She began planning what she'd wear.

"I'm so happy for you," Mimi said, with a pasted-on smile. Inside, she wanted to throw up.

A few days later, Anita called, and there was an upbeat tone to her voice that Mimi had not heard before.

"Amazing news!" she announced. "Rafi is giving us a ton of information on Novak's business dealings. He's found hundreds of documents; more than we ever dreamed of. We're having a press conference next week to lay out our findings."

"That's great. What did you find?"

Anita groaned. "That's the problem. We haven't found anything yet. Retrieving them has taken longer than we expected. Zeke had to work out the technical kinks, and it will take a few days to download everything, and then we have to sift through it all. It's going to be a crazy time getting things ready. Can you come to my place Friday to help out?"

"I'd love to. But Friday is right before the Sabbath, and work is usually crazy busy. How about I come over that afternoon?"

Anita blew up. "Jesus, Mimi. We have tons of material to go through. Isn't freeing an innocent more important than your father's diamond company?"

Mimi always sensed Anita was silently judging her. Now, it seemed, the mask was off. "Whoa!" Mimi snapped. "Do you know how much time I've spent—"

"Let me take that back," Anita jumped in. "I shouldn't have said that. I'm under a lot of stress. This is important to me."

"It's important to me, too."

"I know that," Anita said. "Why don't you come over Saturday? And bring those documents that show Morris Novak owns local real estate. Brandon thinks they will interest the media."

"Okay," Mimi said, without much enthusiasm.

"I'm sorry for what I said before. Brandon and I are really grateful for all you've done. You've been incredible."

"Thanks," Mimi whispered. She appreciated the apology, but it didn't fully remove the sting.

"I consider you a friend," Anita said. "I hope when this is all over, we'll remain friends."

"I consider you a friend, too," Mimi replied, somewhat stiffly, as she wasn't sure how true that was. Mimi viewed Anita as an associate she sometimes jousted with—what they call on TV a "frenemy." Which amused Mimi, as she had never had one of those before.

"How about this?" Mimi said. "My office closes about three-thirty on Friday. I can get to your place by five or so. So, we can work all Friday night."

"Friday night won't work," Anita said. "I'm going out with this guy I'm seeing."

Guy she was seeing? Anita had never mentioned that before.

"I didn't know you were dating someone," Mimi said. "Is it anyone I know?"

"No, no, no," Anita responded, a little too quickly. "It's been going on for a while. It used to be pretty casual, but, you know, it isn't anymore."

Two weeks ago, Anita was lamenting her work left no time for a social life. Now, she was saying she'd been seeing a guy for a while.

"Sounds great," Mimi said. "I'd love to meet him."

"I'm sure you will, at some point," she said. "Maybe. We'll see. He pops in and out of New York, so you might not be able to meet him for a while. But maybe, at some point. I don't know. We'll see." She tittered nervously.

Anita's evasiveness was odd, especially considering she had just called Mimi a friend. She was hiding something. Mimi just didn't know what—or why.

CHAPTER TWENTY

On Saturday afternoon, Mimi gathered all the documents that proved Morris Novak was her father's landlord and headed to Anita's apartment in Williamsburg.

Anita didn't live far from Channah, but her place was in hipster Brooklyn, as opposed to religious Brooklyn, and the two neighborhoods were different worlds.

The hipster area featured trendy bars, sleek experiential retailers, and brunch places that strived for a homey, weathered look. The religious area was packed with kosher supermarkets, Hebrew bookstores, and old-school tailors. They didn't try to look weathered. They actually were.

Hipster-ville was always changing, while the religious area struggled to preserve what was fading away. One felt too modern for the earthy city streets; the other seemed like a relic next to the surrounding neon. Both seemed out of time. Neither truly fit.

Anita's area was on the verge of being gentrified, so it was filled with both grimy bodegas and offbeat restaurants—one served nothing but waffles twenty-four hours a day. Yet, the streets still held a hint of poverty and danger. Her building had a filthy foyer and no elevator—it was a walk-up, in New York speak—so Mimi's calf muscles got a workout as she trod up four flights of stairs.

Anita's place was, like many twenty-something apartments, small and cramped, with bookshelves stuffed with pictures and knickknacks. Her documentary posters were prominently displayed on the wall. The award from the Central New Jersey Film Festival sat on top of the bookcase, next to a picture of her triumphantly hoisting it in the air.

It reminded Mimi of her post-college apartments, when she lived largely on her parents' dime. The memory made her smile, until she realized that her current place was actually smaller than where she lived back then.

Brandon sat at a long table, which was covered by a sea of papers, phones, and laptops. A paper plate held poppy seeds and butter, the obvious remnant of a bagel.

"Pardon the mess," Anita said. "We spent all yesterday looking at documents."

Brandon looked tired, his face lined and grim. The beginnings of a beard branched out of his goatee. Mimi handed him the folder of documents that showed that Novak owned her office building.

He quickly thumbed through them. "Well," Brandon said with a sigh, "at least we have *something*."

"You haven't found anything?"

"Not really." Anita exhaled, sending her bangs skyward. "We've looked through tons of documents, and after all these hours, we've only proved that Novak has extensive holdings in offshore tax havens. Which we knew already."

"Depending on how they're structured," Brandon added, "they may not even be illegal. All they show is normal everyday corruption, and, unfortunately, people have gotten a little too used to that. To make a splash, we need something that will really grab the media's attention."

Anita surveyed the mess on her kitchen table and frowned. "It's impossible to understand these documents without someone guiding you. The only person who can really do that is Rafi. And he won't."

"You can try and convince him," Brandon said.

"Trust me, he won't," Anita said. "He feels he's done his part. We've already asked a lot of him."

Anita rested her elbow on the table and cupped her forehead in her hand. "People think journalism is so glamorous. They haven't spent eight hours trying to make sense of endless rows of numbers on a huge stack of PDFs. Look at these papers. It took hours just to print them. I'm beginning to doubt it was worth the toner."

She picked up her recorder. "Possible documentary subject: Printer toner. What is its environmental impact? Why is it called that? It doesn't really tone anything." She dropped the recorder to the table, without much excitement or energy.

"But didn't Rafi say he witnessed all sorts of incriminating stuff at Novak's company?" Mimi asked.

"I'm sure he did," said Brandon. "The problem is most crooks don't keep written records of their crimes. I am sure that Novak has done terrible things. We just can't prove it. It's also possible that those records do exist, and Rafi is keeping them from us."

"I doubt that," Anita said.

"You never know." Brandon's mouth turned down. "Rafi worked for his father for a long time. He could be implicated, too."

"Then why would he hand over all these documents?" Anita demanded.

"I don't know," Brandon said. "Perhaps he's not complicit, just a coward." He threw Mimi's folder on the table. "The point is, without his help, we're not having a press conference. And Novak will get away with everything."

"I can look though the documents," Mimi said.

"You're welcome to try," Brandon said, without much excitement. "Here's the ones we haven't gone through." He pushed a huge stack of papers toward Mimi.

Anita gave her arms a long creaky stretch. "Brandon and I have been at this for three days. Do you mind if we step out for a quick brunch?"

Mimi smiled, as a bit of a reflex. "Be my guest. How'd it go last night with your boyfriend?"

Brandon's face pivoted toward Anita's. "Did you say—"

"No, I—" Anita flushed with panic. "That didn't—" She waved her hands around. "It wasn't what I thought. I don't have a boyfriend." She let out a strange, unconvincing laugh.

"Okay," Mimi responded. Probably best to drop it.

Brandon shot Anita a glance. "Let's go." As they trotted out the door, Brandon said, "I hope you come up with something. Unfortunately, I doubt you will."

Mimi stared at the tower of documents, determined to prove him wrong.

Before she started, she used the bathroom, and noticed a condom wrapper in the trash can. *Okay, Anita,* she thought. *You may not have a boyfriend, but you got something going on.*

She picked up the first document, and thoroughly inspected it. It was an invoice of diamonds that Novak bought in the African Democratic Republic.

Maybe if Mimi had a record of rough diamond prices from ten years ago, she could tell if Novak was paying fair value for the ADR's resources. A few minutes of Googling revealed no such list existed.

The next five documents were much the same: rows of numbers that took Mimi forever to decode and revealed little once she did. Thoroughly inspecting each page wasn't turning out to be a great use of her time, so she began paging through them quicker. That didn't work, either.

After spending an hour examining dozens of documents, it dawned on Mimi what Anita and Brandon seemed to have discovered long ago—the documents were boring. They showed ordinary, unexciting diamond trades. She'd jotted down a few notes, but that was mostly to feel she was accomplishing something. She had no real idea what any of it meant. She had little to show for her efforts, besides back pain.

One thing did catch her eye, if only because it stood out from the endless lists of gem deals. It was a receipt for a Monet painting from a Beirut art dealer. It was attached to an invoice, shipping it to a woman in the African Democratic Republic.

It wasn't clear why that document was in there until she noticed the business that shipped the painting: New Prometheus, one of the companies that she'd traced to Novak.

She Googled the woman's address in the ADR. It was Windcliff Estates, the home of the minister of mines. Novak had shown Mimi his picture with the minister there, while bragging—in his precise, clipped syllables—of their ex-CELL-ent relationship.

No wonder you're buds, Mimi thought. *If you sent me a quarter-of-a-million-dollar painting, I'd be your pal, too.*

Mimi put that document aside. That might be something.

Two hours after popping out for a "quick brunch," Brandon and Anita returned.

"You guys were right," Mimi said, evading their eyes. "There's not much here. The most interesting thing was this." She lifted the receipt. "It shows a painting being shipped from one of Novak's companies to the home of the ADR's minister of mines."

Anita didn't seem fazed, but Brandon instantly snatched the paper from the table. He brought it to his face, fascinated.

"This woman is the mining minister's wife," Brandon said. "His third wife, actually. And you're saying one of Novak's companies sent her a painting?"

"Yes," Mimi said. "Is that allowed?"

"Absolutely not," Brandon laughed. "This is a bribe!" He held out the document in front of his face. His eyes sparkled. "This is a bribe!"

"Isn't that normal everyday corruption?" Mimi said.

"Of course, but it's *illegal* corruption," Brandon said. "It's against the law for American citizens to give overseas government officials any kind of gift. Technically, he sent it to his wife, but they almost certainly share bank accounts.

"It fits so perfectly that it's a piece of high-value art. That's a huge vehicle for money laundering. Along with diamonds and real estate, of course. I always wondered why the government in the ADR protected Novak for so long. This makes it clear. He paid off its mining minister."

A smile spread across his face. "They put a crime in writing. It's almost too perfect! He could go to jail for this! In fact, I'd be amazed if he didn't. This case would be a slam-dunk for any prosecutor."

Brandon's face shone with delight. "After all these years, I will finally nail him." He thrust his fist in the air. "Morris Novak, you are going down!"

CHAPTER TWENTY-ONE

BRANDON FELT THIS NEW INFORMATION was so damning, it should be released immediately. He decreed they hold the press conference Monday, which was two days away.

The three of them worked all weekend organizing the event. Anita rented a conference room at a Midtown hotel and hired a publicist—paid for with Rafi's money—while Mimi stayed up late meticulously editing Brandon's presentation and compiling an information-packed press kit.

Anita asked Mimi to help check in the media. "If any reporter has a question about the press kit, who better to answer it?"

Mimi reluctantly said yes. It meant she'd have to take off time from her job Monday, but she didn't want to deal with another Anita guilt trip. Her father would probably give her one for missing work, but she could handle that—she'd been getting those all her life.

When Mimi got to the hotel, she was impressed how professional everything looked, especially since it was pulled together so quickly. The room featured a podium in front; blown-up documents resting on easels; even plates of sandwiches. Free food always made reporters happy.

Mimi grabbed a sandwich and greeted Brandon, who was in a side room, reviewing the presentation on his laptop.

Anita was traversing the room with a handful of papers, barking orders to the hired hands. Finally, she stopped and said hello.

"How are things going?" Mimi asked.

"So far, so good," she said, half talking to Mimi, half checking her phone. Her hair was copiously mussed, and her glasses sat a slight angle to the rest of her face. "I'm a little nervous no one will show up, but even if they don't, I'll get awesome footage for my documentary."

Just then, a short pudgy man in a suit appeared. He had an owlish face, a beard, and round glasses, and tightly clutched a leather briefcase.

"This is Mr. Greenfeld, Brandon's new lawyer," Anita said. "Mimi here helped put the presentation together."

The lawyer temporarily let go of his briefcase to offer a dead-fish handshake and a grunt.

Anita frowned. "He's not happy Brandon is holding this press conference."

"It's rule number one," Greenfeld griped. "Defendants should keep quiet."

"Don't worry," Anita said. "Brandon's not dumb. We just want this information out there."

"Trust me, reporters will only come to gawk at the accused killer," said Greenfeld. "They won't care what he says about some obscure billionaire."

Anita was far taller than Greenfeld and gazed down at him. "Brandon will make them care."

Greenfeld groaned and walked away. Anita went back to crisscrossing the floor.

Mimi settled at the press table, and spent a few minutes stacking her media packets into tidy piles. But soon, she was busy. Many reporters *did* show up—maybe just to gawk, but they came. At one point, the line to get in stretched out the door. Mimi handed each reporter a copy of her meticulously assembled press kit.

The journalists were a familiar type to Mimi: they slouched, wore glasses, and couldn't resist wisecracks even when doing a mundane task like checking in for a press conference. They were either chatty and hyper-aware, or quiet and lost in their thoughts, with little in-between. They reminded Mimi of her old newspaper colleagues-slash-drinking buddies, and how much she missed them.

Before the press conference began, Anita and Mimi surveyed the capacity crowd. Anita pointed with pride to one surprise attendee: Detective Matthews. He was standing against the back wall, arms crossed, sporting a suit and his standard scowl.

Anita smiled. "Do you know how long we've been trying to get him to listen to us? He is now!"

A few minutes later, it was showtime. Anita gave a brief, nervous introduction to the assembled reporters, full of "uhs" and hand-waving, instructing them to Tweet with the hashtag #MorrisNovakLeaks. Mimi didn't think that would catch on.

Brandon stepped to the podium, seeming pleased and energized by the large audience. He was dressed in a black suit, his ponytail discreetly tucked in the back of his jacket. He stood ramrod-straight, his hands neatly intertwined in front of him.

Anita hovered nearby, touting her camera, while his lawyer stood to his left, scowling.

"My name is Brandon Walters. I am a longtime human rights activist," he began, his South African accent giving his words extra authority. "Thanks to documents supplied by a courageous whistleblower, I can reveal information about a notorious billionaire named Morris Novak. You might not have heard of him. He stays under the radar and avoids the spotlight. But he's a major landlord in New York City, and perhaps it's time local media started looking into him. I'm happy to begin that process."

He put up a slide showing the New York buildings Novak owned, using Mimi's research.

"Morris Novak's name often appears in the Panama Papers. But the extent to which he hides his money offshore has never been fully documented." Dramatic pause. "Until now."

A slide appeared listing Novak's offshore bank accounts and shell companies. "All that money, hidden from view," Brandon marveled. "It makes you wonder, what else is he hiding?"

A few days earlier, Brandon had dismissed this as standard corruption, not worth informing the media about. At the press conference, he denounced it with such passion, the reporters furrowed their brows and moved their pens. He *was* making them care.

"Let me remind you that Mr. Novak has been accused of dealing in blood diamonds during the civil war in the African Democratic Republic," Brandon intoned, "including possibly buying diamonds from the East Side Kids, one of the most vicious militias during the war."

Mimi felt pained as she remembered that old photo of Reverend Kamora as a child soldier.

On it went, Brandon joyfully dumping basket after basket of trash over Novak's reputation. He took clear relish at the finale—the documents which showed that Novak had sent a painting to the home of the ADR mining minister.

"That's a clear bribe," he declared. "Imagine, sending a government official an expensive and valuable painting, in a country where most workers earn two dollars a day. Think of how much good that money could have done for the people of that country. And consider how much of the country's resources Novak was allowed to hoard for himself, because of that bribe."

He lifted his index finger. "The Foreign Corrupt Practices Act forbids U.S. citizens from offering any kind of payment to foreign officials." The law appeared on the screen. "I should note that the statute of limitations has not expired on this transaction.

"This may not be the worst thing Mr. Novak has ever done," Brandon pronounced. "But it may be what brings him down."

Mimi already knew most of the information in the presentation, but taken together, it was a damning summary, demonstrating that Novak had exploited the ADR for his own thoroughly corrupt ends. And Brandon was the perfect person to deliver the message; he was articulate, fluent, and compelling. It seemed like he had been practicing his whole life for this moment. Anita glimmered with pride; her movie star was delivering an Oscar-worthy performance.

Then came the questions.

"Why should we believe you, given you are accused of murder?" asked one reporter.

Brandon smiled tightly, then lapsed into a monotone. "I am not guilty of the charges against me. My attorney has advised me not to comment beyond that."

The lawyer nodded. He seemed to like that answer—or at least not hate it.

After a few more questions about the murder—which Brandon batted away with crisp non-answers—he grew frustrated. "Are there questions on any other topics?"

"I have one!" a voice called out. "Mr. Walters, why aren't you in jail?"

The speaker was part of a group that had just entered; Mimi was too caught up in everything to check them in. But she instantly recognized the voice, and the accompanying hair helmet and *yarmulke*. It was Morris Novak, flanked by two bodyguards.

Brandon did a double take, then emitted a sly, almost rapacious, grin.

His longtime enemy was standing right in front of him. He looked ready to deliver his death blow.

Mimi wasn't so sure. Novak wouldn't have come without a plan. This could be a trap.

CHAPTER TWENTY-TWO

After hearing Novak and Brandon continually trash each other, it was striking to see them face off in the same room, each determined to bring the other down.

"Ladies and gentlemen," Brandon smiled, "this press conference has been blessed with a special guest of dishonor: The man himself, Morris Novak. You don't realize how rare this appearance is. It's like a sighting of Evil Elvis."

The reporters' faces glowed. The press conference had suddenly escalated to a new level of drama. The photographers all aimed their cameras at Novak. For a man who spent his life avoiding the limelight, it looked like torture. He seemed to flinch with every click.

"Perhaps, Mr. Novak," Brandon declared, "you want to address this clear evidence of corruption."

"All in due course, Mr. Walters," Novak said. He stepped forward, and the photographers parted like the Red Sea. "Perhaps, instead of casting aspersions at others, you should be a little more worried about your upcoming murder trial."

"I'm not worried at all," Brandon said. "I am not guilty. Maybe *you* should be concerned. You had a lot more to gain by killing Abraham Boasberg."

"Are you accusing me of something, Mr. Walters?" Novak said, a slight smile appearing on his lips. "I believe you're the one who's been charged with this crime. Not me."

His lawyer rushed to the podium and nudged Brandon out of the way. "Mr. Walters has pleaded not guilty to all charges," he said into the microphone. "That's the only statement he will make on that subject today."

"How disappointing," Novak said. "I understand Mr. Walters has told people that the police arrested him because they were paid off. Care to comment, Mr. Walters?"

"I just proved you greased palms in the African Democratic Republic," Brandon shouted from behind his lawyer's back. "It's not a stretch to think you'd do it here."

Novak was smiling wider now. "That's quite a charge. I hope everyone heard Mr. Walters accuse New York City police officers of taking bribes. I don't suppose you have evidence for that assertion. I didn't see it on your PowerPoint.

"Making wild claims doesn't help your credibility, Mr. Walters. In fact, it makes you a liar."

Almost at once, the mood in the room changed. The reporters initially regarded Brandon with a certain deference. Now, murmurs and laughter rippled through the crowd.

Through all this, the lawyer's face turned various shades of white and red. Finally, he had enough. He elbowed his client out of the way and moved the microphone close to his face. "Mr. Walters will not be making any more statements today," he said, and yanked Brandon from the stage.

The reporters took this as a sign the press conference was over, and swarmed around Novak, lobbing questions at him. He ignored them all. His guards enveloped him in a circle, and he strolled out of the room, the press trailing behind.

Mimi could see his head poking out of the scrum. He looked pleased. Just like Brandon had blown up Boasberg's big announcement, Novak had blown up his.

As the room emptied out, Mimi could see the pink-faced attorney lecturing a sullen Brandon, while Anita looked on in horror. Mimi thought it best to stay away from that, so she wandered over to Detective Matthews.

Matthews was planted in the same spot he'd stood the whole press conference, scribbling in his notebook. He wore a dark suit and looked pretty much like he did last year, with the same round, bulldog-like face; brown, close-cropped hair; and bulky, imposing chest. Mimi noticed two differences: he had shaved his mustache, and lost weight. Both made him look younger.

Mimi wasn't sure he would recognize her, but he did, though his greeting was both warm and wary.

"So, what did you think of all that?" she asked him.

"What did I think of him accusing me of taking payoffs? You might not be surprised to hear I didn't find that argument persuasive."

Mimi winced. "Okay, that was crazy. Obviously, you would never do that."

"I appreciate that," Matthews grumbled. "I guess."

"That was an awful thing for him to say. I don't blame you for being pissed about it."

Matthews didn't respond, but nodded slightly—and Mimi sensed that, on some level, he really did appreciate her saying that.

Mimi took this as a license to continue. "Though, you have to admit, some of the information he provided was pretty compelling."

"It's difficult for me to comment without examining his purported evidence. What do you think?"

"I believe those documents raise serious questions about Morris Novak's business dealings and show that he's someone you should keep an eye on."

"Perhaps. But Mr. Walters doesn't have a ton of credibility. He might have altered those documents."

"He didn't," Mimi said. "I discovered the shipping invoice for that painting. I have scans of the original documents. I can assure you, nothing was changed."

Matthews cocked his head. "Miss Rosen, I hope this doesn't mean you're investigating again."

"You can call me Mimi. And can't I, as a private citizen, show interest in something like this?"

Matthews thought for a second. "In your case, no."

Mimi put her hands on her hips. "You just asked my opinion. You must think it counts for something."

"I was just being nice."

"That would be a first."

Matthews bristled. "Miss Rosen—Mimi—let me remind you, again, that investigating a murder is serious business. So, my warning you to stay away from this is actually very nice."

Mimi strove for common ground. "Look, Detective, you know I respect you. You saved my life. I can never repay you for that. I'm well aware I'll never be as good a detective as you.

"But you also know I'm trustworthy. I wouldn't doctor those documents. They're real."

A range of emotions crossed Matthews' face. "How about this?" he said finally. "White-collar crime isn't my forte. But if you send me those documents, I will make sure they're delivered to the U.S. Attorney."

They traded numbers, and she texted him what she had.

Matthews checked his phone and nodded. "Great. And now, I hope your involvement in this is over."

"Actually," Mimi said, her feet shuffling, "there's a few more things I want to discuss."

Matthews closed his eyes. "Oh God."

"Why are you so—?" Mimi tried to stay calm. "I have information that is relevant to this case. Right next to the windows in Boasberg's office, someone stuffed a rag in a gap between some bricks. And that rag contains the gold box that held the missing diamond. Not the diamond, just the box. Did you know that?"

Matthews looked stunned. "No, I didn't."

"It was easy to miss," she said, exultant. "The rag was the same color as the brick paste, so you have to really look for it. Good thing I got involved, huh?"

"Actually—" Matthews' eyes grew hard. "I am curious how you were able to see something that close to Boasberg's office window. It seems to me, you could have only done that by illegally trespassing on a cordoned-off crime scene."

Mimi gulped and her mouth turned dry. "I didn't say I personally saw that box," she sputtered. "Someone could have told me about it."

"Someone told you about it? Who?"

"I can't reveal my source." She dropped her voice. "I'm a journalist."

"So, you're telling me you had an alleged source who snuck into a sealed crime scene, and discovered a crucial piece of evidence? Didn't that strike you as odd?"

Mimi shifted her weight from one foot to another. "Well, sure, if you put it that way."

Matthews was visibly struggling to keep his temper in check. "Mimi, I understand that you mean well and just want to help. But I want no misunderstandings from you, or any of your so-called sources. No one is allowed to trespass on, and possibly contaminate, the site of a serious crime. That gets people sent to jail. If I ever catch you or anyone else doing that, you'll discover what I'm like when I'm really not nice. Do you understand?"

Mimi's body was now bathed in sweat.

"I repeat: do you understand?"

Mimi bleated out, "Yes."

"I hope you do. And I hope I've made myself clear." He stormed off.

Mimi caught her breath. *Yes,* she thought. *You've made yourself clear. It's clear you're a dick.*

CHAPTER TWENTY-THREE

THE NEXT DAY IT WAS OBVIOUS what a good job Novak had done at ruining Brandon's press conference.

"Psycho Killer," trumpeted one tabloid headline. "Accused Murderer Insults New York's Brave Men in Blue." Brandon was shown sneering and pointing his finger. The impressive figure at the podium had been made to look unhinged.

The papers interviewed legal experts, who chortled at the folly of a murder suspect holding a press conference, blaming his crime on someone else, then suggesting the police were on the take. "He should sue his lawyer for malpractice," one laughed. Mimi imagined Greenfeld blanching.

Novak's attorney, meanwhile, was having a field day, dubbing Brandon's accusation of murder "ludicrous," "not even worth responding to," and "a desperate accusation from a desperate man."

Plus, his client had an alibi.

"On the night of Abraham Boasberg's tragic passing, Morris Novak was being honored at a charitable dinner for his generosity in supporting the Coltura Garden, a local landmark and one of New York's hidden treasures," he told one reporter. "We also know where Brandon Walters was that night—at Mr. Boasberg's office."

The information Mimi worked so hard to assemble into those press kits garnered little coverage. Only one newspaper asked Novak's lawyer about Brandon's charges, and he barely bothered to answer. "Given the other ridiculous things Mr. Walters had to say, we urge everyone to take his assertions and purported documents with a grain of salt." He no doubt said that with the smuggest of smiles.

"DID YOU SEE THE HEADLINES?" Anita asked Mimi on the phone later that day, sounding near tears. "They made Brandon look like a maniac. I thought what he said might be a problem, but I didn't think it would be *this* bad."

"The reporters totally ignored the substance of the press conference. I don't get it. We gave them so much information. We even gave them sandwiches!

"Brandon's lawyer is furious. He said there's no chance the police will drop the charges now, after Brandon accused them of corruption. And his comments will be used to impeach his credibility at trial. I give Novak credit. He knew what he was doing. It was almost like he was setting Brandon up. How did he know that Brandon thought the police were getting paid off?"

Mimi felt a sudden heaviness in her stomach. "I might have done that."

"What?"

"When I talked to Novak," Mimi said, her voice faltering, "I told him Brandon believed that."

Anita gasped. "How could you say that? You have to be careful with a guy like Novak! He's crafty! He'll take what you say and twist it."

"I'm sorry. I didn't—"

"But you *did*. That's the point."

There was a pause. Mimi could hear Anita sniffle.

"This wasn't entirely your fault," Anita said. "Brandon shouldn't have said what he did. His lawyer was right. We never should have held that press conference. It's destroyed his whole case. And to top it off, Novak had an alibi for the night of the murder. He was at some dinner."

"That's just what his attorney said," Mimi interjected.

"Brandon's lawyer checked it out. It's true."

"Okay. Just because Novak didn't do the actual murder, that doesn't mean that he's innocent," Mimi said. "He's a billionaire. He could have hired someone to do it."

"Of course, he could have," Anita said. "But do we have proof of that?"

"No," Mimi said.

"So basically, all we have are theories. That's not enough to save Brandon."

There was a silence.

"Okay, we've hit a rough patch," Mimi said. "But let's not give up. There's leads we can follow. Like that Merlano company. We need to—"

"Oh, stop it!" Anita snapped. "We have zero. Nothing. At least nothing that will help Brandon. We're just spinning our wheels.

"If you want to keep investigating, go ahead. The only thing you've found is some dumb ADR company that Brandon says is probably a Novak smokescreen. We need to hire a professional."

"Can we do that?" Mimi asked.

"Rafi's agreed to put up the money. We have to. We have no choice anymore." Anita began to cry. "Everything's a mess. This whole time, I only wanted to do good, to shed light on an ongoing tragedy. And all I've done is help create another one. It's so frustrating. I can't do anything right. I try and try, and I never get anywhere."

"Don't be so hard on yourself," Mimi said. "You've accomplished a lot."

"Like what?" Anita sneered through her sobs, as if daring Mimi to compliment her.

"You've made movies on important issues. You're an award-winning documentarian."

"Oh, please. I only won one award. From the Central New Jersey Film Festival. Not even the New Jersey Film Festival. Just one part of the state!

"No one sees my movies. And no one will see this one. Who wants to watch a documentary about a human rights activist when he's an accused murderer?"

Her sobbing grew louder. "I'm sorry. It's been a rough week. We had that disaster of a press conference, and my stupid boyfriend doesn't want to—" She stopped herself. "Never mind. I can't talk about that. That's a whole other mess."

There was another long pause. "Thanks for your help, Mimi, but we're just going in circles. I gotta go." She clicked off.

Mimi didn't blame Anita for getting frustrated. She was, too.

A little later, Zeke called. Mimi had phoned him last week, but he hadn't gotten back to her.

"Sorry I took so long to return your call," he said. "I've been crazy busy. It's been a huge project downloading those old files. It took way longer than expected." He sounded nervous, though he seemed that way the first time she met him.

"Why'd it take so long?"

"At the last minute, Rafi decided he wanted to look everything over, edit out some stuff."

"Hold it? Rafi removed documents? Like what?" Brandon had raised that as a possibility last week, only to have Anita knock it down.

Zeke had clearly revealed more than he should have; he started stammering more than usual. "Nothing. Just personal stuff he wanted to keep private. It wasn't anything to be concerned about."

Mimi considered pressing Zeke further, but doubted he'd say more, and didn't want him to clam up. She had other stuff to get to.

"I want to know about the app that buzzes people into the office from off-site. Who had access to it?"

"I do, Rafi does. Mr. Boasberg did. I think the landlord does, too. That's about it."

"Interesting," Mimi said. "Do you know who the landlord is?"

"A new company just bought the building. Neighborhood Properties."

Mimi's jaw fell. "Neighborhood Properties? That's Morris Novak's company."

"Really? I'd heard rumors of that. But I've never heard it confirmed."

Mimi thought for a second. "Does the landlord control the cameras in the hallway?"

"Sure."

"So, Neighborhood Properties probably handed over the hallway footage to police."

"Probably."

"Could they have altered it?"

Zeke cleared his throat. "It's hard to say without evaluating their audio-visual set-up. But obviously what they call 'deep fakes' could pose a major technological challenge in the future."

He launched into a long monologue on that subject, using information he'd gleaned from a viral Reddit post. He went into way more detail than Mimi could ever want or comprehend, and once he started talking about blockchain, Mimi knew if she didn't interrupt him, he'd never stop.

"All right." She cut him off. "Let's talk about the night of the murder. What time did you leave the office?"

"About six-fifteen."

"Right before Rafi left. Did anything unusual happen that day?"

"One thing," Zeke said. "Mr. Boasberg was worried about this email he'd received. Apparently, the person who sent it wanted their identity kept secret. So, Mr. Boasberg asked me to print out the attachment, then wipe the email from his inbox."

"Did he say why?"

"No. Mr. Boasberg worked in mysterious ways."

"Who sent it?"

"It was from some company. Marlo-something."

"Merlano Resources?"

"Yeah, that's it."

Mimi wrote "Merlano email, with attachment" in her notebook. "Did you see this attachment?"

"No. He made me promise not to look."

"But you printed it. Do you know what Boasberg did with the printout?"

"No."

"How about the email? Can I see that?"

"Oh no," Zeke said. "It's completely wiped from the drive." He described with pride how he used special software to make the email and file irretrievable, even by law enforcement.

"So—" she broke in, not wanting to endure another tech lecture, "you're saying that, unless I find that printout, that email's gone and there's no way to find it?"

"Yeah," Zeke said, his voice rising. "Isn't that great?"

"No," Mimi said. "It's horrible." And hung up.

That night, Mimi mulled things over at home, as Edith Piaf crooned in the background. She jotted the main murder scenarios in her notebook.

The first: Brandon killed Boasberg. That was certainly plausible; plenty of evidence pointed to him.

He just had no motive. Granted, he and Boasberg didn't like each other. But right before the murder, they seemed poised to join forces.

According to the police, Brandon wanted to steal the big diamond. But that didn't make sense. First, they never found it on him. Second, if he wanted to steal it, he picked a really dumb and obvious way to do it. It was hard to imagine a human rights activist—never mind one as smart as Brandon—doing that.

She couldn't rule him out, though. She wrote "maybe."

The second scenario: Rafi killed Boasberg. The timeframe lined up, and he could have used the app to buzz Brandon in the office.

He even had a motive: inheriting his father's estate. Except Rafi didn't seem all that interested in money, and it was hard to imagine him killing his father—though Mimi found that a little more plausible after seeing him wave that gun around.

Rafi also couldn't be ruled out. Another "maybe."

Possibility three: Novak killed Boasberg. Mimi liked that theory. Novak was a bad guy. He had a motive.

She just didn't know how he pulled it off. According to police, the hallway camera didn't show anyone entering the office besides Brandon.

Then again, Novak owned the building; he might have a secret entrance into Boasberg's office. He could have doctored the video. He could have even hired someone to climb in Boasberg's window. That would take skill—but Novak was the kind of guy who had mercenaries for Facebook friends.

Then, there was Brandon's theory: Novak paid off the police, and they're hiding the *real* video. That would mean Matthews was on the take. Again, hard to imagine.

Another "maybe."

Plus, there was Merlano Resources. What Zeke said convinced her it played some role in this. She just didn't know what. She didn't even know who owned it. The most likely candidate was Novak, but she had no way to find out.

Actually, she did have one way, though it was a longshot: she could ask him.

CHAPTER TWENTY-FOUR

Mimi got up at six a.m. the next day, and one hour later she was sitting on the bench in front of NP Inc.'s midtown headquarters, ready to greet Morris Novak. But he and his town car never came. After a few hours mostly looking at her phone, she left.

She did the same thing the day after. And again, he didn't show. To do a true stakeout, she'd have to wait there day and night, and she didn't have enough patience—or life in her phone battery—for that.

Maybe he'd left town. Or maybe he had another way into the building. Time to visit her friend, the receptionist.

Mimi marched into the company office and demanded to speak with Morris Novak.

"He's not here," the receptionist responded in a flat voice. She did not seem happy to see Mimi again.

Mimi crossed her arms. "You told me that last time. And you were lying. I want to talk with him."

The receptionist's stern look suddenly faded. "I'm serious. He's not here. Really."

"Where he is then?"

"I have no idea," she said. "I wish I could tell you."

Mimi suspected she was lying—until she noticed the worry lines on her forehead, her hands knotted in her lap. She was no longer the imperious gatekeeper to a mysterious mogul, simply a person trying to make a living, like Mimi.

"Seriously? You don't know where he is?"

"It's crazy. He's disappeared. No one can find him. You don't know where he is, do you?"

This perplexed Mimi. "No. Why would I?"

"I remember you had those printouts. You seem good at finding things on the Internet."

"Sorry, I don't know any more than you do," Mimi said. "When was the last time you heard from him?"

"He hasn't spoken to anyone at the office in two days."

"That's not long."

"For him, it is. He usually checks in every two minutes. The chief operating officer just called his wife. Even she doesn't know where he is."

Mimi took this in. "When was the last time he was in the office?"

"Tuesday afternoon. Right after the FBI came."

"Hold it. The FBI was here?"

"Yeah. It was like something out of a movie. There was this large group of agents, all wearing suits. One guy even had a walkie-talkie. It freaked us all out."

"Why were they here?"

"Nobody knows. We'd heard there was some kind of press conference about Morris on Monday, but based on what the newspapers said, it was no big deal. Then suddenly, it was like this SWAT team showed up. They talked with him for like three hours, and left with boxes of stuff."

"Did Novak say anything about it?"

"Right after they left, he called a staff meeting. He told us there was nothing to worry about, it was just a misunderstanding caused by that press conference, and it would be quickly resolved. He said the best thing we could do was mind our own business. He always said stuff like that."

"Did he seem worried?"

"Not really. He was cool as a cucumber, like always. But I noticed one thing. Sometimes, when he did big business deals, I'd see this vein on the top of his forehead throb. It was like this tic he couldn't control."

"Was it throbbing during the meeting?"

"Was it ever! It was going ninety miles an hour! Like it was transmitting a code."

"Then what happened?"

"He left, and that was the last time we heard from him. I don't get it. How does a billionaire go missing? I don't even know if I should keep working here. I assume I'll keep getting paid, but I can't say for sure. This business can't go on if the owner's missing. He's this whole operation. I probably should look for something else. You don't know anyone looking for a good receptionist, do you? My name is Margaret. I have excellent references."

Margaret scribbled her personal email on the back of her business card and handed it to Mimi.

"I'll keep an eye out," Mimi said, fingering the card. Then something occurred to her. "Your company owns a lot of buildings. Does it have access to all their security footage?"

"Sure."

"How about Novak? Can he monitor who comes and goes in your buildings?"

"Probably. On my first day of work, someone told me, be careful what I write in emails, Mr. Novak has access to everyone's computer. Speaking of which, I should keep my mouth shut." She lowered her voice to a whisper. "Though, please, let me know if you hear of anything."

Mimi promised she would, though Margaret's question rang in her ears: How could a billionaire go missing?

She glanced at her watch. It was just about noon. There was one other place Novak might be.

Mimi sat on a bench at the Coltura Garden. This was a far more pleasant place for a stakeout. She understood why it was Novak's favorite spot in New York. It was immaculate and well-maintained—just like him.

It was hot and sunny, but Mimi found a cool shady bench underneath a tree. The garden wasn't crowded, and she could enjoy it in relative solitude. The rows of manicured pink and yellow flowers seemed to burst with color. She didn't even look at her phone, a clear sign she felt relaxed.

Mimi was exhausted after getting up so early, and as the gentle garden air wrapped around her like a blanket, she dozed off.

She was awakened by the rustling of grass. She felt a shadow over her. She opened her eyes, and blinked up at Morris Novak.

"You meet the strangest people in these places," he said with a rueful smile.

He stood alone, without a bodyguard, in a tan shirt and slacks, instead of his standard suit. He was trying to blend in, though that's not easy for a six-foot-tall man wearing a *yarmulke*.

"Care to join me?" Mimi scooted to one side.

"I could for a moment," he said, as he lowered himself to the bench.

"I feel honored."

"You shouldn't. You've grabbed the only spot with decent shade."

He sat down next to her, his long knees protruding outward. Mimi was now sharing a park bench with a missing billionaire.

CHAPTER TWENTY-FIVE

As she stared at the flowers, Mimi pondered her options. Should she call the FBI? If so, who would she ask for? And what would she tell them? Novak wasn't wanted for anything, as far as she knew.

It was weird seeing Novak in normal clothes; it made him appear less imposing, more approachable. Granted, his shirt probably cost more than Mimi's weekly wardrobe. Yet, after constantly discussing, investigating, and fearing this man, it was disconcerting seeing him look so . . . human. She spotted the vein on his forehead. It was throbbing a bit. Not a lot. But a little.

Mimi searched for something to say, but there weren't many obvious icebreakers for that situation. Finally, she went with what she'd ask anyone: "How are you?"

"I'm enjoying looking at the flowers. I'm a little peeved that I have to share my favorite bench."

Mimi laughed.

"It's been an interesting week," he said. "I've never been called Evil Elvis before."

Mimi tried to catch his eye, but his face was focused on the flowers.

"What did you think of the press conference?"

He chuckled slightly. "I enjoyed watching Brandon Walters destroy his credibility. I liked the part where he made a fool of himself. I also appreciated how he set himself on fire."

"But what about the other parts? What he said about your business dealings?"

"I am not sure any of that matters. Certainly, the newspapers didn't think so."

Mimi angled her face at his. "Then why can't anyone find you?"

He raised the eyebrow closest to Mimi. He registered surprise as precisely as he did everything else. "What are you talking about? I'm right here."

"You know what I mean. The people at your company don't know where you are."

Novak didn't reply. The vein throbbed faster.

"That tells me," Mimi continued, "that at least some of Brandon's information was true."

Novak removed a piece of paper from his front shirt pocket, which he unfolded and read. "I steadfastly deny Mr. Walters' allegations." Then he refolded it and placed it back in his pocket.

"But seriously," Mimi said, "what about his information?"

"I'd be pretty stupid discussing that with a journalist."

"As you keep reminding me, I'm an ex-journalist."

"And you keep trying to convince me otherwise. How do I know you'll keep this, as they say, off the record?"

She raised her hand. "My word is my bond."

"Famous last words."

"You called my father a decent person," Mimi said. "I am, too."

He inhaled and frowned slightly. "What did I think of that press conference? First, your friend the murderer has a vendetta against me. I'm not sure why. It's a bit of mystery, frankly.

"He painted me as a criminal for having offshore accounts. That's absurd. They are a standard part of financial planning today. They limit your tax exposure and legal liability. I'm nowhere near my investment advisor's biggest client."

"So those arrangements are all completely above-board?"

"That's what my lawyer says. I have no reason not to trust him. Other than him being a lawyer."

"Brandon also said you dealt in blood diamonds."

"Again, I deny that. But I will point out that, for much of the period he referenced, they were not called blood diamonds. They were just called diamonds. The activists came up with that lovely term.

"Before that, if someone wanted to sell a diamond, and someone wanted to buy it, that was fine. That was business. There was no judging if the diamonds were quote-unquote 'good' or 'not good.' The only thing that mattered was how shiny they were."

Mimi thought a bit. "I spoke with Reverend Kamora."

Novak lifted his chin. "Ah yes. How is the Reverend-Commander?"

"He told me about his time in the militia. He was conscripted when he was fourteen. He did whatever he had to, in order to survive."

"That was common back then," he said, with an air of detachment.

"Right, but you bought diamonds from the people who forced him to do those things."

Novak didn't react.

"I'm just saying," Mimi said, "there was a cost to what you did."

His voice sped up. "Again, I deny the allegations. But for the sake of argument, I fail to see why I should be responsible for the behavior of every person I've ever dealt with. Do you know where the diamonds that your father sells come from? Do you know anything about the production of your shirt, or your pocketbook? Do you think they were made under lovely conditions? Because I can assure you, they were not."

His face turned to granite. "Despite all the lovely words companies now speak about corporate social blah-blah-blah, business is all about money. Always has been, always will be. Money doesn't have a smell, it doesn't have a personality, and it sure doesn't have a conscience." He took a breath. "Anyway, the ADR civil war was a long time ago."

Mimi decided to drop the subject. Novak wasn't going to have a sudden attack of remorse on a park bench.

"How about the painting and the mining minister?"

"Well, again I—"

"I know, you deny the charges."

"Speaking generally, doing business in countries in a place like the ADR is very different than doing it here. On my first visit there, the Customs officer wrote 'one-hundred-dollar tip' on my entry form. Not only did he expect a so-called tip, but he also put it in writing. And God help you if you didn't pay up. There, they jail you if you *don't* bribe.

"All the big mining companies, the ones that today show off all their social programs, used to pay government officials what they called facilitation fees. You can imagine what they facilitated. They even used to be tax deductible. And I assure you, those payments haven't stopped. The big players have just gotten better at hiding them." He frowned. "Better than me, apparently." He cleared his throat. "Of course, I never engaged in such practices. Just putting them in proper context."

"Which brings me back to my original question," Mimi said. "If everything you did was common and above-board, why can't anyone find you?"

He scrunched his face. "I have always kept a low profile. Granted, generally not *this* low."

"I heard that the FBI came to your office."

"Yes, I did enjoy the pleasure of their company." The vein throbbed faster. He looked like the sixty-year-old man he was.

"Apparently, they have some, shall we say, misconceptions, based on certain documents that appeared in Mr. Walters' presentation. I tried to explain to them that you can't trust anything that Walters says, but apparently they've seen documents they feel are legitimate. The whole thing is completely without merit, of course. But you know how these prosecutors love to take down big targets to get their name in the papers."

He shifted in his seat. "It's also possible that once they start looking into my affairs, they may find certain other things that could perhaps be misconstrued. Mind you, there's nothing to any of it. I don't behave differently than any other successful businessman. But apparently I have become their target of the week."

"So, what are you going to do?" Mimi asked.

"If they ever do bring charges, I could hire fancy lawyers, who will probably be able to drag things out for a few years, for a mere five million dollars. Without any guarantees, of course. One friend who's been through it says it will feel like a three-year proctology exam. Not my idea of a good time.

"My current plan is to move to one of those Caribbean islands that aren't big on fulfilling extradition requests. They will grant you residence if you donate money to the government—they call it 'citizenship by investment.' It is less flatteringly known as 'passport for sale.' I told you, some locales like bribery.

"I'm not really suited for doing nothing in a tropical paradise for years, but the beaches may be nice. There are a few diamond industry criminals who have fled to those places, so I'll have some interesting new friends."

For a moment, neither spoke. Time for the big question. "As you know, I'm looking into the murder of Abraham Boasberg. Right now, you're in trouble and you have nothing to lose. Is there anything you want to get off your chest about that?"

He stared at her in disbelief. "What could I possibly have on my chest about Abraham?"

"I just wonder about certain things. For instance, the main evidence against Brandon Walters is the video footage of him entering the building. Did your company supply that?"

"I assume so. It happened in our building."

"But couldn't that be a conflict of interest, given you're a possible suspect?"

"My Lord, Miss Rosen, you *have* been brainwashed. The only person who's called me a suspect is the one who's been arrested for the crime. What possible reason would I have for killing Abraham?"

"Maybe you didn't want the information about your business getting out."

"If that was my plan, it didn't work out too well, did it?" He shook his head. "I suppose I have my wonderful stepson to thank for that. I guess that's my reward for helping and protecting that boy. I'd stop speaking to him if I hadn't already done that three years ago."

Mimi inched forward on the bench, trying to catch his eye. "Don't be upset with Rafi. He just did what he thought was right."

He didn't look at her.

"Remember," Mimi said, "you told me that Reverend Kamora tried to sell the Hope for Humanity to a local business. I've found out that company's name was Merlano Resources. Is that one of your businesses?"

"No."

"You swear?"

"As they say, my word is my bond."

"So, who owns it?"

"You're the investigator. You find out."

"I can't. It's connected to a company in Saint Phoebus. There's no ownership information."

He crossed his legs. "Ah, Saint Phoebus. Beautiful island. I may have a company or two located there. It has many interesting things to see, plus many interesting things you can't."

"Is there any way to determine who owns businesses there?"

"For you, no. For me, I have close associates in the department of finance who will supply that information for the cost of a little, shall we say, facilitation fee."

She fully leaned over so he couldn't avoid her gaze. "Could you find out who owns Merlano Resources? Please."

"I'm not sure you want to go down that rabbit hole. You might find some nasty little bunnies."

"That company might hold the key to who killed Abraham Boasberg."

"We *know* who killed Abraham Boasberg."

"A Merlano employee was killed, too. He was stabbed in the middle of a street. He was a young father with three kids. His murder might be connected to Abraham's."

Novak seemed unmoved.

"When we first met, you told me, contrary to what Brandon Walters says, you are a human being. Maybe it's time you acted like one."

Novak looked taken aback, like he wasn't used to being talked to that way. After a moment of silence, he said, "How about this? I will consider your request. Will you excuse me for a moment while I collect my thoughts?"

He rose from the bench. He strolled through the main flowerbed, slowly and deliberately. Then, his long legs started moving faster. His body grew smaller and smaller, and soon, he was gone.

Mimi stayed on the bench for a few minutes but knew he wasn't coming back. She was gathering her things when her phone shook. It was a text, from a hidden number.

"Sorry I couldn't chat longer," it said. "I don't like to stay in one place for too long these days. I will work on getting you the requested info. In the meantime, here is something that I wanted to bring to your attention."

A document was attached. Mimi opened it expectantly.

It was an invoice, noting her father's rent was due next week.

When Mimi got home, she called Anita.

"You'll never guess who I spoke with today," Mimi said with a touch of pride.

"I can't talk now." Anita again sounded on the verge of tears. "Rafi was just attacked. He was coming home, and this guy jumped him and started pummeling him. Luckily, someone saw it, and started yelling for help, and the guy ran away. Otherwise, Rafi would have been killed."

"My God," Mimi said. "Is he okay?"

"Physically, he's all right. Mentally, he's a mess."

"Is he in the hospital?"

"No, we're at his father's house in Brooklyn." She paused. "Listen, why don't you come to his house tomorrow? We need to discuss some things."

"Sure." Mimi was in shock. "I can't believe this. Who did it?'

"We don't know. But this was not some random attack. It was deliberate. Somebody wanted to kill Rafi."

CHAPTER TWENTY-SIX

THE NEXT MORNING, THE TEMPERATURE TOPPED one hundred degrees. By the time Mimi arrived at Boasberg's mini-mansion in Williamsburg, she was soaked with sweat.

Anita greeted her at the door without much of a smile or even eye contact. Mimi found that disconcerting, but she was more focused on the welcome blast of air conditioning.

Rafi and Brandon were sitting in the spacious living room Mimi remembered from the *shiva*, but the rows of chairs were gone, replaced by two adjoining white sofas and a glass coffee table.

Brandon was sprawled out on one couch, his feet clad in socks and propped on the table. Anita sat next to him, her legs tucked under her waist. The table was covered with coffee mugs, phones, and plates of half-eaten food. It was almost the standard scene of twenty-somethings enjoying a leisurely morning, expect one of them had just been beaten to a pulp.

Rafi lay on the other couch, his face a medley of black and blue, with occasional bursts of red. A damp cloth lay on his forehead, and he held an ice pack against his cheek. It was the first time Mimi had seen him without a *yarmulke*.

He beamed when she entered, which was both sweet and disheartening, since his grin was bracketed by swollen lips.

"Nice to see you," he said, his words slightly slurred. "Though it might not be so nice seeing me." He chuckled, then cringed. "Whoops, I shouldn't laugh. Makes my cheeks hurt."

"I am so sorry about this." Mimi sat next to him and put her hand on his knee. "How are you feeling?"

"Beat up, in every sense of the term," he answered.

"Tell me what happened."

"I was coming home last night at around seven-thirty. I was about to open the door, when this big dude came up behind me, threw me to the ground, and started punching me in the face. He just kept wailing and wailing, until someone who works at the deli across the street screamed at him to stop, and he ran away. That deli guy saved my life."

He dabbed at his face with an ice pack. "Everyone says I'm lucky, but I don't feel that way. Lucky people don't get the crap beaten out of them." He laughed, then gritted his teeth. "I keep forgetting: no laughing."

"Do you know who attacked you?" Mimi asked.

"I have no idea," Rafi said. "The deli guy said he was wearing a mask and had an animal tattoo on his arm. Maybe a lion."

"What did the police say?" Mimi asked.

"Not much. They took a report, and that was about it. I doubt they'll find the guy. I just have to be more on guard."

"I notice your gun didn't help," Anita scoffed.

"It didn't last night, but I won't get caught by surprise next time," Rafi said. "If someone comes after me again, they'll get what's coming to them." He padded his belt. That seemed to be where his gun was—though, thankfully, he didn't display it this time.

Anita rolled her eyes, exasperated.

"I know my stepfather did this," Rafi said, his face drawn. "He just can't leave well enough alone. He had to get his revenge."

"You know," Mimi said, "I spoke to your stepfather yesterday."

"Really?" Rafi sat up a bit. "Where'd you find him? Even my mom doesn't know where he is."

"He told me he liked to go to the Coltura Garden," Mimi said. "So, I paid a visit, and there he was."

"Probably won't be back for a while," Rafi said. "What he say?"

"Not much," Mimi said with a shrug. "I did find out that federal authorities are investigating him. The FBI came to his office the other day."

"Really?" Brandon brightened. "Woo-hoo." He and Anita gave each other high fives.

"Don't get too excited," Mimi said. "He already has an escape plan. He's jetting off to a Caribbean island."

"I wouldn't necessarily believe him," Brandon said. "He probably said that, assuming you'd tell the authorities, so he could lead them on a wild goose chase.

"I've studied his type for a long time," he continued. "Even if he does hide out for a while, he'll be back in New York soon enough. Guys like him can never stay away from the action. Did he tell you anything else?"

"We talked about Merlano Resources," Mimi said. "He insisted that he didn't own it, but said he would find out who did."

"Oh, please." Brandon waved his hand. "That company is obviously his, and he's trying to throw you off the trail. I wouldn't believe a word he says. Look what he did to our friend here." He put his finger to his chin. "Did he mention Rafi?"

"No. He just said he had Rafi to thank for leaking the documents."

Brandon stared at her. "And what did you say to that?"

"Nothing, really," Mimi said. "I said that Rafi did what he thought was right."

Brandon raised his eyebrows. "You didn't deny Rafi leaked those files?"

"No." Mimi began to feel uncomfortable. "There wasn't any point. He seemed to have figured that out."

"I'm sure he suspected it," Brandon said. "That's why he brought it up. To test you. And you confirmed it." He stared at her, his gaze unyielding. "Did he say anything else about Rafi?"

"Not much. He said that he would stop speaking to Rafi, but he'd already done that three years ago. Then he said, 'this is my reward, for helping and protecting that boy.'"

"Oh Jesus," Brandon said.

Mimi was puzzled. "Is that bad?"

"You have to understand," Brandon said, wagging his finger. "Guys like him speak in code. He was saying he's done protecting Rafi. And now he's throwing him to the wolves. *His* wolves. That was a clear threat."

This stunned Mimi. "It didn't come across that way."

"Of course not." Brandon clenched his hands. "That's the code part. Do you think it was coincidence that right after you spoke with him, Rafi got attacked?"

Acid rose in Mimi's throat. "You can't blame me for that!"

"No one's blaming you for anything," Brandon said. "You meant well. But you're dealing with a dangerous man."

Brandon and Anita swapped glances. Rafi stared at the floor.

Anita sat forward. "We had a long talk last night. You've helped a great deal in the last few weeks."

Mimi sensed a "but" coming. No sentence that began with "we had a long talk about you last night" ever ended well.

"But," said Anita, "now that Rafi's funding Brandon's defense, we can afford a private detective."

"Great," Mimi said. "I'll help that person however I can."

"Perhaps we're not being clear," Brandon said.

Anita finished his thought. "We appreciate all you've done. But we no longer want you involved."

Mimi was too stunned to respond.

"It's nothing against you," Anita said. "In a lot of ways, you're an incredible journalist."

Never has the phrase "you're an incredible journalist" sounded more condescending, especially when preceded by the words "in a lot of ways."

"And don't worry," Anita said. "We'll give you a credit on the documentary. Like a thank you."

Mimi had gone from "head of research," to a "thank you." She couldn't help but feel smacked in the face. The cool kids were kicking her out of their club, or family, whatever it was.

Mimi swallowed her hurt and muttered, "fine." But the more she thought about it, the more she decided it was not fine. She had gotten too involved with this to back out.

"I didn't ask to help out here," she said finally. "Anita begged me to. And since then, I've accomplished a lot. I put your presentation together. I discovered which buildings Novak owns. I found those documents that showed he bribed the government." Mimi felt stupid defending herself, but couldn't help it.

"Yes, we appreciate all that," said Brandon. "Unfortunately, you also told Novak that I thought the police were getting paid off. That hurt my case tremendously. I know you didn't mean to, but you did. And what you said yesterday, may have hurt Rafi."

"This is high stakes," Brandon continued. "Rafi could have been killed last night. I might go to jail."

Brandon and Anita's eyes drilled into Mimi, making her feel trapped and claustrophobic.

"We never said you haven't been helpful," Anita said. "But we need to up our game. We can't have you out there, making mistakes."

Mimi understood their point—somewhat—yet it all seemed so sudden. Last week, Anita told her she'd been "incredible," and Brandon called her "amazing." Granted, that was after he tried to kiss her. Perhaps Anita found out about that—or maybe just sensed it. Mimi had long suspected that Brandon was Anita's mystery boyfriend. Something about this seemed off.

Mimi thought about continuing to make a case for herself, but there was little point. She was getting fired from a job she wasn't getting paid for.

"Whatever," she said. She rose from the couch and hoisted her purse on her shoulder.

"Don't be upset," Rafi said. She could see a glint of compassion in his face, as bruised and banged-up as it was. "You're a great person."

Mimi couldn't help but like him right then. He'd just gotten the hell beaten out of him, but retained his humanity.

"I hope you'll help with the auction," he added. "I know your friend Channah is planning to come."

"I'm sure she will," Mimi said. "She likes you."

"God," Anita moaned. "That girl needs to take a hint."

Rafi glared at Anita. "Don't say that."

Anita plucked her recorder from her purse and held it to her mouth. "Possible documentary subject: Why women who grew up in repressed backgrounds have low self-esteem."

Mimi never hated Anita more than at that moment.

"Hey, Anita," Mimi snapped. "I have a documentary subject." She held her fist under her chin. "Why failed filmmakers spew nonsense into tape recorders."

Anita glowered at Mimi. She rose from the couch, fists clenched, like she wanted to brawl.

Mimi has never really been in a fight before, but she was mad enough to give it a go.

Brandon leaped from the sofa and stepped between them. "Everybody calm down. It's stressful times and we're all feeling frayed. But this squabbling doesn't solve anything. Let's walk away friends."

"Actually," Mimi declared, "I'm not walking away. I promised Reverend Kamora I'd help find his diamond. I intend to keep that promise."

"Great," Anita said. "Another person who can't take a hint." She fell onto the couch, scowling.

Brandon walked toward Mimi. "I can't tell you how to live your life. But I'd be careful if I were you. Consider what Novak did to Rafi, what he did to Boasberg, what he's doing to me."

Mimi kept her arms folded against her chest.

"Novak knows you're digging into him," Brandon said. "Do you think he's okay with that? Don't you think he'll do something to you, too?"

"And he's the kind of guy who won't just hurt you," Brandon continued. "He'll hurt your family."

Mimi couldn't believe what she what she was hearing. "Come on. You're exaggerating."

"Has he ever mentioned your family?" Brandon asked.

"No. I mean, he did send me a text about my father's rent."

Brandon smashed his fist against his hand. "That's what I'm talking about. That was your warning. These guys speak in code. They don't say things outright; they're too smart for that. But he was telling you, he's watching your father.

"Right now, Novak is like a cornered animal," Brandon continued. "He has nothing to lose. You should be careful."

Silence filled the room. Mimi tried to comprehend what Brandon was saying. It was terrifying.

"Nice seeing you, Mimi," Anita announced, in a way that made it clear that it not nice seeing her.

Mimi murmured a half-hearted goodbye, and they mumbled the same in return.

Mimi trekked back to the train in the hundred-degree heat. The three-minute walk took forever.

Mimi's mind reeled as she rode the subway back from Brooklyn. She felt badly treated by her now-former friends. She fretted that she had gotten Rafi hurt. And she worried that Novak would hurt her family. Not that there was any evidence he would, but the prospect scared the hell out of her.

When Mimi arrived at the office, her forehead dripping from the heat, she was greeted by a stricken Channah.

"Mimi, I don't know how to tell you this," she said. "But I can't find your father. He's missing."

Mimi was seized by a wave of fear. "What do you mean?"

Channah's face turned gray. "He called this morning to say he was delivering that two-carat pear-shape to Sol. That was four hours ago. I haven't heard from him since. He usually borrows someone's phone to check for messages. But he hasn't. And of course, I can't get ahold of him, because he refuses to get a cell phone."

For the millionth time, Mimi cursed her father for not having one.

"Did you contact Sol?"

"Yes!" Channah's face fell. "I talked to him two hours ago. He said that your father dropped off the diamond, then said he was heading back to the office."

"So, hold it. No one's heard from my dad in three hours?"

"A little more than that."

"My God, Channah. Why didn't you call me?"

"I was hoping he would show up and I didn't want to panic you." She rubbed Mimi's back. "How are you feeling?"

Mimi's shoulders slumped. "Panicked."

CHAPTER TWENTY-SEVEN

MIMI BREATHED DEEP, she clenched and unclenched her fists, she closed her eyes and counted backwards. She tried every trick therapists taught her to keep calm. She even popped one of Channah's Valiums. Nothing eased her mind. It kept going to scary places.

She tried to stay rational. Her father hadn't called in a little more than three hours. That wasn't normal, but there had to be a logical explanation. She just couldn't think of one. If Brandon hadn't warned that Novak might target her family, she might not have gotten quite so panicked. She would have worried, but not like this.

She rang Sol, and he told Mimi the same thing he'd told Channah: Max had left his office over three hours ago, and he hadn't heard from him since.

"He hasn't called?" Sol said. "I'm surprised. I hope nothing happened to him."

That didn't help.

She paged through her dad's Rolodex and phoned a few names she recognized. No one had heard from him. If she weren't so crazed, she'd have rolled her eyes that her dad still used a Rolodex.

Every now and then, Mimi would check in with Channah, who assured her everything would be okay. Mimi could tell she was nervous, too. She considered calling her sisters but didn't want to panic them.

She kept thinking about Brandon's warning. She longed to call Novak and ask if he knew what happened to her father. There was no proof that he did, of course, but she couldn't think of anyone else who might.

She just had no way to reach him. His text was sent from an unknown number.

She remembered Rafi had given her his mom's number. She debated whether to call, then decided she had no choice.

No one picked up, so Mimi left a message.

"Hi, Mrs. Novak, this is Mimi Rosen. My father Max is missing. I have no idea if your husband knows anything about it, or had anything to do with it, but if he did, please ask him, if he has any kind of conscience or humanity, to bring my father back. I swear I won't report him or have anything else to do with him. I may be off base here, and if I am, I apologize, but please, I'm begging you, if he knows anything, tell him not to hurt my father. Thank you."

Sonia Novak would likely think her nuts for leaving that message. Mimi felt nuts leaving it. She could only imagine what Detective Matthews would say.

That was it. That was who she needed to call: Detective Matthews.

"Hi, Detective. This is Mimi Rosen. I'm sure you remember—"

"Yes," he grumbled. "What is it now?"

"Please, Detective, this is serious. My father is missing "

"Okay." His tone shifted. She now had his full attention. "When you say your father is missing, how long has he been gone?"

"Over four hours. I know that doesn't sound like much, but he's an older man and it's not normal that we don't hear from him for that long. I've called his friends. No one knows where he is."

"All right," Matthews said. "I understand that people get nervous when they don't hear from family members, especially older ones. But it's a little early for us to conduct a major manhunt. Do you have any indication that something may have happened to him?"

Mimi swallowed. "No."

"Have either of you received any kind of threats?"

"Morris Novak sent me a text about my father's rent. Brandon Walters says that was a warning in code."

She wondered if Matthews would confirm that, but he just uttered a skeptical "uh-huh."

"I don't know if it was," Mimi added. "Investigations make you paranoid."

"Correct. That's one reason I've warned you not to do them."

Mimi whispered, "I know."

"Is your father answering his phone?"

"He doesn't have a mobile."

"No?"

"I've told him a million times to get one. He won't listen."

"Sounds familiar."

"Please, Detective—"

"I'm sorry. I shouldn't have said that." He sounded genuinely contrite. "I'll email you a missing person's report. It'll ask for information on what your father looks like, any distinctive features, when you last heard from him, any places he might be. Fill it out as soon as possible and email it back with a couple of recent pictures. And then we'll start a search."

His voice softened. "For what it's worth, it could be a million things. I know it's hard not to panic in this kind of situation, but it doesn't do much good. Fill out the form I'm sending you, and we'll start looking. If he's out there, we'll find him."

After she hung up, Mimi felt glad she'd called him. Something about his tone soothed her. Or the Valium had kicked in.

Within seconds, she received the missing person's report by email. She was examining it when Reverend Kamora called.

"Miss Rosen," he said. "Thank God I have reached you. I am sitting here with your father."

Mimi nearly jumped out of her seat. "Oh my God. Where is he?"

"He's at Lenox Hill hospital. He's fine but he had an incident. He was walking down Forty-Seventh Street and fainted."

"Why?"

"The doctors said he was dehydrated. They've examined him and think he's fine. I apologize for not calling sooner, but I didn't realize he hadn't been in touch."

Mimi called out to Channah that her dad had been found and sent a quick email to Matthews. "Call off the search party," she wrote. "My father's okay."

She took a long deep breath. "This is such a relief," she told Reverend Kamora.

"Miss Rosen, I was thinking," he said. "Your father should probably get a cell phone."

Mimi almost screamed, "I know!"

Twenty minutes later, Mimi was standing at her father's bed at the Lenox Hill Hospital emergency room. He had a prominent bandage on his head from where he fell, and an IV sticking out his arm. The whole scene conjured unpleasant memories of visiting her mom in the hospital.

Reverend Kamora was sitting in a chair next to his bed, one leg crossed over the other. They seemed to have been chatting amiably.

Max appeared frailer than usual, but personality-wise, he was much the same. Now that he had a phone to borrow, he'd called Channah three times for messages.

"What happened?" Mimi asked.

He shrugged and his mouth formed a semicircle. "I was walking to the office after I dropped off the diamond at Sol's. It was really hot, and I started feeling dizzy, and a little nauseous. I thought maybe I should sit on a curb or something, but before I could, I blacked out. The next thing I knew, I was on the ground with all these people staring at me, and an ambulance was coming. The doctors say I'm okay. I just got dehydrated. They think it was a combination of the hot weather, and me skipping breakfast."

"Why didn't you eat breakfast?" Mimi asked.

"I was so happy I was unloading that pear shape for a good price, I rushed out of the house before I ate anything."

Mimi couldn't believe she'd spent the last hour panicked because her father got over-excited about a diamond deal.

"Thank God, you're okay," she said. "And I hope this proves, once and for all, you need a mobile phone. This wouldn't have driven me quite so crazy if you had one."

Max flicked this away. "I've told you, a million times, I don't want one of those things. I see people with them, they pay more attention to their phones than to their own family. I don't need one. I'm not that important."

"Dad, you *are* important," Mimi said. "You're important to me. You know how scared I was today? I was worried that you were hurt, or someone did something to you."

"Who's going to hurt me?" Max said. "I'm a nice guy. Aren't I, Reverend?"

"You certainly seem like one, Max," Reverend Kamora smiled.

"This was an unusual thing," Max said. "It's super-hot out there. On the radio, they said it's a record."

"There's going to be other hot days!"

"So what? Next time, I'll eat breakfast. I don't need a stupid phone."

"We'll discuss it later." Mimi didn't want another argument; this day had been stressful enough. "Reverend, thanks again for your help. I don't know what I'd have done if you hadn't called."

"My pleasure. I have enjoyed talking with your father. We follow different religions but are both men of faith."

"Hold it," Mimi said. "I don't think you two have ever met. How did you recognize him?"

Reverend Kamora and Max laughed in unison.

"Go ahead," Max smiled. "Tell her."

"When I spoke at the conference, your father was the only person in the audience who was asleep. So, when I saw him on the ground, he looked exactly as I remembered him. He had his eyes closed." He laughed again.

Mimi laughed too. It felt good. It had been a long time since she'd laughed about anything.

"Unfortunately," Reverend Kamora continued, "I didn't know he was your father. Otherwise, I would have called sooner. They wouldn't let me ride in the ambulance. I had to take the subway to the hospital."

"Well, thanks, for all you've done. How is everything else?"

Reverend Kamora's face drooped. "Not good, sadly. We haven't yet found the diamond. And the auction's on Monday."

"That's three days away," Mimi said. "Shouldn't you cancel it?"

"I have faith the diamond will turn up," he said.

"But it might not," Mimi said. "Who knows where it is? I found the gold box that held it, but the diamond wasn't in it."

Reverend Kamora perked up. "Where'd you find the box? Maybe the diamond is near it."

"I doubt it. It was hidden in a rag, which was stuffed in a gap between some bricks outside Boasberg's window."

"How'd you know the box was there?"

Mimi's cheeks flushed. "I briefly went in Boasberg's office, and saw it when I looked out the window. I put it back in case the police want to examine it."

Kamora grinned. "Max, I must say, your daughter is an excellent investigator."

"Hold it." Max sat up on his bed and all the weakness seemed to flow out of him. "Did you just call Mimi an investigator?" He turned to her. "Are you investigating again? How many times have I told you not to do that?"

Mimi cringed. "I agreed to help Reverend Kamora find the missing diamond. It's not a real investigation. Just a little one."

"A little investigation? What's that mean?" He jabbed his finger in the air. "I've told you a million times, I don't want you investigating anything. Big, little, it doesn't matter."

"Dad, that's—"

"Don't 'Dad' me. You know how dangerous these things are. No wonder you were worried about me getting hurt. Who knows what kind of sick people stole that diamond?"

"Dad, you are in no position to lecture me. You're the one who had me terrified because you refuse to get a cell phone."

"What's that got to do with anything?" Max snapped. "I don't want to be a nervous wreck worrying you're gonna get killed."

"And I don't want to be a nervous wreck worrying where you are," Mimi responded.

"I'll be fine," Max said. "I don't need you managing my life."

"And I don't need you managing my life," Mimi shot back.

Mimi and Max scowled at each other and grumbled under their breaths.

A long uneasy silence followed, which was finally broken by Reverend Kamora. "Well, it was nice seeing you two."

After Max was discharged, he wanted to go to his office. Mimi told him absolutely not, and warned him if he tried, she'd have Channah lock the doors so he couldn't get in. They finally agreed he'd take an Uber home. Mimi tried to ride with him, but he insisted she didn't need to. She let him win that fight.

As she put her father in the car, she gave him a kiss on the forehead. "I'm glad you're okay."

"Me, too," he said. He held up his hand. "As God is my witness, I'll never skip breakfast again."

Her father was definitely better; he was making bad jokes.

Mimi was walking back to the office when her phone rang. She picked up and heard an ear-splitting New York squawk. It was Sonia Novak—Morris' wife, and Rafi's mom.

"Is this the woman that left the message about her missing father?"

"Yeah, I—"

"Look, I don't know anything about your father, and I doubt my husband does either, and it doesn't matter because no one can get in touch with my husband anyway. That's all I can tell you."

"Actually, Mrs. Novak, I'd like to apologize for that call. They've found my father. I shouldn't have bothered you."

"How'd you get my number anyway?"

"Your son gave it to me."

"You know Rafi?" Sonia said, her tone shifting. "Are you a friend of his?"

"Sort of," Mimi hedged.

"Have you seen him lately?"

"I saw him this morning."

"I have a serious question for you. Is he okay?"

Mimi wasn't sure how to respond. "I don't know if you heard, but he was badly beat up last night. He seems fine, if a little shook up."

"I know that. I'm talking about something else. Is he okay in the head?"

Mimi stopped walking. "What do you mean?"

Sonia Novak was breathing heavily. "I'm worried he's about to do something crazy. Like hurt somebody."

CHAPTER TWENTY-EIGHT

MIMI STOOD IN THE MIDDLE of the hot sidewalk, trying to understand what Sonia Novak had just said about her son.

"Why do you think he might hurt somebody?" Mimi sputtered.

"Never mind," Sonia responded. "I shouldn't have mentioned it. Goodbye."

Something told Mimi that this woman would be worth talking to.

"Please, Mrs. Novak, don't hang up. I've spent a lot of time with your son lately. I can give you insight on him. We should meet."

Sonia Novak said she'd be at her apartment all afternoon. "Just come before *Shabbos*." Fortunately, she lived on Fifth Avenue, not far from Lenox Hill Hospital.

"I'll be over in ten minutes," Mimi said.

THE LOBBY OF THE NOVAKS' APARTMENT building was massive, highlighted by a glittery chandelier the size of Mimi's dining room table. Its floors were made of marble, and the walls looked bathed in gold—but, having seen her share of jewelry, Mimi recognized it as fake gold; it was too yellow, too shiny, too perfect, to be the real thing.

The doorman sent her to the twenty-second floor. "What's the Novaks' apartment number?" she asked the elevator operator, who was dressed in a red uniform with oversized brass buttons—something she had only seen in movies.

They don't have an apartment number," he said. "They own the whole floor. Plus, the two above that."

This would be interesting.

Mimi had never been to a billionaire's penthouse before and tried not to gawk.

A maid—dressed in black, with a white-frilled headdress, another thing Mimi had seen only in movies—led her to the "sitting room," which was as large as a tennis court. It was surrounded on all sides by windows with a spectacular view of Central Park. Its walls were dotted with paintings—apparently, Novak collected art that he didn't send to African mining ministers. A cream-colored sofa sat in the middle of the room, next to a red silk-upholstered chair and a side-table so ornate it could have been owned by Marie Antionette.

Otherwise, it was empty. In a city notorious for cramped living arrangements, this room took up a massive amount of space, simply because it could.

Mimi spied a terrace outside one of the windows and asked the maid if she could walk out on it. The maid shrugged and Mimi took this as a tacit okay.

Mimi stepped on the balcony—tentatively at first. She was high up enough that, on this sweltering-hot day, she felt a cool, sweet breeze. Over the railing, she could see Central Park in its lush summertime glory. The afternoon crowds looked like dots, small and far below her. She felt like a queen looking down at the commoners. Even the skyscrapers on the other side of the park no longer seemed like imposing structures, but peers, on her level.

Mrs. Novak's arrival was announced by the clip-clopping of her heels from the next room. Mimi dashed to the sofa.

Sonia Novak was small and buxom, with sharp, angular features, and walked with a hurried stride. Like many Orthodox women, she wore a *sheitel*, a wig to preserve her modesty—though hers was bright red, so it was arguable how much of her modesty was being preserved. She was clad in a long blue dress and chic black shoes and had gold bracelets up and down her arm.

The moment Sonia sat in the red chair, the stone-faced maid placed a cup of tea and purse on the nearby table. Neither acknowledged the other, and they both seemed fine with that.

Sonia Novak glared at Mimi. "So, what's your name again?" Her accent was even sharper in person.

"Mimi Rosen," she answered in a small voice.

Sonia took a sip of tea. "You said your father was missing."

Mimi blushed. "Yes. We found him. He'd fainted, and I couldn't get ahold of him, and I called a lot of people, and you were one of them. I didn't mean to accuse your husband of anything. I hope I didn't upset you."

Sonia made a face. "You didn't upset me, it just seemed so off-the-wall. Why would Morris have anything to do with your father being missing?"

Mimi's body clenched. "I don't know. Someone put the idea in my head."

"It's all conspiracies today." Sonia took another sip of tea. "You think people would have a little more *seychel* than to believe this stuff. But everyone's lost their minds. You should see the crazy text I got from my son last night." She called the maid to bring her phone, and it promptly appeared on the table, along with her glasses.

Sonia donned her specs and sourly scrolled through her messages. "This is what he wrote me. Imagine. This is my own son talking. 'Mom, I just got beat up and nearly killed. Tell your husband thanks. Let him know he won't get away with it. I have a gun.'"

She moved the phone away from her face and peered at Mimi over her glasses. "I've been calling him all morning, and he refuses to call back. It's insane. He's convinced Morris is some kind of monster."

She took off her glasses and rubbed her eyes. "Who puts this *narishkeit* in you people's heads? And now Rafi says he's friends with this Brandon Walters, which is also crazy. Why's he spending time with his father's killer?"

"Mrs. Novak," Mimi said, choosing her words carefully, "Brandon Walters has only been *accused* of killing your ex-husband. He hasn't been convicted of anything."

"Yeah, yeah, yeah. *Accused*. Arrested. Whatever. Let's just say he's not a person I'd want over for dinner. The craziest thing is, Rafi has no problem spending time with this murderer, but won't say a word to my husband. And now he thinks that Morris had him beat up. Why would he think that?"

"I don't know if you're aware," Mimi said, "but your husband blames Rafi for releasing those documents."

Sonia gave a small shoulder shrug. "I'm sure he does. I do, too."

"Don't you think Mr. Novak might—" Mimi hunted for the right phrase. "—do something about that?"

Sonia looked appalled. "Morris would never hurt my son, if that's what you're implying. Sure, he's angry at Rafi. Mind you, I'm not thrilled with what he did, either. That's not how I want my son to treat my husband. That doesn't mean Morris would send a hit squad after him. You think I married a psychopath?"

"No, but—"

"Never mind." She waved her hand. "I'm wasting my breath. You're all insane. Rafi is convinced that Morris not only tried to kill him, but he killed Abraham, too. Why do you people believe such nonsense?"

Mimi's leg bounced. "Mrs. Novak, you must admit, Abraham Boasberg possessed lots of information that could be harmful to your husband."

Sonia's expression stayed blank. "So?"

"Maybe he was worried that Abraham would reveal it."

"Oh please. I know both these men. First of all, Abraham would never release that information, because that might open that whole can of worms with Rafi—" Her hands fluttered. "Well, never mind. The point is Abraham wouldn't want his son to look bad. Whatever you want to say about Abraham—and God knows, I've said plenty—he would never do anything to hurt that boy. And Morris wouldn't either."

Mrs. Novak threw her shoulders back. "You're looking at me like I'm some kind of moron. I'm well aware my husband is no angel. You realize, I have no idea where he is right now."

"You don't?" Mimi asked.

"Of course, I don't. He's disappeared. The government started probing his affairs and rather than face up to it, he ran away. It's been two days and I've spoken to him maybe fifteen minutes. He says he can't talk long because the government might trace his calls."

"He told me he might go to a Caribbean island."

"He told me that, too. I have no idea if that's true or not. All I know is I wasn't invited. Though, honestly, I wouldn't have gone. My family's in New York. I'm not running around the world hiding like a criminal. I haven't done anything wrong."

She drank more tea. "My husband is not a stupid man. He knew this day would come. If it wasn't these documents, it would be something else.

"A few years back, when he had that issue with the smuggling, the U.S. Attorney started looking into his business, but didn't bring any charges. Morris' lawyers told him he was now on whatever list they have over there, and it was only a matter of time before they went after him again.

"Why do you think he was so ready to jet overseas? He had a plan just in case there was trouble. He was well aware, at some point, your luck runs out. Especially with that Walters bad-mouthing him all the time.

"I never understood why that kid was so obsessed with my husband. Morris is not the worst person in the world."

"Mrs. Novak," Mimi said, "you yourself said that your husband is no angel."

"Of course, he isn't," Sonia said. "I can also tell you, he's not even the biggest crook in this building. You think all these rich people made their money by being nice and honest? Some magazine said Morris was the world's six-hundred-and-second richest person. You know what that means? There's six-hundred-and-one bigger crooks than him."

Mimi craned her neck. "Forgive me if this is a personal question, but it seems like your husband acted in a way that invited trouble. If he knew the government might come after him, why did he keep all those offshore accounts?"

Sonia stared off into the distance for a moment, then her attention snapped back to Mimi. "I've never been able to figure that out. Morris is brilliant, but he often acted stupid."

"Like me, he came from modest circumstances. His father was a Torah scholar, who studied all day and never provided for his family. He and his brothers had it pretty rough growing up. He always said he never wanted to be that way."

"At some point, he became obsessed with money. It was like a sickness. He would say, the more he made, the more he could give, but that was nonsense. He donated a little money to some park uptown, and a few other things. The reality is, he couldn't stop. Everything was business with him. Business and money."

"He'd do business with these terrible dictators. They were monsters, some of these people. He'd go into meetings where everybody carried machine guns. I was always worried he'd get killed. I'd ask him: why do you need this nonsense? You have enough money to last ten lifetimes. You can only eat one breakfast."

She fixed her hair and adjusted her blouse. "In our old neighborhood, the local *yentas* said I married Morris for his money. Did I like the fact that Morris was successful? Of course. This is America, and money is an important thing here. But the truth is, both Morris and I were in bad marriages. Abraham was so crazy and excited all the time. It was exhausting. Morris appeared calmer. Once I got to know Morris, I realized he was just as crazy, maybe more so. He was just better at hiding it.

"In a way, Rafi did me a favor. Morris is gone, and I can get on with my life. Our marriage wasn't working. For whatever reason, I don't have the best taste in partners." Her mouth turned flat. "I tell you, it hasn't been easy."

Mimi almost laughed at this. "Come on, Mrs. Novak. I understand that you have problems. But you have a pretty sweet deal here. This is a great apartment."

It was Sonia's turn to look at Mimi like she was an idiot. "You do realize, not everything in life is money. People think it's glamorous being the wife of a billionaire. Trust me, it gets old quick. Half the time, my husband is galivanting around the world, while I sit home, watching TV. I don't need to be rich to do that." She gestured to the windows. "Even this view, it's nice. But after a while, you think, I could buy a postcard and see the same thing.

"I don't even know how long we'll keep all this. I talked to our lawyer this morning. He said if the government really goes after us, they'll take everything, this furniture, this apartment—" She glanced at her arm. "—these bracelets. You can spend all the money in the world fighting the government, but they have unlimited resources, and they'll win in the end."

She massaged her forehead. "At this point, I don't care. The place I grew up in had two rooms. This has seventeen. Who needs so many? This was nice for a while, but I can live without it. My biggest concern right now is my son."

Mimi pursed her lips. "Then let's talk about Rafi. Why do you think he'll hurt someone?"

Sonia thrust out her hands. "Why do you think? All the things he's been saying, about a gun, about Morris. Plus, that private detective. He scared the life out of me."

"What private detective?"

"That Walters kid hired some investigator. Rafi asked me to talk with him. I said fine. So yesterday, he came over, and I thought he'd question me about Morris. He only wanted to know about Rafi."

"He didn't ask about your husband?"

"No. Just Rafi. Has he ever been violent, did I know he bought a gun, what did he think of his father, what did he think of Morris? He asked about his arrests. He made him seem like a ticking time bomb. It left me petrified. And then when I saw Rafi's message this morning, I thought, 'my boy's really gone off the deep end.'"

Sonia moved forward on her chair, and locked eyes with Mimi, and for the first time, Mimi felt they were talking woman-to-woman. "Rafi has always been a sensitive boy. When Abraham and I split, Rafi blamed himself. I told him a million times it wasn't his fault, but he always felt responsible.

"He acts like everything's a big joke, like he's always laughing. Trust me, the world isn't funny to him. Underneath, he's very serious. Intense, even." She took a sip of tea.

"Is there any way I can help?" Mimi asked.

"Just watch him. Let me know if something's wrong. The last time I talked to him, I felt he was hiding something."

"Like what?"

"I have no idea. It's so strange. For a long time after I married Morris, Rafi and I barely spoke. At one point, he basically ran away from home. It was a terrible thing. I'd wake up in the morning and have no idea where my son was.

"But over the last few weeks, after Abraham died, we started talking again. I thought, maybe something good can come out of this.

"Then, in the last week or so, out of the blue, he changed back. Now, he isn't talking to me again, and sending me these crazy texts. You have no idea what those messages do to me. They break my heart, every single time." Her eyes reddened. She called out, "tissue please."

The maid speedily brought her a handkerchief.

Sonia dabbed at her eyes and blew her nose. "I know things haven't been easy for Rafi. And maybe I made some bad choices. But if you see him, please tell him that his mother loves him, and always will, no matter what." Her voice broke. "I don't care if he leaked those documents. He can always come to me for help. If the government leaves me with just one dollar, I'll spend that dollar helping him. He needs to know that."

She finished her tea and placed the cup on the saucer, which was instantly fetched by the maid.

"I just spoke to Morris. I told him you were coming. He asked me to give you a message. Let me find it." Sonia rummaged through her purse and pulled out a small, crumpled piece of paper. "It says, tell her, 'his last day, Abraham got a passport, and she should look for it.'"

This set Mimi's brain swimming. "Abraham got a passport. What does that mean? Did he want to leave the country?"

"How should I know? I told you, he couldn't speak long on the phone." She shook her head in disgust. "What a life I have." She teared up again. "I've talked enough. I need to lie down." She slumped in her chair, her arms dangling over its sides—a sad, small woman in a large, empty room.

That was Mimi's cue to leave—but, before she did, she promised Mrs. Novak she'd pass on her message to her son.

Once she left the apartment, Mimi phoned Rafi, but got voice mail, and left a message.

She saw she had a message from Matthews and called him back. He sounded genuinely pleased her father had been found. "I had a feeling he would turn up. And I hope this has convinced to you stop investigating."

"Actually, there's something I'm curious about."

"Oh God," Matthews said.

"It's just one question!"

It was spurred by comments Sonia Novak made. She'd mentioned Rafi's *arrests*. Mimi only knew of one. And what was that "can of worms" she hinted at?

"A friend of mine has a crush on Boasberg's son, Rafi. I know he's had a few scrapes with the law. I was wondering, is there some kind of database where you can see what Rafi did, so I could tell her? She's a little nervous and wants to make sure there's nothing to worry about."

Matthews groaned. "Give me a bit."

He called back a few minutes later. "Rafi Boasberg's most recent arrest occurred four years ago, when he was collared on a misdemeanor charge of selling a small amount of marijuana in Durham, North Carolina."

"Doesn't sound like a big deal," Mimi said.

"You are correct, usually it's not. But in this case, Rafi Boasberg was on probation for another crime. Two years earlier, he'd pled guilty to smuggling diamonds into the United States."

Mimi nearly dropped her phone. "Really?"

"Yep. He was nabbed at JFK airport. He had just arrived back from Africa, accompanied by Morris Novak. He was lucky to have escaped jail both times. Must have had good lawyers."

Mimi stood in the street, stunned.

"Does that answer all your questions?" Matthews asked.

"Not really," Mimi said.

After a few minutes pacing up and down the street, Mimi decided to go home. This new information made her head hurt.

On her way to back to New Jersey, Mimi called her father to see how he was doing.

"*Baruch Hashem*," he responded. "I'm fine. All I did was faint. I'm not suddenly an invalid."

"I know that. I'm checking in. I don't think that's unreasonable, given you were just in the hospital."

"Okay, *bubelah*. You're right. I appreciate the call. You're a good daughter. Except for your ridiculous investigating. Please stop that, by the way."

"Yes, Dad. You've made your feelings clear on that."

"Hey," he said, sounding brighter, "you know who called to see how I was doing? Reverend Kamora. We had a nice long talk. He's depressed, the poor guy. He kept moaning they couldn't find his diamond. I told him, 'look, it's bad when a diamond gets stolen, but it's not the end of the world. Maybe there was insurance or something.' But nothing I said cheered him up."

God, Mimi thought. *The Reverend must be in bad shape if my dad's giving him pep talks.*

A little later, Mimi called Reverend Kamora, and he sounded as down as Mimi had ever heard him.

"I always believed that God would return the diamond in time," he said. "But the auction is in three days, and it hasn't turned up. For the last four weeks, I have been praying for a miracle. It looks like my prayers will not be answered.

"It makes no sense. When I was young, I did bad things, and no one stopped me. Here, I'm trying to do good things, and am unable to. I know that God has a plan for each of us, that we cannot comprehend." He paused. "Because right now, I cannot understand what is happening."

"So," Mimi asked, "what are you going to do?"

"We'll probably hold the livestream, and if we don't have the diamond, I'll explain what happened to the people of my country and hope they'll understand."

"Do you think they will?"

"No."

"What are you going to say?"

He was silent for a moment. "I am praying for the answer to that question."

"Is there anything I can do? Maybe I can look around, or—"

"No, Miss Rosen. You should not investigate."

"Did my father tell you to say that?"

"Of course," Reverend Kamora laughed. "But I have decided he is correct. I'm sure you're aware of the terrible thing that happened to Rafi Boasberg. He could have ended up like my friend Farhad. I do not want to see anyone else hurt.

"The fate of that diamond is in God's hands. You have done your part. Go and relax."

Mimi sighed. She wanted to keep investigating, but it seemed like the entire world was asking her to stop. A little relaxation might not be the worst thing.

MIMI SPENT THE WEEKEND in her air-conditioned cocoon of an apartment. Periodically, she'd muse about the murder, and try to put the puzzle pieces together. Then, she'd scold herself, and turn her attention back to the crossword she was solving, or the show she was binging, or her early-evening walk around the neighborhood.

Monday morning, Mimi woke up refreshed.

Her mood soured when she saw Rafi's post on the Hope for Humanity's Facebook page. "I'm sorry to announce that it looks like tonight's auction will be cancelled," he wrote. "I don't have anything to add right now except we are all terribly disappointed." Mimi could only imagine how Reverend Kamora felt.

She was about to leave for the office when the phone rang. It was Paul.

"Long time no speak," she grinned.

"This isn't a social call," he said coolly. "I need your help with something. Remember that big diamond that was stolen? I think it may have landed in my lab."

Mimi felt her heart jump in her throat. "The Hope for Humanity?"

"Yes. Someone just submitted a sixty-six carater that I'm pretty sure is a D flawless. You don't see a stone like that every day. Those were its coordinates, right?"

"Yes!" Mimi clutched the phone. "Do you know who submitted it?"

"The name of the person was—" Paul typed and murmured to himself. "Rafi Boasberg. Isn't that the same last name as the guy who was murdered?"

"Listen, Paul," Mimi barked. "Don't do anything with that diamond until I get there."

Mimi hung up and rushed out the door.

CHAPTER TWENTY-NINE

MICHELSON DIAMOND GRADING ASSOCIATES was located just down the street from Mimi's office, though she had never visited before. She was immediately struck by its size and scale. It was filled with serious people peering into serious microscopes. Diamonds were continually being submitted, unwrapped, sorted, graded, and re-wrapped. Not bad for one year in business.

Mimi didn't have much time to marvel. She was quickly ushered into Paul's office. His desk was stacked with papers, and his creased face showed the burden of overseeing this vast operation.

Now that Mimi no longer had a romantic interest in Paul, she felt far more relaxed around him. She had been friends with Paul on the grade-school playground. If this ended with them being friends again, she'd be okay with that.

He greeted her with a wan smile and half-hearted handshake, then turned his perpetually furrowed brow to the big rock on his desk. It was the Hope for Humanity, sitting on an open set of blue parcel papers. After a year working with diamonds, Mimi had become quite jaded about them. Yet, there was something bewitching about this one.

It was the biggest gem she had ever seen, about the size of a ping-pong ball. It was positioned near the window, so light continually swam through it; every time Mimi looked, a swirling kaleidoscope of color would appear, then vanish, like magic. It was obvious why this big rock had become the receptacle of so many people's dreams. It was so beautiful. She couldn't imagine anything bad being associated with it.

"Yeah, that's definitely it," Mimi said. "No doubt about it. And you said Rafi Boasberg submitted it?"

"His name was on the slip."

"Could someone else have turned it in?"

Paul shrugged. "It's possible."

"Is there any way to check?"

"Not really. It was delivered by a messenger. I could try and call the messenger service, but they're usually not upfront with information."

"Doesn't it strike you as strange, though?" Mimi said. "Rafi knows the industry. If he stole it, he would have had it recut. It seems like someone sent it in to make him look bad."

"That's possible," Paul said. "The point is, it's here now."

"True," Mimi said. "I'll get it to Boasberg's office, in time for the auction."

Paul held up his hand like a stop sign. "I can't let you do that."

Mimi was stunned. "Why not?"

"This is a stolen diamond," Paul said. "I have a call into my attorney. I'm waiting for her to get back to me. I assume she'll say if it's stolen, I should hand it over to the police and they'll determine who its true owner is."

Mimi's body grew stiff. "But we know who owns it: Reverend Kamora. He discovered it. He has his heart set on auctioning that diamond tonight. He said if it doesn't show up, it could cause unrest in his country. You don't want that, do you?"

Paul stared at her, incredulous. "It doesn't matter what I want. I have to follow my attorney's advice."

Mimi had a sudden brainstorm. "You said that Rafi Boasberg submitted it. If he asked for it back, would you return it?"

A groove deepened in Paul's brow. "Ordinarily, yes. But not if it's stolen."

"But how do you know it's stolen?"

"You just said it was."

Mimi put her index finger to her lip. "Actually, now that I've looked at it more, I was wrong about that. It looks nothing like it. You should return it to Rafi."

Every vein on Paul's neck seemed to pop. "You told me there was no doubt—" He tried to calm himself. "Never mind. You're acting crazy."

"Come on, Paul. You have no proof that diamond was stolen. None."

"You told me it was!"

"Correct. You also said I'm acting crazy. Why would you listen to me?"

Paul clutched his forehead. "You know what? That's a good question. I can research the diamond by myself, thank you." He gestured toward the door. "Have a good day."

"Paul, I saved your life last year. You owe me one."

"Are you really going to play that card?"

Mimi's shoulders slackened. "I don't have many left."

He didn't react.

"Didn't you say that you never wanted to get involved in any more murder investigations?"

"Sure, but—"

"If you call the police, you'll end up right in the middle of this. The police will question you all day. You may have to go to court. You don't have time for that. You have a lab to run."

Paul sat at his desk, his back turned to Mimi. "Let me speak with my attorney."

"Why? I'm just saying that if Rafi Boasberg, who submitted the diamond, asks for it back, you should return it to him. That's something you do all the time. You don't need anyone's permission for that."

"Well, first of all, Rafi Boasberg hasn't contacted me."

Fair point, Mimi thought. "What if I get him to ask for it? Will you return it to him then?"

Paul seemed at the end of his rope. "If I don't give him that diamond, you'll probably never leave me alone."

Mimi chuckled. "You know me well."

He rubbed his temples. "My attorney will get back to me soon. I can't ignore her advice. If, by some miracle, Rafi Boasberg reaches me before my attorney calls, I will consider returning it to him."

Mimi's face lit up. "I'll call him now. Thank you so much. You're doing the right thing."

"Probably not. I just listened to you."

Mimi dashed out of Paul's office. She phoned Rafi and got voice mail. Come to think of it, he hadn't returned her call from the other day. He seemed to be ignoring her, though she wasn't sure why.

She texted him. "Rafi. Call ASAP. It's about the Hope for Humanity. I know where it is. You need to call now."

No response. She phoned again, and again got voice mail.

She fired off another text. "I repeat. I can get the diamond back, but you have to call me RIGHT NOW."

Mimi peered through Paul's office window. He was typing on his computer.

She paced around the back of the lab, waiting for Rafi to call. Finally, his name popped up on her phone.

"What's this about?" Rafi demanded.

"Did you submit the Hope for Humanity to Michelson Diamond Grading?"

He sounded mystified. "Of course not. I haven't seen that stone in weeks."

"It doesn't matter. You need to ask for it back."

"How could I ask for it back if I didn't send it in?"

Paul picked up his phone. He might be talking to his attorney. Mimi's anxiety level shot through the roof.

"It was submitted in your name," she told Rafi.

"But I didn't submit it!" he shouted.

"We'll figure that out later," Mimi said. "All I know is, if you don't ask for it in about two seconds, we won't be able to sell it tonight. So, you either ask for it now, or the auction isn't happening. Do you understand? Ask for it now."

"But—"

"Ask for it now!" Mimi shouted.

Rafi continued to protest, but Mimi was done with this discussion. She sprinted to Paul's office.

As she burst in, he was talking on the phone. He glanced at her and mouthed the words "my attorney," then went back to his call. "So," he said, "this morning, we got this—"

Mimi ran up to Paul and smacked his phone out of his hand. It flew into the air and fell to the ground. Paul looked at it lying on the floor, then turned to Mimi, his mouth open. She pressed her phone in his hand. He stared at it, stunned.

"Rafi Boasberg's on the line," she declared. "He wants his diamond back."

CHAPTER THIRTY

A FEW MINUTES LATER, RAFI ARRIVED at Paul's lab, wearing sandals and a puzzled look. Mimi greeted him at the door.

"I don't understand this," he said. "I didn't submit that diamond."

Mimi shushed him and hooked her arm through his elbow. "Don't ask questions," she said under her breath. "Just get the diamond. We'll sort it out later."

She escorted him into Paul's office. "Okay," she announced. "Here he is. Rafi Boasberg. He submitted that diamond, and he would like it back."

Paul's lips turned down. Mimi held her breath as he typed what he needed to type, then held it again as Rafi signed what he needed to sign. Finally, Paul, not quite sure what he was doing, handed the diamond to Rafi, who looked just as confused.

Mimi thanked Paul; he responded with a grunt. She hurried Rafi out of the office before anyone asked any more questions.

It was only when they were out the door, heading down the hall, Rafi clutching the twenty-million-dollar diamond in the pocket of his cargo shorts, that Mimi allowed herself to smile.

"We got it back!" she crowed.

"Whatever." Out of his house, away from his friends, Rafi showed little of his standard good cheer. He was as angry and jumpy as you'd expect of someone who'd just been beaten by a guy with a lion tattoo.

"Be happy!" Mimi prodded. "We got the diamond back. We can have the auction tonight."

"Yeah, I know," he grumbled. "I'm just freaked out that someone submitted this diamond in my name. It had to be my stepfather. He's trying to frame me, and to make me look like a thief. But what do you expect? The man's a monster. He tried to kill me last week."

Mimi slowed her pace and turned toward Rafi. "Speaking of your stepfather, I have a question. It's about something that happened long ago. After your trip to the ADR, did you get arrested at the airport for smuggling?"

Rafi looked shocked. "How'd you find out?"

"I can't say," Mimi responded.

He avoided Mimi's gaze. "It's true. When we got back, I was so disgusted with everything I saw, I knew I couldn't keep working for my father's company. Except my dad would never let me quit. I made it blatantly obvious I was smuggling goods, hoping they'd catch me, and Novak would give me the boot. Which is what happened. I got caught, then I got fired. I went through hell, but it worked."

Mimi nodded. "And you also had Zeke remove the files about that from your father's papers?"

"Yeah," Rafi said, his eyes downcast. He stopped walking. "I didn't want Anita and Brandon to know. You know how hard-core they are. Please don't mention this to them."

"I won't," Mimi said.

They began walking again. As they headed into Boasberg's building, Mimi lowered her voice. "You know, I talked with your mother yesterday."

"So that's who told you! My mom. She can't wait to make me look bad, after what I did to her husband."

"No, no, no. It wasn't her, I swear. She doesn't feel that way at all. Exactly the opposite. In fact, she wanted me to give you a message."

"I don't want to hear it," Rafi snapped. "I no longer want her in my life. I hate her."

Mimi gasped at this. "Rafi! Don't say that!"

He didn't respond, just rushed to the elevator bank, where he stood staring at the descending numbers. His face was covered by a web of scars and bruises, and a forest of facial hair, but through it all, Mimi could see eyes lit with rage. His mom was right; he could be quite intense.

"Rafi, listen to me," Mimi said, almost pleading. "I understand your relationship with your mom hasn't been perfect. But she wanted me to tell you—"

"I don't care what she said. I want nothing to do with anyone who'd marry Morris Novak." Rafi spit out of his stepfather's name with contempt. "And soon, my mother will want nothing to do with me."

"Why not?"

"I'd rather not say."

Rafi was obviously in no mood to talk. They rode the elevator to his father's office in silence.

When they reached Abraham Boasberg Diamonds, they were greeted at the door by a security guard, with a gun conspicuously hanging from his belt. He had slicked-back hair, thick wrists, even thicker arms, and a rock-like face that looked like it hadn't smiled in years. He asked Mimi for an ID and glared while she fished it out of her purse.

"Brandon convinced us to hire security," Rafi said. "We figured it would make people worry less."

"Sounds good," Mimi said. As Channah was coming later, it made Mimi worry less.

They walked to the conference room, where Brandon and Anita were sitting at the table, thumbing their phones.

"Good news," Rafi said. "We got the diamond back."

Brandon and Anita looked shocked, but when Rafi produced the glimmering gem from his pocket, they both cheered.

"Where's Reverend Kamora?" Mimi asked. She hadn't told him the diamond had been found; she didn't want to get his hopes up. But his reaction was the one she most wanted to see.

"Last time I checked," Rafi said, "he was in the back."

Rafi and Mimi entered the small storage room in the rear of the office. Reverend Kamora was sitting cross-legged on the small patch of yellow floor between the door and the heating unit. His head was bowed, his eyes were closed, and his lips were moving, though they didn't produce a sound louder than a whisper. He seemed to be muttering some endless private prayer.

"Hello, Reverend," Mimi said.

He stopped whispering, opened his eyes, and looked up at Mimi.

"We have good news," she said.

He offered a meager smile, as if the concept of "good news" was now foreign to him.

Rafi's face twinkled with anticipation. "Look what we got," he said, and pulled the diamond from his pocket.

Reverend Kamora's mouth fell open. He stared intently at the gemstone in Rafi's hand. His breath grew quicker as he grabbed hold of the wall and lifted himself up, eyes never leaving the diamond. He moved his face next to it, like he wanted to kiss it. His head jerked up. "Is this—?"

"It is," Rafi said. "Want to hold it?"

Reverend Kamora just stared.

"Take it," Rafi said. "It's yours."

Before he could respond, Rafi handed him the diamond.

He gingerly touched the triangular stone's pointy tip, then rolled it around in his palm with his index finger. "Amazing. I never thought I'd see this again."

"Really?" Mimi said. "You said you had faith that you would."

"I did say that." He lowered his head. "I wanted to believe it. I wanted others to believe it, too. I didn't want the auction to be cancelled. But deep down, I always feared I would never see this again."

He clutched the diamond in his fist. "This is incredible. God has now blessed me with this gift, not once, but twice." The corners of his eyes were red. "Where did you find it?"

"It's a long story," Rafi said. "But you can thank Mimi."

He turned to Mimi. "You didn't put yourself in any danger to find this, do you?"

"No," Mimi said.

"Then thank you very much. Can I hug you?"

Mimi got a lump in her throat. "Be my guest."

He stood up and gave her a tight embrace. His body shook as he wept over her shoulder. When he let her go, his cheeks were wet. "You have no idea how much this means to me."

"I think I do," she smiled.

Rafi turned to Reverend Kamora. "We need to get the diamond ready for the auction."

This seemed to startle him all over again. "That's right," he mumbled. "God be praised." He plucked the diamond from his palm with two fingers and handed it to Rafi. "If you'll excuse me, there's something I need to do."

He headed out of the room, but turned to Mimi before he left. "Once again, Miss Rosen. Thank you, and may God bless you."

Rafi pumped his fist. "Let's do this." He followed Reverend Kamora out the door.

Mimi stood by herself in the small room. This investigation had been grueling and mostly thankless, but watching Reverend Kamora get his diamond back gave her a small tinge of pride.

Just then, she heard a familiar voice: Channah's.

Mimi stepped from the back room to see her friend sweep into the office. She was dressed up and trying to get Rafi's attention.

"You look nice today," Channah cooed.

Rafi's mouth curdled. "How could you say that? My face is covered with bruises."

"Yes, but you look good otherwise," Channah chirped.

Rafi turned away from her. "You should go help my friend Zeke. He's running the video tonight."

He pointed to a desk in the corner of the room. It held three laptops, an oversized mixing board, and a tangle of cords and wires. Zeke popped his face up from behind one of the laptops. He shyly attempted a smile.

Channah tittered, like Rafi was joking. Then Rafi left for the conference room, and it hit Channah that she really was being banished to the desk with the *nebbishy* computer guy. Her mouth turned squiggly, and she dragged herself to Zeke's workstation.

Right after she sat down, Zeke began teaching her the fine points of running a livestream, which Channah greeted with obvious disinterest. Mimi shot her a smile. Channah rolled her eyes and shrugged.

Rafi's behavior puzzled Mimi. When Channah said she was coming to the auction, he'd sounded excited. Now, he was acting like he didn't want her there. Granted, Channah was coming on pretty strong. But Rafi seemed to be pushing away everyone who reached out to him.

Mimi looked at her watch. It was four-thirty. Everyone was readying the six o'clock livestream, but Mimi hadn't been given anything to do. Which was fine. It had been an intense day. She needed to take a walk and get some fresh air.

On her way out, the security guard said a messenger had just delivered an envelope for her.

"For me? How does anyone know I'm here?"

The guard looked annoyed. "Beats me, lady. Just take it."

She glanced at the return address. It said just, "M.N." Morris Novak. He *could* monitor the cameras.

Mimi walked back in the office and tore open the envelope. It contained a certificate of ownership from the finance department of

Nivens, stamped "private." It listed the owner of Merlano Resources as Arnold Remley.

Arnold Remley? Mimi wondered. *Who's that?*

Mimi whipped out her phone, and Googled "Arnold Remley"—and found, to her dismay, that many people had that name, most of whom weren't that interesting—except for one.

A six-year-old article from an ADR newspaper reported that an overseas dealer with that name had been arrested for trying to smuggle diamonds over the border to avoid taxes. He was released on bail, and when he didn't show up for any court dates, they lost track of him.

Yet, if Novak's info was right, he was still active in the African Democratic Republic.

But who was he? How did he fit into this? Was that even his real name? Brandon had warned her not to trust anything from Novak, but this looked legit.

Then she heard a noise, coming from Boasberg's office. The door was still covered in yellow tape, but was half open. When Mimi left, she was careful to keep it open only a crack.

She put her ear to the door. She heard rustling. Someone was in there. Someone who shouldn't be.

She looked around. No one was nearby. By this point, Mimi was an old pro at breaking into Boasberg's office. She jiggled the door handle with her elbow, then crawled under the yellow tape. After she crossed into the dark room, she rose from the floor, and closed the door with her back.

A figure stood at the window. He must have heard her enter because he gasped and turned around. Mimi pointed her phone light at him.

It lit up the sad, scared face of Reverend Kamora.

CHAPTER THIRTY-ONE

Reverend Kamora and Mimi stood there gaping at each other for a second.

Mimi didn't know what to say, so she blurted the first thing that came to mind. "Why are you here?"

"I am getting the gold box," he said with a slight tremor in his voice. "You told me it was outside the window."

Mimi wasn't sure she heard him correctly. "You're trying to take it?"

"Not for me," he said. "For the auction. The box belongs with the diamond. It was produced with locally-mined gold. Mr. Boasberg talked about it at the conference."

"Reverend, with all due respect, you shouldn't touch anything in here. We shouldn't be in this room. It's considered trespassing."

"But you said you came in here."

"Yes, but I shouldn't have done that. Detective Matthews warned me to never come in here again."

"Oh." Reverend Kamora appeared confused. "Then why are you here now?"

This flustered her. "I heard someone inside and wanted to see who it was. But we both have to leave."

"Miss Rosen, I can't just leave that box out there. It's valuable."

"I know, but—" Mimi stopped. A realization hit her like a hammer. "Come to think of it, that's a good point. It doesn't make sense that someone would leave an empty gold box in a gap between bricks."

She started putting the pieces together. "And chances are the person who left that box there, killed Abraham Boasberg. Because that box was deliberately hidden inside that rag. Why would that person hide the box, and take the diamond? Wouldn't they take them both?"

"I do not know."

"It's weird, though," Mimi said. "Here's something else I always found strange. You had a handshake deal to sell the Hope of Africa to Merlano Resources, correct?"

"Yes."

"And you said *Mazal* on it?"

"I did."

"If there's one thing that I've learned working at my father's office, it's that once you say '*Mazal*' on a diamond deal, it's binding. But Merlano Resources didn't pursue that. Why not? They had a legitimate case. There was lot of money at stake."

"Mr. Boasberg always found that odd," Reverend Kamora said. "He was constantly worried they'd come after us."

"Why do you think they didn't?" Mimi said.

"I do not know. Mr. Boasberg believed that whoever owned the company didn't want anyone knowing they were associated with it."

"Right," Mimi said. "That's the most logical explanation. Which means it probably wasn't owned by Morris Novak, or anyone connected with him, because it wasn't exactly a secret that he owned companies in the ADR. He'd been involved there for years." Mimi thought more. "I've heard that Merlano was owned by someone named Arnold Remley. Ever heard of him?"

"No," Reverend Kamora said. "I must say, Miss Rosen, you ask a lot of difficult questions."

Mimi started connecting the dots. Boasberg received a "Merlano email, with attachment." Then he texted Brandon, "I have shocking information we need to discuss." What was that info? Maybe Novak had the answer: "Abraham had a passport."

Mimi shone her light on Boasberg's big black vault. It was bolted to the floor, which was probably why the police hadn't removed it. Its door was open, as it had been the night of the murder.

"That's where Abraham Boasberg kept his important items, right?" she asked.

"I believe so."

She rushed toward it, cracking the door open further, and flashed her phone inside. She feverishly rummaged through the endless piles of boxes of diamonds, hunting for an object that was even more valuable.

"What are you doing?" Reverend Kamora asked.

"Looking for something," she said, without stopping her sifting.

"But you told me not to touch anything in this office."

"I just want to find one thing," Mimi said quickly.

"So did I!"

Mimi had no time to argue. After sorting through what seemed like dozens of boxes on shelf after shelf, she found it: a brown manilla envelope taped to the vault floor. She plucked it from the safe and opened it with trembling hands. It held a printout of a passport, the evidence that cost two people their lives. She gulped, quickly closed it, and tucked it under her arm.

"We should go," she told Reverend Kamora.

"You're leaving with that?" He sounded incredulous. "You told me not to take anything."

"This is important."

"What I wanted was important, too!" His voice grew peppery. "If you are taking what you found, then I will take the gold box. It belongs with the diamond."

"No," Mimi cried out. "Please don't. We need to get out of here."

It was too late. Reverend Kamora was headed toward the window.

Mimi's heart raced. If that box turned up at the auction, Matthews might blame her. "Please, listen to me!" she screamed. "Do not take that box. Do not even touch it. That would be a very bad thing to do."

At that moment, it struck Mimi that screaming at someone, while trespassing on a crime scene, was also a very bad thing to do.

But it was still a shock when the office door flew open to reveal the security guard's unmistakable hulk-like frame.

"What are you doing in here?" he barked. One hand held a flashlight, the other a gun.

Mimi's body felt like ice. She had no response.

Fortunately, Reverend Kamora spoke first. "It is my fault, sir," he said. "I was looking for the gold box that held the diamond."

The guard ducked under the yellow tape. "I don't care what you're looking for," he snarled. "You are not allowed in here. Don't you see the room was sealed off?"

"I understand," said Reverend Kamora. "I just need this box."

"I'm not letting you steal that," the guard shot back.

"I am not stealing it." Reverend Kamora stamped his foot. "It belongs to me."

"Listen, moron," the guard growled. "This is a crime scene. You are not allowed in here."

"I will leave in a moment," Reverend Kamora said.

"No, you idiot. You will leave now. I used to be a cop. I got friends on the force. I can have you arrested right now. If I were you, I would stop talking and start walking." He aimed his flashlight at Mimi. "What's that in your hands?"

Mimi grew stiff. "Nothing."

"You got that from here, right? Let me see it." He walked up to her, snatched the envelope, opened it, and looked inside.

The light gave Mimi a glimpse of his bulging arm. It showed why she didn't want to mess with him.

"Stealing from a crime scene," he growled. "You could face serious charges for this." He towered over Mimi. "I want you two not only out of this office, but gone from these premises. You are officially banned from this auction. If you leave right now, I might be nice and not call my friends on the force. You have ten seconds to get your butts out of here. Go!"

Reverend Kamora started walking to the door. Mimi yanked his shirt, stopping him.

"We're not leaving," she told the guard.

Reverend Kamora turned around and gaped at her.

"What did you say?" the guard said.

"We will leave this room." Mimi said. "But we're not leaving the auction. Reverend Kamora found that diamond. This sale is his dream. We will watch it in person."

Reverend Kamora sounded confused. "I don't—"

Mimi put her hand on his shoulder, so he wouldn't say more.

The guard's chest puffed out. "I just caught you stealing from a crime scene. I was going to be a nice guy, let you off easy, but now you're gonna face serious jail time. You think I'm bluffing?"

Mimi considered this. "Actually, yes. I think you're bluffing."

There was a brief silence. Mimi could hear all three of them breathing.

"Okay, lady," the guard said. "You're gonna regret this day for the rest of your life. It's your funeral."

He shut off his flashlight, shrouding the room in darkness. He marched through the police tape, leaving it in shreds, and slammed the door so loudly the whole office shook.

"Miss Rosen—" Reverend Kamora said, "I cannot comprehend your behavior."

"He's full of it," Mimi responded. "If he was going to call the cops, he would have held us here. He just wants us to leave the auction."

Reverend Kamora sounded shell-shocked. "I don't know about you, Miss Rosen, but I am from another country. I don't want to get into trouble in the United States of America. I might not be able to return home."

"Then, leave," Mimi said. "I'm staying."

Reverend Kamora looked at Mimi with amazement. "But that man seemed dangerous. He has a gun. Aren't you worried about what he might do?"

"Of course, I'm worried. But at this point, I'm in danger no matter what I do."

"What do you mean?"

"The guard saw what was in the envelope. That's why he grabbed it from me. It shows who killed Abraham Boasberg."

"So, what are you going to do?"

"I'm still figuring that out." Mimi sighed. "Mostly, try not to get killed."

CHAPTER THIRTY-TWO

Mimi and Reverend Kamora crept to Boasberg's office door, then snuck under what was left of the police tape. Mimi expected to see the guard waiting for them in the reception area, but he was nowhere to be found. Mimi wasn't sure if that was good or bad.

She did spot Channah sitting in the corner with Zeke, the computer guy. Zeke was droning on about the livestream, while Channah nodded politely and tried to look interested.

Mimi rushed up to her. "Do you know where the security guard is? Is he outside?"

Channah seemed eager for a distraction. "I don't know. I haven't seen him."

"How about Rafi?"

"I believe he's in the conference room," Zeke said.

"Let's go," Mimi said to Reverend Kamora, as she hurried to the conference room. Reverend Kamora limped behind her, mystified.

Rafi and Anita sat at the long table in the conference room, their eyes glued to their laptops, typing furiously. The Hope for Humanity diamond stood in the middle of the table, a gleaming triangle that seemed to power all around it.

Mimi closed the door and took the chair next to Rafi. "We need to talk."

Rafi looked annoyed. "We're getting the auction ready. Can't it wait?"

"No," Mimi responded.

"It has to," Rafi said. "The auction's in an hour!"

"This is way more important." She stared at Rafi, until he stopped typing and swiveled toward her with an exasperated eye roll.

"What is it?"

"A few minutes ago, I was in your father's office when I—"

"You were in my father's office?" Rafi stared at her in shock. "It's sealed with police tape. How did you get in?"

"I crawled under the tape. Anyway—"

Rafi raised his voice. "You're not allowed to crawl under police tape! The cops warned me a million times about that."

"I know," Mimi said. "I was only in there for a second."

Rafi slapped his hand on the table. "The issue isn't how long you were there. You're not allowed in there at all. I've been dying to go in that office. But I never did, because the cops told me not to. And you just waltz right in."

Mimi felt her muscles grow taut. "I only went there because I heard someone inside and wanted to see who it was."

"Hold it," Rafi interrupted. "Somebody else was in there? Who?"

Mimi sucked in her breath. "Reverend Kamora." Mimi didn't look at him as she said this. She felt like a snitch.

"*Really*?" Rafi swerved his head to look at Reverend Kamora. "You were in my father's office, too?"

Reverend Kamora's chin dissolved into his neck. "Yes. But I had a good reason. I wanted to retrieve the gold box from outside your father's window."

Disbelief washed over Rafi's face. "How did you know the gold box was there?"

Reverend Kamora appeared sheepish. "Miss Rosen told me."

Rafi pivoted back to Mimi. "And how did you know?"

Mimi felt her stomach flip. "I saw it the first time I was in your father's office."

"Hold it. You were in there, *twice?*"

"Yes, but—"

"It just kills me," Rafi said. "So many times, I wanted to go in that room, just for a minute. But I never did."

"That must be difficult," said Reverend Kamora, placing his hand on Rafi's shoulder.

"Please!" Mimi felt ready to burst. "Can we stop talking about who was in your father's office? I agree, I shouldn't have been in there. But there's something far more pressing to talk about."

The room grew silent.

"Rafi, do you remember the first time we met, at the conference? Brandon asked your father how he could sell the Hope for Humanity diamond without revealing all he knew about Morris Novak. That question upset him, right?"

Rafi thought a bit. "Sure. He didn't think it was fair. But what's that go to do with anything?"

"The next day, your father texted Brandon that he had shocking information. We all assumed that your father wanted to show Brandon information about Morris Novak. But he couldn't have. All that material was stored on the cloud, and it took Zeke days to get it down."

Rafi squinted at her. "Then, what did he want to show him?"

Mimi looked him in the eye. "I believe your father wanted to show Brandon information about—" She took a breath. "Brandon."

At this, Anita, who appeared to be only partially paying attention, stopped typing.

Mimi continued: "Right before your father died, he asked you to wire money to Merlano Resources. That was the company that originally tried to buy the diamond. It was owned by someone named Arnold Remley. And in your father's vault, I found an envelope with a copy of Arnold Remley's passport. And you know whose picture was on that passport?" Mimi hesitated, because part of her still found it hard to believe. "Brandon's."

Rafi stared at her, blankly.

Mimi almost bounced in her chair. "Don't you understand? Brandon is not his real name. It's Arnold Remley. He owned a company in the ADR that dealt diamonds. It took me a long time to put it together. But your dad figured it out before me."

"And how did he know?" Rafi was struggling to get his mind around everything.

"My guess is, when Novak and your father talked at the conference, Novak warned him that Brandon might alert the media about your smuggling bust. And, as you know, your father was very protective of you.

"So, what does he do? He'd always wondered why Merlano never contested the diamond sale, since Reverend Kamora said *Mazal* on it. So, the next day, he called up the company and spoke to the person who worked there, a gentleman by the name of Farhad Sultan. A few weeks ago, that man was murdered in cold blood, but we'll get to that in a second.

"What I believe is, Farhad and your father struck a deal: your dad would wire him money, and in return, Farhad would email him Brandon's passport, which showed he had two identities. When your father got that, he texted Brandon and said he had shocking information."

She pointed her finger at Rafi. "That was why your father asked you to leave that night. He'd gathered that information to protect *you*. And when Brandon arrived, your father basically told him: 'if you release information about my son, I'll tell the world about you.'"

Rafi looked like he couldn't believe what he was hearing. Reverend Kamora and Anita appeared deep in thought.

"That should have ended things but—well, you know there's always a but." Mimi paused to collect her thoughts. "Imagine that you're Brandon—or Arnold, whatever his name is. That passport proves that he's living a double life. It shows he's a fraud. If that got out, his diamond and human rights careers would be over, he wouldn't be the star of a movie, he might even face criminal charges. Someone having that information was a serious threat to him."

Rafi gazed at Mimi levelly. "So, if what you're saying is true, then isn't it possible—" He didn't want to finish the sentence.

Mimi didn't want to, either. "Yes," she said. "It's more than possible. I believe it's true." She inhaled slowly. "Brandon killed your father." That wasn't easy for Mimi to say, but once she did, she knew it was right, and there was no turning back. "He also hired someone to kill Farhad Sultan. He has two people's blood on his hands."

Rafi sat with his jaw open, taking this in.

A heavy silence descended on the room. Until Anita declared, "come on, Mimi! You have no proof of this!"

"It's true!" Mimi said.

Anita eased back on her chair with a syrupy smile. "Obviously, there's some bad blood between you and Brandon. He said you had a thing for him, and he blew you off. And I guess this is your attempt to get back at him. Still, accusing him of murder is going a little far, don't you think?"

Mimi was so shocked, she could barely respond. "First of all," she sputtered, "Brandon made a move on me, when we were both in Boasberg's office."

"Hold it," Rafi threw up hands. "Brandon was in my father's office, too? Didn't he realize it was sealed?"

"Yes, but—" Mimi paused. "Let's not get on that subject again."

She turned to Anita. "Brandon kissed me, not because he liked me, but so I'd back away from him and I wouldn't see him removing the diamond from the gold box. Then, once he had it, he sent it to the lab to frame Rafi."

"Again," Anita sniffed, "you have no proof of any of this."

"There *is* proof." Mimi was getting exasperated. "I saw Arnold Remley's passport. It had Brandon's picture. How many people have two identities?"

"So, let's see this passport," Anita said.

"I don't have it. The security guard took it from me in Boasberg's office."

"My God!" Rafi shouted. "The guard was in the office, too? Was the whole world in there?"

"Can we please not get back on that topic?" Mimi snapped.

"If the guard has the passport," Anita said, "let's ask him for it."

"He won't show it to you," Mimi said. "He works for Brandon."

"So, basically," Anita said, "you have no proof."

Mimi didn't want that guard anywhere near her, but figured talking to him would provide the final bit of proof, as it had for her. "Okay," she said. "Get him."

Rafi stood up, walked to the door, and stuck his head out. "Hey, Jack. Can you come in here a sec?"

The guard lumbered in. When he saw Mimi and Reverend Kamora, his lips curled into a snarl. "What are these two doing here? You know I caught them trespassing in your father's office? Trying to steal stuff."

"Yes, they know all about it," Mimi said. "Didn't you say you were calling the cops? Where are they?"

"Oh, don't worry," he snarled. "They're coming."

"That's weird, because you said you were calling them ten minutes ago," Mimi said. "They'd usually be here by now. But before they come, can you return that folder you snatched from me?"

"I don't have to give you nothing, lady," the guard shouted. "I don't know what you're talking about."

Mimi sensed his growing discomfort. "Actually, you *do* know what I'm talking about. The folder you took from me, that you said I was stealing. Which you then stole yourself."

His nostrils flared, like a bull. "I didn't steal nothing. And you weren't in there to steal a folder. You were there to steal diamonds."

"Look," Mimi said, "I know Brandon is paying you, but you don't have to be such a pathetically obvious liar."

The guard moved toward Mimi, invading her space. "I don't have to take lip from you, lady. I can just kick you the hell out of here." He stuck a hot-dog-sized finger in her face.

Mimi's insides lurched, but she kept cool. "Why don't you try it, tough guy?"

This seemed to goad him into a fury. "Okay, lady, I've had enough of you." He grabbed a big chunk of Mimi's hair and squeezed it. Mimi felt a quick jolt of pain, and shrieked. Before she knew what was happening, he'd yanked her out of her chair. Her chin received a nasty bump as she hit the floor.

The whole room started screaming, but none louder than Rafi, who popped up from his seat, and shouted, "let her go!"

"Why should I?" groused the guard. "You hear how she's talking to me?"

"Touch her again, I'll call the cops," Rafi yelled, his voice firmer. "Understand?"

The guard waved his gorilla arms. "This lady's a crook and a liar."

"Yeah," replied Rafi. "And you know what? I'll deal with her myself. I want you out of here. Now."

The guard gritted his teeth. "Sorry, buddy. I answer to Brandon. He's the one paying me."

Rafi's face turned so pink it looked like one big bruise. "This is my office. And if you don't leave this minute, I'll have you arrested for trespassing. Understand?"

The guard seethed. "I've had enough of you people." He pointed his eyes at Mimi. "Don't worry, lady. You'll get yours." He banged the door open with his fist and stormed out of the conference room.

Rafi sat down, all the color drained from his face.

"You saw it, didn't you?" Mimi said from the floor, as she rubbed her wounded chin.

"Yeah," he said in a low voice. "It was on his arm. The lion tattoo. You are right about everything." He sat for a second, his stomach heaving. "I'm getting my gun." He leaped from his chair.

"No, Rafi," Anita cried. "Don't."

But Rafi wasn't listening. He had already dashed over to the long brown cabinet at the far end of the conference room.

"Please," Anita begged, her voice sinking to a sob. "Don't do anything crazy."

At that moment, Brandon strolled in the conference room, acting like he didn't have a care in the world. "What's going on here? The security guard said you asked him to leave. Shouldn't we have someone keeping watch, with a valuable diamond up for auction?"

Rafi's eyes became balls of fury. "I made him go. I want you gone, too."

"Why should I leave?" Brandon asked. "I haven't done anything wrong."

"You know what you did." Rafi growled back. "And you'll get what's coming to you. But right now, I want you gone."

Rafi threw open the top drawer of the cabinet. He looked down, his eyes wide with disbelief. "What the—" He slammed it shut. He started feverishly opening and closing the other drawers.

"Looking for something?" Brandon asked with a taunting grin. He pulled Rafi's gun from his pocket. He regarded it for a second, then pointed it at Rafi. "It's here."

Everyone in the room froze. Just then, the security guard re-entered the room. He had his gun out, too.

"Hey, lady," he called to Mimi, still lying on the floor. "Remember I said you'd get yours?"

He lifted his gun and pointed it at her.

CHAPTER THIRTY-THREE

THE GUARD FLASHED A CROCODILE GRIN, like he would relish killing the woman who dared talk back to him. He looked ready to pull the trigger when he was distracted by Brandon's shouting.

"Everyone keep cool," Brandon barked, "and no one will get hurt."

"Give me my gun back!" Rafi roared at him.

"Sorry," Brandon said. "I don't give guns to criminals." He seemed relaxed and confident—unnervingly so.

"I'm no criminal," Rafi said.

"Of course, you are," Brandon said. "You've been caught smuggling diamonds and dealing drugs. I believe those are criminal acts.

"I was quite disappointed, though, by what I've learned from my friend Jack here. You really had us fooled, Rafi. Jack has amassed an impressive amount of evidence that you killed your father."

"What are you talking about?" Rafi screamed.

"You were the last person to leave the office before your father was killed. You also had a clear motive, standing to inherit your father's estate."

"I don't care about the damn inheritance!" Rafi said. "It's mostly blood money anyway. And none of that is evidence."

"Correct. But here *is* evidence: you sent the Hope to Africa to the Michelson Gem Lab."

"I did not!" Rafi shouted.

"Really?" Brandon smiled. "Then why'd you sign for the diamond this morning?" He giggled. "I have to say, even I couldn't believe that. It's not often you see a criminal signing for a stolen gemstone.

"My trial should be fun. Do you really think a jury will convict a well-known human rights activist when all the evidence points to the man's drug-dealing, diamond-smuggling son?"

His voice turned officious. "Anita, I advise you to leave this room. It's full of criminals. There's Rafi, who killed his father, and Mimi and Reverend Kamora, who were just caught breaking into Abraham Boasberg's office trying to steal diamonds. They're all going away for a long time. You shouldn't be in here. It's not safe."

He smiled. "Our movie will have one hell of an ending. All these people will be arrested, and we'll win an Oscar."

All eyes turned to Anita, who sat, stunned and speechless.

"Seriously, Anita," Brandon said, his smile growing strained. "You need to get out of here. You shouldn't be near these people."

Anita looked right at him and spoke slowly. "Brandon, what you're saying makes sense. And yet—" She paused. "I know a load of crap when I hear one."

Brandon's smile faded. "What are you talking about?"

"It's over Brandon," Anita said, her voice calm and even. "You need to give up."

Brandon's nostrils flared, and his face flushed. "Really, Anita? You say that, after all we've been through? All the work we've done together? We could make an incredible documentary. You're going to throw that all away?"

Anita showed little emotion. "It's over, Brandon. Give up."

Brandon's face turned bright red. "It is not over. My fight is never over! I've planned this perfectly. Just tell the police everything I tell you to. It will all work out. From there, the sky's the limit. Our movie will be huge. We'll make tons of money, and we can donate it all to good causes."

Anita shook her head. "It's over, Brandon. Or should I say Arnold?"

This seemed to unsettle him. "All right. I know I'm not perfect. I might have done some borderline things. When you go against an evil guy like Novak, you have to play rough. What's done is done. We have to move on."

"I repeat," she said, "it's over, Brandon. Give up."

Brandon's face grew stiff with malice. "I warn you, Anita, you're either with me, or against me. And you do *not* want to be against me. All the people around you, they are all going down. You do not want to go down with them."

Anita didn't change her expression. "It's over, Brandon."

He gripped his gun. "Actually, you are wrong about that. It is not over for me. Only for you." He lifted his gun and pointed it at her. "It's a shame. We could have made beautiful movies together."

"Don't you dare!" Rafi moved toward him.

"Rafi, a few words of advice." Brandon aimed the pistol at him. "Don't anger a man with a gun."

The room grew silent, except for some voices from the next room.

"Who's that?" growled the guard.

"There's two of the religious out there," said Brandon.

Mimi's anxiety shot sky-high. *He's talking about Channah.*

"Should I take care of them?" asked the guard, in such a clinical way, it gave Mimi chills.

"Keep 'em calm," Brandon said. "Don't shoot them. I don't want a huge pile of bodies."

God. Mimi thought. *Does that mean he's okay with a small pile?*

The guard said, "okay," and left. Mimi didn't trust him to hold to that.

Brandon waved the gun around. "Now everyone relax." He reached across the table and grabbed the Hope for Humanity. "First, I will take this little beauty—"

"You cannot steal that!" Reverend Kamora suddenly blurted. He limped away from the wall, toward Brandon. "It belongs to my country!"

Brandon looked over his shoulder. "Sorry, Rev. This diamond belongs to me. You agreed to sell it to my company. Then you reneged. That's bad business. So now, it's all mine." He dropped it in his shirt pocket.

"I cannot let you have that," Reverend Kamora said, coming closer.

Brandon pointed his gun at Reverend Kamora, who stopped in his tracks.

"There's nothing you can do about it, old man," Brandon sneered.

Mimi later wondered if Brandon regretted calling Reverend Kamora an old man, since he wasn't, or suggesting there was nothing he could do, as that wasn't true either. Reverend Kamora raised his fist and smashed it into Brandon's hand. Brandon yelped in pain and dropped his gun on the ground.

Brandon lunged at Reverend Kamora, but apparently didn't see his other fist hurdling toward to his face. Brandon's arms flailed in circles, as he reached for help that wasn't there. Then he toppled over like a fallen statue. He hit the ground with a bang so loud and merciless it made Mimi wince.

Brandon's head was gushing blood, yet he sat up, his face aflame. Reverend Kamora crouched down and gave Brandon a quick elbow jab to his jaw. He executed it calmly and precisely, as if he'd calculated the exact amount of injury that would knock Brandon out without causing him excess pain. Brandon crumpled to the floor. Reverend Kamora plucked the diamond from Brandon's shirt pocket and clutched it in his hand.

Mimi peered at Brandon's body, which lay on the ground, unconscious but breathing. She walked over to Reverend Kamora, who did not look happy.

He tilted his head toward the sky. "May God forgive me."

Mimi put her hand on his shoulder. "I think you'll be okay."

Outside the door, a deafening gunshot rang out.

"Oh my God," Mimi screamed. "Channah!"

She rushed to the door and swung it open. The security guard lay on the ground, motionless and gushing blood. Detective Matthews was standing at the door, holding a gun.

For the next hour, the office was swarmed with police and EMTs. The security guard was pronounced dead on the scene. Everyone watched in shock as Brandon was carried out on a stretcher in handcuffs, his face ghostly white. Brave crusader Brandon had regressed to scared rich kid Arnold.

Matthews took statements from everyone. Mimi went last. She dreaded talking to him, as she'd have to admit that she'd broken into Boasberg's office on two different occasions. She weighed creatively editing out that information, but couldn't tell the story without it. She decided to just admit it and accept any consequences.

When she relayed that part, her voice grew soft. Matthews registered no rection, except to twist his lip in seeming disgust. Otherwise, he scribbled in his notebook.

When Mimi finished her statement, she sat quietly as Matthews kept writing. She needed to address the elephant in the room, or at least the one trampling through her brain.

"Detective, you haven't said anything about me going into Boasberg's office," she said.

He looked up. "You're right. I haven't." His blue eyes—piercing and unreadable—bore into her. She felt pinned to the chair. "What do you expect me to say?"

Mimi knew she should probably shut up, but couldn't help herself. This man had saved her life—twice. And she'd let him down.

"I'm sorry. My curiosity got the best of me. I know you told me not to go there. And I did." Her pulse sped up. "You know I respect you. If you want to arrest me, fine. I mean, it's not fine. I don't want to be arrested. No one wants to get arrested. Maybe I should get a lawyer or something.

"Should I get one? I don't know any. I mean, my ex-husband was a lawyer. Should I call him? We don't talk much."

She caught her breath. "Remember how I told you when I get nervous, I babble? I guess that's what I'm doing now." She studied his face. "I should stop talking, right?"

"Yes. And I never thought I'd say that to someone actively incriminating themselves." He reclined on his chair and sucked in air through his nose. "I'll repeat what I told Reverend Kamora. Given that I'm now dealing with a number of serious crimes, your little trespassing escapade is not top of my list."

Mimi exhaled.

"However," Matthews said, his brows moving closer together, "that doesn't mean what you did was okay. It most assuredly was not. I don't want to hear about you doing anything like that again. Or for that matter, being involved in any kind of investigation."

"I understand," Mimi said.

After a long silence, she whispered, "Can I speak frankly?"

Matthews threw up his hands. "What the hell."

"I know you don't like when I investigate. But you have to admit, I have good instincts. I helped a lot with this case. You now have solid proof that Brandon was guilty."

"We *had* solid proof," Matthews growled. "Four weeks ago. That's why we arrested him. I also have good instincts. Otherwise known as two decades of law enforcement experience."

"Okay," Mimi whispered.

Matthews exhaled noisily. "I will grant that, as there are now multiple witnesses to Mr. Walters' conduct, you have clarified his motive, and helped crack the question of his identity, you have perhaps—*perhaps*—

bolstered the case against him." He muttered the last few words out of the side of his mouth, like he hated saying them.

"However, please, stay out of these investigations. They are dangerous! I'm saying this for your own good."

Mimi slouched in her chair. "I know. You're right. I *shouldn't* investigate murders. But give me a little credit. I work hard at these things. You act like I'm useless."

"Oh, for God's sake!" Matthews' hands turned into claws. "It's not about you being useless or not useless! Detective work is a skill. It takes years to learn. It's just like—" He thought for a second. "I play clarinet. But I didn't get good at it overnight. It took me years—"

"You play clarinet?" Mimi interrupted.

"Yeah. It's a hobby. The point is—"

Mimi's eyes widened. "You don't seem like the type of person who plays clarinet."

Matthews crossed his arms. "Well, obviously, I am that type of person, because I do play clarinet. It helps blow off steam. I don't want my life to be all murder, all the time."

"Do you ever play in public?"

"I'm in a jazz band with some friends. We have gigs every now and then. It's just for fun, real amateur stuff. But the point is—" He grew flustered. "Actually, I forgot the point."

"You were saying, I shouldn't investigate," Mimi said. "And I promise you, I will never do it again."

Matthews chuckled mirthlessly. "I feel like I've already heard that a million times."

After that, Mimi returned to the conference room, where Rafi, Anita, and Reverend Kamora sat, along with Channah and Zeke.

Mimi was proud of Channah; she was the day's secret hero. She had called 911 when she heard Mimi screaming after the guard attacked her. If she hadn't done that, it's possible more people may have been killed.

Mimi later discovered the day had another secret hero, though he kept his role even more under wraps. The security guard had locked the office door, requiring Matthews to bust it down. Then, out of the blue, Matthews was buzzed in—but not by someone in the office, by someone with access to the app, who was watching the action on the hallway camera. That could only be one person: "M.N." Novak undoubtedly acted out of self-interest, like he always did. Yet, by letting Matthews catch the guard unaware, he probably saved their lives.

Everyone sat around the table, bewildered and numb, recovering from the day's traumas. They were mostly silent, though at one point, Anita broke into tears, and was comforted by Rafi.

Through it all, the diamond remained perched on its pedestal, the afternoon light sailing through it. It looked as beautiful as ever—even if its promise had once again been unfulfilled.

Mimi glanced at her watch. It was five-forty-five. The auction was due to start in fifteen minutes.

"So," she called out to no one in particular, "are we going to do the livestream?"

Everyone looked at her, blankly.

"What are you crazy?" Rafi asked. "After what we've been through? We all could have died today. I don't think anyone is in the mood to do the auction." His eyes bounced among the various faces in the room. "Right?"

For a moment, no one spoke.

"It might be nice," said Reverend Kamora. "One ray of hope on this dark day."

"I wasn't expecting to," Anita added in a soft voice. "But I wouldn't be against it."

"How about you, Channah?" Mimi asked. "You want to do it?"

"Sure," she replied, in a cracked whisper. "It beats going back to Brooklyn."

Rafi blew out air. "I know my dad would want us to. Zeke, is it possible?"

"Well," Zeke said, "there's many factors we have to consider—"

Everyone braced for a long technical explanation. Zeke must have sensed this, because he stopped talking mid-sentence, and bounced his shoulders up and down. "Sure."

Rafi sat up in his chair. "So, does everyone want to do it?"

The rest of the room murmured their assent.

Rafi glanced at his watch. "We have about fifteen minutes. Let's get going."

Suddenly, the room, which minutes before had been eerily quiet, sprung to life, with everyone getting ready for the big event.

Zeke pointed the webcam at the diamond. Rafi opened his computer to the Hope for Humanity's Facebook page, narrating his update as he typed. "The livestream is on. It's happening at 6 p.m. Hope you can join us." He hit the return button with a loud tap and did something Mimi hadn't seen him do all day: he smiled.

Detective Matthews walked in amid the clamor, trailed by a police officer. "What's going on?"

"We're getting ready to auction off the diamond," Mimi said.

"There is one problem with that," Matthews pronounced. "We're taking the diamond."

All the activity ground to a halt.

"What?" Rafi asked, flabbergasted.

Matthews shot him a stern look. "That diamond is stolen property. We should have taken it earlier, but with everything going on, didn't get a chance. We need to determine who it belongs to."

Reverend Kamora snatched the diamond and clutched it to his breast. "We know who it belongs to. The people of my country."

"Reverend, I've been quite fair to you," Matthews said, in a gravely baritone backed by the weight of the New York City Police Department. "But this is not negotiable. Assuming everything you've said is true, the diamond will be returned to its rightful owner. For the moment, you must hand it over."

Mimi looked at Reverend Kamora. "We can sell it later."

His arms sagged, and he grudgingly placed the diamond on the table.

The officer wordlessly scooped it up, and placed it in a sealed Ziploc bag.

After that, all the energy seeped out of the room, like air from a balloon.

Reverend Kamora's lips trembled. "I guess I'll go on the livestream, and explain to the people of my country why the diamond can't be sold tonight."

Zeke adjusted his tripod. "Okay. We'll point the camera at you. Channah, please place a chair against the wall."

Channah fetched a seat. Reverend Kamora grimly sat on it.

"Do you know what you're going to say?" Mimi asked him.

"Not really." He bowed his head and closed his eyes.

"Okay," Zeke shouted. "One minute and we're live."

Rafi turned to Mimi. "Before, you said my mom wanted to tell me something. What was it?"

Mimi smiled slightly. "Just that she loves you, and she will always love you no matter what you do."

Rafi softly chuckled. “Yeah, I thought so. That’s the kind of thing a mom would say. Or at least the kind of thing *my* mom would say. It’s taken me a while to realize that.” He sprang from his seat. “You know what, Reverend? You don’t have to do the livestream. I’ll take care of it.”

Reverend Kamora was aghast. “With all due respect, I believe I am best equipped to explain this situation to the people of my country.”

“I’ll handle everything,” Rafi said, with more confidence than before.

Puzzled, Reverend Kamora ceded the chair to Rafi.

“All right,” Rafi said. “How long ‘till we’re live?”

“Two seconds,” Zeke answered.

And with a sense of purpose Mimi had never seen in him before, Rafi faced the camera.

CHAPTER THIRTY-FOUR

"GOOD EVENING," RAFI SAID, his voice briefly veering into a squeak. He straightened his back and smiled unconvincingly. "Greetings to everyone watching tonight, especially to our friends in the African Democratic Republic.

"My name is Rafi Boasberg. My father was Abraham Boasberg. He came up with the crazy idea to sell Reverend Kamora's diamond as the 'Hope for Humanity.' It's safe to say that things didn't work out the way he planned. But I guess that's true with a lot of things in life. You try to do something good, and it gets messed up."

He retreated into himself for a moment, then seemed to remember he was on camera, and began speaking again.

"My father believed that even when things go wrong, you should try to make them right. So that's what I'm doing tonight.

"We don't actually have the diamond we wanted to auction. The New York City police have it. It's a long story. We trusted someone we shouldn't have, but that doesn't matter now. We'll get the diamond back. Anyway, this auction has always been about more than the actual gemstone. It's about what we do with the proceeds. Which is why we are still going to sell it. That's right, we are holding a diamond auction without the diamond."

Mimi looked around. Everyone wore the same baffled expression, wondering where he was going with this.

"Our goal was always to sell this diamond so that your resources benefit you." He took a breath. "I hoped to find a buyer who understood that. But I've decided I don't have to look for that person. It's me."

Rafi raised his voice. "I hereby commit to buy the Hope for Humanity for thirty million dollars. That's the bulk of my father's estate. It's also one and a half times what we had originally hoped to get for it. Everyone will agree that's a great result."

"So, you may wonder, why do I want this diamond? It's a decent investment, I guess. But that's not why I'm buying it."

"A lot of people from the ADR are watching tonight. One thing that Reverend Kamora taught me is that many people who spend their lives digging for diamonds don't understand why people in the rich countries want them."

"So, I'll tell you. In the United States, diamonds are a symbol. Traditionally, one person gives a diamond to another when they get engaged. It means they want to spend the rest of their lives together. It's a big moment. And right now, this is a big moment for me."

He kept his eye on the camera. "For the last few weeks, I've kept an important part of my life secret from those around me. And I've witnessed how terrible it is to live a lie. It eats people up, turns them warped and twisted."

He inhaled, and his voice broke. "Recently, I started seeing someone, but because I grew up religious, we've kept it quiet because of how my family might react. But when you've faced death like I did today, you understand what's important in life."

"So, when we get the diamond back from the cops, I'd like to place it on the finger of someone I care about. Someone who's compassionate, brilliant, and one of the bravest people I've ever known." He lifted his chin. "I know we've only been seeing each other for a few weeks but this has been such a crazy time, it's felt like years. Anita Vaz, will you marry me?"

Everyone turned to Anita, whose face was frozen in shock.

Rafi tensed up. "I know this is sudden," he added quickly. "Feel free to say no. You can even keep the diamond. I don't care. It just feels right for me. I hope it does for you, too. Because I love you and always want to be with you."

The room waited for Anita to say something, but she stayed silent, the surprise visible on her face. Mimi worried Rafi was about to get publicly humiliated.

Suddenly, Anita's face filled with dimples. "Of course, I'll marry you," she said, and rushed to give him a big showy kiss, that nearly knocked him off the chair.

The crowd chorused congratulations and *Mazal Tovs*. Zeke whipped out his phone to take a picture of the happy couple. Rafi was covered with bruises, but at that moment, his face shimmered so much the wounds didn't show.

Rafi clutched Anita. "Well, that's it folks," he grinned. "I've had a terrible day, and a terrible month, but right now, I am the happiest man in the world.

His gazed straight at the camera. "I only wish my father was here were to share this moment with me. But the best way to honor him is to fulfill his dream, and that of Reverend Kamora. I pledge that all proceeds from this diamond will help the people of the African Democratic Republic. This diamond came from your land. It was unearthed by your labor. You should benefit."

And with that, he signed off, having delivered one hell of a livestream.

Mimi heard someone weeping behind her. She turned around. It was Reverend Kamora.

Mimi sidled up to Channah, who was standing in the corner. "So," she asked in a soft voice, "how do you feel about this?"

Channah gave a listless shrug. "You mean Rafi getting engaged? *Eh.* Considering I nearly got killed today, I can't get all that upset about it." She started twirling her hair. "For a long time, I thought I'd never have feelings for another guy. I know I can now. That's progress."

Mimi took her hand. "You'll find someone."

"Actually—" Channah pulled Mimi close, and spoke in a conspiratorial whisper. "I'm kind of crushing on Zeke."

Mimi's jaw dropped. "Zeke, the computer guy?"

"Who would have thought, right?" She unleashed an earthy chuckle. "At first, I wasn't into him. But he's really sweet and smart. You learn a lot about someone when you're held at gunpoint together."

Channah dropped her voice further. "Anyway, I gotta go. Zeke and I agreed to take the subway home together. We can talk tomorrow." She winked and wriggled her eyebrows.

Channah and Zeke trotted out of the office, chatting excitedly.

Mimi turned around to see Rafi smiling. His *shiddach* had worked.

Mimi walked up to Anita, and congratulated her on her engagement.

"Thanks." Her eyes were red. There was an awkward moment as they stared at each other.

"And when I say thank you," Anita said, "I mean thank you for everything. You're an amazing person. I'm sorry I doubted you." She gave Mimi a firm, tight hug.

When they broke apart, she added, "I'm also sorry for what I said about your friend Channah. It's been so long since I've had anything like this, that—"

Mimi broke in. "It's okay."

"If Channah is a friend of yours, I'm sure she's a great person."

"She is," Mimi smiled. "Anyway, you must be feeling good now. You're the proud owner of the Hope for Humanity diamond."

"I am," she sighed. "Though I don't know if I could wear that thing. It's way too big." Her mouth curled and she walked away.

Mimi saw Detective Matthews heading for the door. She ran up to him. "Detective, thanks for saving my life. Again."

"It's my job," he growled. He was about to exit when he touched his scalp and blurted, "Actually, Miss Rosen, I mean, Mimi—"

Mimi turned around.

"This case will probably wrap up in about a month. If you want me to brief you for an article—"

"You don't have to," she interrupted. "I'm not writing about this, remember?"

"Oh, that's right." He seemed disappointed, like that had become their post-case ritual.

"But I'd like to see your band play," Mimi said.

Matthews brightened. "All right. We have a gig in a few weeks."

Mimi started laughing.

Matthews looked confused. "What's so funny?"

"I'm sorry. It's been a hard day. Something struck me funny. Everyone involved with this had a secret, including you. But your secret was that you play clarinet. Which is a pretty small secret in the scheme of things." She laughed again. "I'm sorry. I'm a little punchy. I'm not mocking you. It's a good secret."

Matthews smiled and looked confused. He did have one more secret, that Mimi hadn't found out yet.

CHAPTER THIRTY-FIVE

As Matthews predicted, Brandon Walters' case wrapped up quickly. Given the now-towering mountain of evidence against him, he had little choice but to plead guilty—which he did, under his real name, Arnold Remley.

Soon, his *real* origin story became clear, and it was quite different from the tale he'd spun in the conference room. It was true, he came from a wealthy oil family. It was also true, he didn't get along with them, but not because he was an activist. They just didn't trust him.

Seven years ago, he was working in the ADR on family business, but looking to break out on his own. He started dabbling in diamond trading. He was a quick study and became quite good at it. He could make nice money because he took lots of risks. He soon became an extremely skilled smuggler.

When Rafi was nabbed sneaking diamonds into the United States, the ADR cracked down on local dealers. Brandon—then Arnold—was among those caught in the net. While Rafi got probation—thanks to Novak's lawyers—Brandon had to spend three terrifying weeks in an ADR jail, which he never forgot. Nor did he forgive Novak, who, Brandon believed, used his juice with local authorities to have him arrested, to scare off a rising competitor.

When Brandon complained about this in a report he posted online under a pseudonym, it caused such a stir, a new career was born.

Along with this new career and new name came a new background—he wasn't really a Rhodes Scholar. He had barely graduated college. Mimi should have known that credential was "too good to check."

Brandon's reports were so detailed, so comprehensive, and so on-point they drove many of his competitors out of business. And the more rivals he eliminated, the more his business grew. Few questioned where he was getting this information—except for his targets, and they were crooks, so no one listened to them.

The more dealers he nailed, the more he learned to evade detection. He had soon socked away millions in offshore accounts, which he expertly kept his fingerprints off.

The only person better at that was the ADR's biggest dealer, Morris Novak, who Brandon longed to bring down. He finally did, but destroyed himself in the process.

When Anita learned all this, she took it hard. She and Mimi hadn't spoken much since the auction, but after Brandon pled guilty, she texted Mimi, "I feel so betrayed."

Later, they talked on the phone. Anita was ashamed she'd not only bought into Brandon's con, she had helped perpetuate it—nothing enhances a person's prestige like being trailed by a camera crew. They spent hours discussing how they'd gotten Brandon so wrong. He seemed so sincere and committed. Was it all an act?

At one point, Mimi combed through Brandon's old reports. One included damning info about Merlano Resources—which, of course, omitted the fact that he owned it. What kind of a person trashes his own company? The same kind who seemed shocked when Anita smacked down his half-baked escape plan. Brandon was such a good con man, he'd even conned himself.

One afternoon, Mimi heard from Brandon's attorney, pitching an exclusive interview.

She was skeptical. "Why are you asking me? I haven't had a major byline in years."

"You uncovered this," said the attorney, in pitchman mode. "You have a personal connection to the story. That'll make it more interesting to editors. In fact, I don't think this will be just an article. This could be a book. A movie. Maybe even—" He dropped his voice. "—a podcast."

He was right. It could be all of those things—and they'd garner tons of interest. That made this an easy decision.

"I'm not interested," Mimi pronounced.

The attorney sounded shocked. "Why not?"

"Arnold, Brandon, whatever his name is, always liked attention. He doesn't deserve more."

The attorney grumbled something about her being crazy, this could be a gold mine. Mimi didn't care.

"Why don't you ask Anita Vaz?" Mimi said. "She has plenty of material on Brandon."

"We did." The pitchman slowed his patter. "She wasn't interested. She wants nothing to do with him.

"She won't even sell us the footage she has. This film company offered her a fortune for it. She wouldn't budge. We were hoping that if you wrote the article, you'd convince her to release it. That would, in fact, be a precondition of you doing the interview."

Ah, Mimi thought, *so that's why he's asking me.*

"It's the craziest thing," the attorney went on. "Brandon said she was this aggressive career-focused filmmaker. She has the makings of a great movie here. But she wants to destroy any film she has of Brandon, all out of bitterness. Can you believe that?"

"Yes," Mimi smiled. "I can."

On the other hand, Brandon's nemesis, Morris Novak, was still trying to avoid the spotlight, but wasn't having much luck at it. His bribe to the ADR's mining minister became a major scandal in that country, causing its government to fall, and sweeping a reform slate to power.

As Sonia Novak predicted, once the feds began combing through her husband's empire, they found enough shady business to start dismantling it. Most of his real estate holdings were sold off, and the industry worked with the city to bring "friendlier" landlords to Forty-Seventh Street. That ended the plan for a middle-of-the-block hotel. The Diamond District was safe—for now.

Rafi gained temporary stewardship of his stepfather's business, and granted Max a generous break on his rent. Eventually, another company took over, and Max's rent rose five percent. Which he still complained about—but at least he could afford.

Novak himself kept, as he told Mimi, a "low profile." There was talk of an international manhunt, but his whereabouts remained a mystery; every few months, reports would appear placing him on a Caribbean island or Dubai or somewhere else.

One afternoon, Mimi was visiting Novak's favorite spot in New York, the Coltura Garden. She'd spent a lot of time there lately. After all she'd been through, she found its well-ordered rows of pink and yellow flowers extremely calming. *If I got nothing out of this whole experience,* she thought, *at least I discovered this place.*

Then one afternoon, she heard a voice in her ear.

"I told you not to trust him."

She turned around to see Novak, wearing the same nondescript summer outfit as last time, and the same smirk.

Mimi sputtered a response, but before she could say anything, he walked away.

A month after the case wrapped up, Reverend Kamora was ready to return to the ADR. Before he did, he visited Max's office, accompanied by Rafi and Anita.

Max and Reverend Kamora greeted each other warmly. They had become pals ever since the Reverend discovered Max on the street.

They came from such different backgrounds that their friendship at first puzzled Mimi. But the more she thought about it, the more it made sense. They were both gentle. They were both religious. They were both confused by modern technology—though Reverend Kamora came from a poor country, so at least he had an excuse.

Reverend Kamora wasn't as old as Max, but had been through so much he seemed like an old soul. As for her father—Mimi had seen pictures of him when he was younger, but remained convinced he'd emerged from the womb an old Jewish man.

While the two of them chatted, Rafi and Anita updated Mimi on their marriage plans.

Anita had the Hope for Humanity diamond recut into several smaller stones, including a modest one-carat heart-shape that sparkled on her finger. Mimi was about to comment that might hurt its resale value, when she recoiled. She was starting to think like a diamond dealer.

Rafi said his mom has been "surprisingly cool" about their upcoming wedding, and they were having the ceremony conducted by both a Rabbi and Reverend Kamora.

"So Reverend Kamora will fly back here for it?" Mimi asked.

"No," said Rafi. "We're having it in the ADR. We've decided to move there."

Mimi was shocked. "Really?"

"Sure," Rafi said. "The Reverend and I are setting up a foundation to make sure all the diamond money goes where it should. And I figured to do that, I need to be there. I don't want to just parachute in there and throw money around. I want to really understand how it could be put to best use. With guidance from Reverend Kamora and the locals, of course. I'm also going to train the miners there how to value and sell diamonds, so they don't have to keep relying on guys like me."

"Plus," Anita said, "I've figured out what my next movie is going to be. A profile of Reverend Kamora."

"Wow," Mimi said.

"Yes," said Anita. "I want to tell the story of Africa through the eyes of someone who lives there. It probably won't attract as much interest as a movie about Brandon, but it will be a better film. It won't just show the bad side of Africa, but also the positive aspects, like the culture and the spirit of the people. The Reverend promised to talk about his time as a child soldier. It's going to be amazing." She took a beat. "Harrowing but amazing."

Mimi admired Rafi and Anita's commitment to what they were doing. She also realized she didn't share it.

She wished she did. Maybe someday she would again. But after all she'd been through, she was too worn out to try and solve any social ills. She just wanted to live her life. Let someone else fix the world.

She didn't feel great about that, but figured for every burned-out idealist like herself, there were young people like Rafi and Anita who had the drive to make a difference. That gave her hope for humanity, and the world.

After the auction, Channah and Zeke started seeing each other. Mimi enjoyed watching them together; they were always smiling and laughing and playfully arguing. Channah was even able to reign in Zeke's endless tech talk. When he'd start on some esoteric tangent, she'd blurt out, "Zeke, no one cares." Then Zeke would stop, nod, and say, "you're probably right." And that would be that.

One day at lunch in Bryant Park, Channah said that Zeke wanted to get married, and she did, too, but—well, there was always a but . . .

"Part of me thinks I'm being unfaithful to Yosef—even though, it's not like me and Zeke—or me and Yosef—"

Mimi cut her off. "I get it. I think that's why my father's never dated anyone since my mom died. He feels like he'd be cheating on her. But you know what? My mother would want him to be happy. Yosef would want you to be happy, too."

"Of course, he would." Channah's head bounced back and forth. "That's the only thing he would want. I care about Zeke a lot. It's just—" She sighed. "I'm scared. Getting married is a big step. You saw what happened the first time I tried.

"Everyone in my community always gets engaged super-fast. And ordinarily, I would, too. But I don't want to rush this. I'm not ready. I need more time." She chuckled. "Last year, I was pressuring Yosef to get married. This year, it's me with the cold feet.

"Of course, my parents are nagging me to do it. And don't get me started on your father." She looked away. "Actually, Mimi, if you don't mind, could you tell your dad to stop asking me when I'm getting engaged? I know he means well, but I'm dealing with enough pressure as it is."

Mimi put her hand up. "Say no more. Nothing would make me happier than to ask my father to stop bugging you."

"Thanks," Channah smiled. "I can't take one more mention of his new suit."

As promised, Detective Matthews invited Mimi to his band's next gig, at a small dark bar in Queens. All his bandmates were roughly the same age and body type. The audience appeared to be all friends and family, yet the band was surprisingly good. The music was smooth and listenable and played with clear affection.

On stage, Matthews looked as she'd expected—down to the way his cheeks grew red and puffy when he blew his clarinet, to how his bulky frame swayed to the music, like a metronome. One thing surprised her: he appeared to be having fun. He continually smiled, joked, even laughed—and not his standard weary this-world-stinks laugh, but one that lit up his face.

After the show, they went for a drink. He was looser than she'd ever seen him, especially when he asked Mimi about her life, which he did quite a bit.

He wasn't surprised to learn she still had nightmares about her last investigation, though it happened a year ago—or that she was now having them about this new one. He said that even after twenty-plus years of police work, he occasionally got them, too. Mimi finally felt understood.

The second time they went out, Matthews was even more relaxed. He talked about his ex-wife, his daughter, his elderly mom, and his job.

"For all the good and bad things that people say about the police," he said, "and believe me I can talk for hours about that, I believe I'm doing important work, which genuinely helps people." Beneath his gruff exterior there was yet another idealist.

It turned out they had more in common than she thought. They both liked to read. He even liked crossword puzzles—the same puzzles he once disparaged.

At the end of the night, Matthews confessed he had long had a "thing" for Mimi. "It started the second time I met you," he said.

"Not the first time?" Mimi asked.

"No," he said. "The first time, I thought you were nuts."

Mimi laughed, and felt flattered. She asked herself, "could I be interested in this guy?" Weeks ago, the answer would have been a definite "no." Now, it was definite "maybe."

At the end of the summer, Max invited Mimi to dinner at the Wolf and Dragon, a kosher steakhouse on Forty-Seventh Street. That was generally a sign that he had a big announcement, though it took a while for him to make it.

"You'll never believe it! I'm getting a mobile phone. Reverend Kamora convinced me to get one."

"Really?" Mimi said. "How?"

"He told me, they have these things on them, applications."

"Apps," Mimi broke in.

"Apparently you can make calls on them. Absolutely free. No long-distance charges or anything. So, every now and then, he and I can *kibbitz* a bit."

"That's definitely something worth toasting to," Mimi said.

They clinked glasses.

Max pointed his finger at Mimi. "Though I'll only get it on one condition. You must promise never to investigate again. I have enough to worry about."

Mimi rolled her eyes. "Of course, I won't, Dad. I've told you that a million times."

Max grimaced. "Yes, I know. And for some reason, you keep doing it anyway."

Mimi shrugged.

Max adjusted the napkin on his lap. "There's something else I want to talk about. We need to go big into this responsible sourcing thing. Really push it."

Mimi peered at him suspiciously. "You always said it was too impractical."

"Yeah, I know, but I've been talking to Reverend Kamora. Do you know that there are whole villages, whole countries, where the main work is mining diamonds? That's millions of people. And the conditions for some of these small-scale guys are very difficult, and sometimes their communities barely benefit."

"Yes, Dad. I knew that. I actually paid attention during the conference."

"I knew it, too. Everyone in the industry knows it. We always figured, that's the way it is. But when you hear from someone who actually lives it, it's different. We have to make sure those people are taken care of."

He held up his finger. "Don't get me wrong. The diamond business does a lot of good. There are countries that we've helped a lot, and we do a lot of charity work. But you can always do better. Reverend Kamora said he's trying to organize cooperatives of local diggers. I figure we can sell those goods in a way that really helps the people there."

Mimi turned her eyes to the tablecloth. "Dad, I'll be honest. This sounds like a great project. I'm really glad you're doing it."

"I'm sensing a 'but.'"

Mimi couldn't even look him in the eye. "I don't know if I can do it."

Max was startled. "I thought you'd be happy about this. You were the one who got me into it."

"I know. But you saw all the crazy stuff that happened with the diamond auction. We tried that responsibly sourced brand, and I gave it everything I had, and barely made any progress. Maybe I'm just old and tired. I don't know. It's just so hard to do good in the world."

Max put his fork down. "Of course, it's hard. If it wasn't, someone would have done it already.

"Listen, being a good person—a true *mensch*—is never easy. And it shouldn't be. Because if it is, that means you're not stretching yourself. But what other choice do you have? What else are you going to do? Be rotten? Be a person who doesn't care?"

"You've always been a compassionate person. I remember, as a little girl, you'd go to the supermarket, and insist your mother buy damaged cereal boxes. You were worried no one else would buy them, and you didn't want them to feel unwanted."

Mimi laughed. "Right. That was nice of me."

"Yeah. It wasn't so nice for us. Our cabinets would be full of ripped cartons with cereal falling out of them."

He thrust out his hands. "The point is, anyone who had the *verkakte* idea to do that, can give this another shot. We are never going to make this world perfect. We just need to make it better. There's a saying in Hebrew: 'You are not obligated to finish the work. Nor are you free to ignore it.'

"It's no secret the diamond industry has issues. I've tried in my way to improve it. I hope you will, too."

Mimi sighed. Like Reverend Kamora, her father was hard to resist. "Okay, Dad. You've convinced me. Old, tired me will try again."

"Hey," smiled Max, "no one's more old and tired than me."

They clinked glasses again.

After that, they pivoted to other topics.

"So," Max asked, "what's happening with Channah and Zeke? I don't understand why they haven't gotten engaged yet. We need a little *nachas* around here."

"I think they'll do it eventually. Channah just has a few issues to work out. Be patient."

"That's easy for you to say," Max said.

Mimi wasn't sure what that meant. "It'll be fine. And I appreciate you not bugging her. I know that's not easy for you." Her nose twitched. "I just realized something. You haven't asked me about my personal life lately." She suspected her father had given up on her.

Max arched his eyebrows. "Why would I? You always tell me not to."

"I know, but you never listen and do it anyway. I've come to expect it." She took a sip of wine. "How about this? I'll let you ask once in a while."

Max looked surprised. "Once in a while? What does that mean?"

"I don't know. Maybe once every two months."

"Once every two months, huh?" Max stroked his forehead. "Do I have to wait two months, or can I ask now?"

Mimi laughed. "You can ask now."

"I appreciate you granting me this privilege. So, can you update me on your personal life? Channah says you've gone out a few times with this Detective Matthews."

"Yeah," she nodded. "I'm not exactly sure where it's going. But we'll see."

Mimi nervously gulped wine. She and Matthews hadn't even kissed. Though, if things kept going well, they might—soon. That made her both excited and anxious. Like Anita, it had been a long time since she had something like this.

Mimi took a breath. "I notice you didn't ask if he was Jewish."

"If I thought he was, I'd have asked."

"It turns out, one of his grandparents is," Mimi smiled. "He's part Jewish. You can only be part upset."

Max didn't laugh. She could sense his disappointment. That was the downside of giving your father question privileges.

"You have to live your life," he said finally.

Mimi nodded. "I am."

She spent the rest of the dinner giving her father a tutorial on his new phone. Some things he got, others—well, this would be a process.

On her way home, Mimi realized she felt happy she was getting involved in responsible sourcing again.

This time, she knew better what to expect. She had always put activist types on a pedestal. Now she understood they were just people, like everyone else. She would encounter plenty of phony Brandons, messianic Boasbergs, corrupt Novaks, and judge-y Anitas—as well as lots of sincere folks who were really trying to make a difference.

There would be days when she'd want to give up. She would put in a lot of time and effort, and experience mostly disappointments, setbacks, and—if she was lucky—the occasional little victory. And that would make it all seem worthwhile.

Mimi slept well that night, knowing that, the next day, she had a lot of work to do.

GLOSSARY

of Yiddish/Hebrew/Diamond Industry Terms

(But Mostly Yiddish)

Baruch Hashem*—Hebrew.* Translates to "blessed be the name," or "thank God."

Bashert*—Yiddish.* Fated. Ordained by God, or providential.

Bubelah*—Yiddish.* Sweetheart, term of endearment.

Bupkis*—Yiddish.* Nothing, or virtually nothing. Its original meaning was "beans."

Carat*—Diamond industry.* The unit of weight that measures diamonds, as well as other precious stones. It is believed to have been derived from the carob bean.

Chazeri*—Yiddish.* Junk, garbage.

Conflict diamonds*—Diamond industry.* The official definition of *conflict diamonds* is gemstones "mined in areas controlled by forces opposed to the legitimate, internationally recognized government of a country, that are sold to fund military action against that government." Many, including some in the diamond industry, feel that definition is too narrow, as it doesn't include human rights abuses perpetuated by governments (as opposed to rebel forces), and there have been efforts to broaden it. They are often called *blood diamonds*, though that term has no official definition.

Daven*—Yiddish.* Recite the traditional prayers.

D Flawless*—Diamond industry.* D (colorless) is the highest color grade on the standard diamond color grade scale. It means the diamond has no body color, that it's perfectly "white." Flawless is the highest clarity grade on the diamond clarity grade scale. It means the stone has no flaws that a skilled grader can see using 10x magnification.

Frum*—Yiddish.* Devout, pious.

Ganef*—Yiddish.* A thief, a dishonest person, or someone with low morals.

Haredi*—Hebrew.* Ultra-religious Jews, known for strict adherence to religious traditions. It translates to "those who tremble," meaning it refers to people that live in constant awe of God.

Hawker*—Diamond industry (Forty-Seventh Street)*—A person (generally a man) who stands in the Diamond District and tries to lure passers-by into a store, to either buy something or trade in their used jewelry. Most people consider them annoying. The author does too.

Kibbitz*—Yiddish.* To engage in friendly chat or small talk.

The Kimberley Process*—Diamond industry.* The United Nations-sanctioned certification scheme that was established in 2003 to stop the flow of conflict diamonds (see entry above). Rough diamonds must be accompanied by a Kimberley Process (KP) certificate to be legally exported or imported.

Loupe*—Diamond industry.* A small handheld magnifying glass that lets dealers examine diamonds at 10x magnification.

Macher*—Yiddish.* Translates to "one who makes." It refers to an important person, or sometimes, a self-important person.

Mazal und Brucha*—Hebrew/diamond industry.* Translates to "luck and blessings." Along with a handshake, it is used to seal deals in the diamond industry. It's often shortened to *Mazal.*

Mazal Tov*—Hebrew/Yiddish.* Translates to "good luck." It is uttered as a form of congratulations at happy occasions.

Mamzer*—Yiddish.* A bastard, both literally and figuratively.

Mensch*—Yiddish.* A person who is mature and has integrity and honor. Someone to emulate.

Meshugana*—Yiddish.* Crazy.

Mishigas*—Yiddish.* Craziness, nonsense. The noun firm of the above.

Mitzvah*—Hebrew.* Translates to "command." It generally means a good deed.

Naches*—Yiddish.* Something you derive pride or pleasure from.

Narishkeit*—Yiddish.* Foolishness.

Nebbishy*—Yiddish.* A nerdy, weak person.

Olav ha-shalom*—Hebrew.* It translates to "may peace be upon" the person—basically "may he (or she) rest in peace."

Oy/oy vey*—Yiddish.* An expression of dismay.

Payis*—Hebrew.* Side curls worn by some religious men and boys due to the Biblical injunction against shaving the "corners" of one's head.

Pear-shape*—Diamond industry.* A popular diamond cut.

Pisher*—Yiddish.* An insignificant person, a nothing.

Putz*—Yiddish.* A jerk. Kind of like a *shmuck.*

Rebbe*—Hebrew.* A Jewish spiritual leader, particularly in the Hasidic movement.

Schmuck*—Yiddish.* A jerk. Kind of like a *putz.*

Seychel*—Hebrew/Yiddish.* Wisdom, common sense.

Sheitel*—Hebrew.* A wig worn by some married Orthodox Jewish women, in line with the edict that married women cover their hair, in order to preserve their modesty.

Schnook*—Yiddish.* A fool, someone easy to dupe.

Shabbat/Shabbos*—Hebrew.* The Sabbath is the traditional day of rest and prayer in Judaism. It starts Friday night at sundown and ends at sundown Saturday night.

Shiddach*—Hebrew.* A match/love connection.

Shiva*—Hebrew.* The proscribed seven-day mourning period in Judaism.

Shul*—Yiddish.* Synagogue.

Tefillin*—Hebrew.* A pair of black leather boxes containing Hebrew parchment scrolls, that are worn by religious Jews when they say their morning prayers.

Tachlis*—Yiddish.* The bottom line, the "gist."

Verkakte*—Yiddish.* Complete crazy, nonsensical.

Yarmulke*—Yiddish.* The skullcap generally worn by Orthodox Jewish men, as well as by less observant Jews during prayer and visits to synagogues. While there are different theories as to why this has become customary, it's generally considered a symbol of that God is always above everyone. Known in Hebrew as a *kippah.*

Yenta*—Yiddish.* A gossip.

Yeshiva*—Hebrew.* A Jewish educational institutional that focuses on religious teachings.

AFTERWORD AND ACKNOWLEDGEMENTS

THIS BOOK DEALS WITH SERIOUS TOPICS that have long been discussed in the diamond and jewelry industry. I don't have room to give my opinions on all of them here, but as I hope I've laid out, they lack easy answers, and changing the industry in sometimes-fraught, troubled countries is a difficult process. And yet the issues in these places shouldn't be ignored, and the people there shouldn't be left behind. Fortunately, there are dedicated people working on them.

One notable resource on the subject of this book is the Diamond Development Initiative (ddiglobal.org), which aims to improve the lot of artisanal diamond miners. For a broader view, I recommend Ethical Metalsmiths (ethicalmetalsmiths.org), which addresses not just issues with diamonds but other jewelry materials, including gold and other gemstones. There are many industry associations and non-industry NGOs that do great work on these topics, and I don't have the space to name them all, but I plan to post a list of resources on my website, robbatesauthor.com.

As I hope I've also laid out, plenty of diamonds and other jewelry materials do help the communities in which they're found, and provide a living to some of the poorest people on Earth. But, unfortunately, not all of them do as much as they could, or should, and, it's no secret, some have had harmful effects. So, if you're looking to buy jewelry, you should ask questions about origin and social impact. (That goes for lab-created products, too.) The replies may vary, given that most jewelers are cut off from the source, and the jewelry supply chain remains complex. But it's important the trade knows that buyers care.

This book was heavily informed by papers and research written by Ian Smillie, Estelle Levin-Nally, Rachel Lichte, NGOs like IMPACT (formerly Partnership Africa Canada), and many, many others. I'd also like to give a shout-out to Martin Rapaport, who not only gave me my first diamond-writing job, but took me on an eye-opening trip to Sierra Leone, where I saw the kind of diamond mining described here first hand. He has always been a staunch advocate for a better industry.

This plot is based on a real gem that apparently did a lot of good—and thankfully, didn't lead to any murder mysteries. Needless to say, all the characters and events that occurred here are completely fictitious.

And now, for the thank yous:

Thanks to my regular writing group, for your great, constructive, and lively suggestions. And thanks to all who bought the first book in this series. If you're reading this, I assume you've bought the second. Which means a lot to me.

Thank you to my magazine and publishing colleagues, at *JCK*, Advance Local, and all the other places that have tolerated me over the years. And thanks to all my industry friends and colleagues—especially those that really do show the honest and humane side of the business.

My patient and helpful editor, Jennifer McCord from Camel Press, offered great feedback that improved this book enormously. And I couldn't be writing these acknowledgements without my agent, Dawn Dowdle, of Blue Ridge Literary Agency.

Much of this book was written during that strange time known as COVID-19 lockdown. I don't think that I could have survived all that craziness without my two best friends: my awesome, kind, beautiful, and—needless to say—patient wife Susan, who is also a great critic; and my lovely son, Mikey, who is not a great critic yet, but hey, give him time. For now, I'll just have to settle for him being sweet and smart and funny, a real New York City kid, down to the accent. I love you both, so much.

And thanks to my parents, sister, friends, and family—in-laws included (and how many people can say that?) I feel these thank yous have gone on so long the orchestra is about to play me off, but to all those I owe a debt of gratitude, I hope I can one day pay you back.

Rob Bates
New York City

ROB BATES HAS WRITTEN ABOUT the diamond industry for close to 30 years. He is currently the news director of JCK, the leading publication in the jewelry industry, which just celebrated its 150th anniversary. He has won 12 editorial awards, and been quoted as an industry authority in The New York Times, The Wall Street Journal, and on National Public Radio. He is also a comedy writer and performer, whose work has appeared on Saturday Night Live's Weekend Update segment, comedycentral.com, and Mcsweeneys He has also written for Time Out New York, New York Newsday, and Fastcompany.com. He lives in Manhattan with his wife and son.

CPSIA information can be obtained
at www.ICGtesting.com
Printed in the USA
BVHW060301110322
630955BV00004B/18

9 781942 078180